Compliments of
Topsail Township
Friends of the Library

PLEASE JOIN

Dragons of Silk

GOLDEN MOUNTAIN
CHRONICLES: 1835–2011

Also by Laurence Yep

The Star Maker
The Dragon's Child
A Story of Angel Island
The Earth Dragon Awakes
The San Francisco Earthquake of 1906
The Dragon Prince
Dream Soul
The Rainbow People
Sweetwater
When the Circus Came to Town

The Tiger's Apprentice Trilogy
The Tiger's Apprentice, Book One
Tiger's Blood, Book Two
Tiger Magic, Book Three

Golden Mountain Chronicles
*The extraordinary intergenerational story of the Young family
from Three Willows Village, Kwangtung province,
China, and their lives in the Land of the
Golden Mountain—America.*

The Serpent's Children (1849)
Mountain Light (1855)

Dragon's Gate (1867)
A Newbery Honor Book
The Traitor (1885)
Dragonwings (1903)
A Newbery Honor Book
Dragon Road (1939)
Child of the Owl (1965)
Sea Glass (1970)
Thief of Hearts (1995)

Dragon of the Lost Sea Fantasies
Dragon of the Lost Sea
Dragon Steel
Dragon Cauldron
Dragon War

Chinatown Mysteries
The Case of the Goblin Pearls
The Case of the Lion Dance
The Case of the Firecrackers

Edited by Laurence Yep
American Dragons
Twenty-Five Asian American Voices

Awards
Laura Ingalls Wilder Award

LAURENCE YEP

Dragons of Silk

GOLDEN MOUNTAIN
CHRONICLES: 1835–2011

HARPER

An Imprint of HarperCollins*Publishers*

Library of Congress Cataloging-in-Publication Data

Yep, Laurence.

Dragons of silk / by Laurence Yep. — 1st ed.

   p. cm.

Summary: Four generations of Chinese and Chinese-American girls, beginning in 1835, are tied together by the tradition of raising silkworms and the legacy of the legendary Weaving Maid.

   ISBN 978-0-06-027518-1

   [1. Silkworms—Fiction. 2. Chinese Americans—Fiction. 3. China—History—Fiction.] I. Title.

PZ7.Y44Dqu 2011   2011016553

[Fic]—dc23   CIP

                                           AC

Typography by Tom Forget

11 12 13 14 15   CG/RRDB   10 9 8 7 6 5 4 3 2 1

❖

First Edition

To my maternal grandmother, Paw-Paw, my sister-in-law, Terry Yep, and to my fellow banana slugs Katharine Gilmartin and Barbara Chatton

 **PREFACE**

China's history is tied together forever with threads of silk, and so is its mythology. Legend says that silkworms were the children of a marriage between a human princess and a magical creature. Perhaps this is true in the way myths are at a deeper level, for silk is a magical fabric, so light, so cool, so soothing, so tingling to the touch.

Another legend says that an empress 5,000 years ago first thought of weaving the silkworm's threads into cloth. More likely some observant woman looked at a bush and saw loose threads dangling from cocoons left behind by silkworms that had metamorphosed into moths.

Whoever invented it, silken cloth has definitely been found in a Chinese tomb from more than 4,500 years ago. From ancient times, Chinese silk traveled over mountains, through arid deserts and steaming jungles, across stormy seas, past bandits and pirates to clothe the nobles and rich folk of many other lands. It was as precious as gold.

Another story tells of a woman so skillful with silk that she wove the robes for Heaven itself. Humans and magical spirits identified her so much with her marvelous creations that everyone refers to her simply as the Weaving Maid.

There are many versions of how she met and married her husband, the Cowboy. Whatever the beginning, all the stories agree that it was a happy and passionate marriage. Once she was married, she spent all her time with the Cowboy. Her loom gathered dust; the robes of Heaven became old and shabby. His herds wandered free.

It was a situation that Heaven could not tolerate, so the two were separated by a great river, the Milky Way, able to see one another but no more. And so they remain in the sky. She is the star we call Vega, and he is the star called Altair. And the Weaving Maid's sisters are the Pleiades.

The magpies, though, felt sorry for the lovers, and so on the seventh day of the seventh month of every year, these birds gather, linking their wings to form a feathered bridge over the Milky Way. And the Weaving Maid and the Cowboy run toward each other, balancing on the shifting, uncertain path of warm, ticklish bodies.

And Heaven relented enough to allow this, but not very far. If it rains, the birds do not come, and in China, the seventh month belongs to the monsoons, when storm clouds sweep daily over the land.

PART ONE
(1835)

Silk is as soft as tears on a cheek.

CHAPTER | I

*7th day of the 6th (intercalary) month of the era
Way of Honor*
August 1, 1835
*Bird Hill, Shun-te District, Kwangtung Province,
China*

Author's note: An intercalary month is an extra
month added to the Chinese lunar calendar to
bring it more into alignment with the solar
calendar. In this case, the intercalary month had
twenty-nine days.

Lily

Nimble as the Monkey King, Lily pulled herself onto the thick branch of the mulberry tree. The monsoon had rained so much that she had been stuck inside the house for the last three days, so she felt as if she had been released from prison.

The summer sun magically transformed the canopy of leaves into a green cloud through which Lily began to move upward, her hands and feet finding the holds instinctively while her mind drifted away again, imagining that she was now a sunbeam flashing through a brilliant jewel.

"Get back down here," her older sister, Swallow, scolded. "You'll break the branches."

"I haven't yet," Lily called back, ignoring how the branch beneath her feet bowed under her weight.

The tree itself was kept pruned, so it was about at the eye level of an adult, but Lily was short for a ten-year-old, so she had to climb to reach the top. The years of pruning had created knobs where branches had been cut, so that tree was covered with the wartlike bumps.

She savored the moment when her head rose out of the leaves, breaching like a freshwater dolphin she had seen once in the river.

The mulberry groves spread across the hillside and down across the clan's island like a billowing emerald sea. They had the right to harvest about a hectare of mulberry trees, scattered in six groves across the clan lands, in exchange for a share of the silk that they would reel. All around her, the trees in the other mulberry groves rustled noisily as women and children picked the choicest leaves.

Immediately below her, men and boys moved about the fishponds, the water shining mirror-bright in the sunlight. As she watched, one of the fish leapt out of the surface, its iridescent scales flashing as it flapped its tail before splashing back noisily. A small rainbow appeared momentarily in the spray.

The rainbow seemed to hover like a good omen near their farmhouse. The whitewashed walls gleamed, and a ribbon of smoke curled above the thatch roof. She sniffed the air and thought she could smell meat dumplings steaming, her favorite lunch.

Lily thought she would burst with happiness. She would have invited Swallow up into the tree with her, but she knew her sensible sister would just snort and remind her again to get back to work. All the village praised Swallow for being a girl with her feet planted firmly on the ground. Lily, on the other hand, was always walking in the clouds—and that was not meant as a compliment by the pragmatic villagers.

Lily's gaze swept beyond the mulberry sea. The village's territory was surrounded on all sides by streams and channels, and beyond them were more villages on their islands in the delta like fat, fuzzy green caterpillars swimming in the mud. The Pearl River itself was just a brown smudge on the eastern horizon.

"Swallow," she called.

"Hmm," Swallow said absently.

"Do you ever wonder what's out there?" Lily asked.

"No, because I know it's the river," Swallow insisted. "It's always *been* the river. And it will always *be* the river."

Lily swept her arm in a wide arc in a gesture indicating the world, and the motion made the knobby branch beneath her sway. "No, I mean, beyond the river," she said, feeling a little frustrated that she couldn't find the right words for her far-reaching thoughts. "You know, the world. What are the foreign countries like? And what about the people there? And . . ." In the rush of questions pouring out of her, she lost her breath for a moment. "And what would it be like to sail there?"

Swallow parroted what Mother often told Lily. "Wondering won't get food on the table."

Lily made a face down at her sister. "Don't you ever dream?"

Her sister gazed up at her reprovingly. "I do what I have to do, Monkey-face. And so should you."

Lily straightened so fast that she almost lost her footing. "Look! Look!" she cried.

She could just make out the tips of a foreign ship's masts as it glided up the Pearl River. Steam rose from an unseen funnel.

Swallow barely spared it a glance before she went back to picking the broad green leaves from the mulberry tree, the picture of quiet efficiency. Holding the tip of one small branch in one hand, she stripped the broad leaves quickly but left the young ones to mature for a later harvest. The branch hardly stirred at her gentle but thorough touch.

"Remember what that ship may be carrying," Swallow said.

Lily lowered the hand that she had been intending to wave. "Demon Mud."

The Demon Mud granted sweet dreams to those who smoked it and misery to their loved ones, who watched the smokers waste away and die. It seeped from the foreign warehouses in Canton across the Middle Kingdom, or China as the foreigners called it, blighting whole provinces.

Suddenly the foreign ship seemed more like some sleek, deadly viper creeping toward Canton to poison not just one victim but thousands.

It hadn't always been that way. Mother said that once, the foreigners had come politely seeking tea and silks and paying gratefully with silver. Then some evil genius had thought to pay with the addictive Mud. A few poor souls had tried it, and then more and more, until the need for it had spread like a plague across the empire. No, the ship was far crueler and more dangerous than any viper.

Lily spat in the direction of the ship. "They ruined Father."

"Father ruined Father," Swallow snapped impatiently. "Now hurry up. The silkworms have to be fed."

Lily plucked some choice leaves from the middle branches, twirling the stems as she admired them for a moment. They shone like paper-thin slivers sliced from a giant green emerald. With the leaves in hand, she shinnied back down to the lowest branch and dropped them into her basket. "I was just finding the tastiest ones for your pets."

"They're not *my* pets," Swallow snorted. "If we didn't need the money, I'd feed every last one of them to the pig."

Lily moved back and forth among the swaying branches, picking the leaves that had dried quickly in the morning sun. She arranged them into a stack with the stems all pointing in the same direction before she climbed down, cradling the leaves as if they were her children. The ground was still damp from yesterday's rain, and the silkworms, who were as fussy as little old men, would object to mud on their meal.

The problem was getting her started, but the village said no one worked as hard as she did once she began. She soon had filled half of her big, broad basket. She made sure to arrange each stack of leaves with the stems pointing to the center. A space had to be left there so the leaves wouldn't heat up and begin to ferment or get moist.

"Let's get more than usual," Swallow said. Leaves rose a third of a meter beyond her own basket's rim. "It looks like rain again tomorrow."

Lily's sister was thin, with high cheekbones that made her small eyes seem even higher up on her head. It was her sister's fingers that Lily envied—long and slender, so nimble when they braided Lily's hair and so skilled at sewing and embroidering. Mother had just started to teach Lily, but so far her stitches were ugly and clumsy.

"Got to make those baby silkworms fat and sassy," Lily said. Together, they moved on to another tree, where Lily clambered up into the branches again.

With Swallow helping, it wasn't long before Lily knocked on a branch and said it was enough.

As Lily climbed down onto the ground, she used her dark cotton sleeve to brush some grit from her sweaty face. A new fancy had taken her. "I wonder what it would be like to wear a silk blouse."

"Cotton's good enough for me," Swallow grunted as she lifted her basket. "What good is silk to a farmer?"

Lily liked to stroke the silk thread that her mother reeled from the silkworm fibers. "But it's so soft and cool, just like a breeze. Wouldn't it be nice to wear silk in the summer when it's so hot and sticky?"

Lily hefted the basket up to her waist and rested it against her hip. "Well, do you ever wonder who buys our silk? Maybe it's some lady on the other side of the world." Lily's eyes widened, and she spoke more rapidly. "And maybe it goes in a big boat just like I saw. And . . . and . . ." Once Lily's imagination had seized her, it was capable of soaring anywhere—like a falcon with a mouse in its claws.

"That's a nice trade. We give them our silk and they give us . . ." Swallow's voice choked on the words. Even though the whole clan knew, Swallow still could not bring herself to talk about such a shameful thing.

Lily blinked her eyes innocently. "Maybe people don't realize what the Mud is doing to China. I mean, not the sellers, but the other people back in their countries. If they knew, maybe they'd stop selling it."

"Oh, they know," Swallow insisted. "And they don't care." She glanced up at the sun and pivoted impatiently. "Now get your basket. We don't want the pigs getting at it."

Lily grinned mischievously. "But this is heavy, and that's the long way."

"We'll take a short rest by the stream," Swallow promised as she set off.

CHAPTER | 2

Swallow

Lily had been abnormally chatty even for her. Swallow had barely crossed the threshold of her family's home before Lily had begun talking to her and had barely paused since.

At sixteen, Swallow had followed the clan's custom and lived in the girls' house, where she would stay until she married. Her mother had done the same in her village, just as her grandmother had done in hers. But Swallow came home every day to help her family.

Left to her own devices, Lily would have simply babbled all day, so Swallow did what she always had to: be practical. Swallow was the one who'd seen that the morning's dishes had all been washed and the other chores done. She'd gotten the baskets and herded Lily—still chattering like a magpie—out the door and down to the mulberry grove. But they were later than usual.

Swallow just wished Lily would concentrate on picking leaves, but Lily insisted on asking questions—her flights of fancy wilder than the birds who had drunk from the pool of whiskey when Uncle Prosperity had dropped the jar during a festival. Though Swallow kept her answers short, even rude, Lily would not take the hint that her older sister was listening for someone else's voice.

No one would have suspected Swallow of being flighty. Swallow was the reliable one. Swallow had her feet on the ground. Swallow was boring.

And yet here she was, ears straining to hear *him* and feeling disappointed when she didn't. But they were late, so perhaps she had missed him.

At this point, they should have returned home to the mountain of chores that awaited them, and yet she did not want him to misunderstand. Unable to resist that urge, she decided to do something even bolder and go looking for him.

Her feet quickening, she tried to stroll rather than run. However, her eyes searched through the green groves for a glimpse of the stream.

Part of her felt guilty for being so impatient with Lily. To Lily, talking and speculating were as natural as breathing. They were what made Lily Lily.

And when Lily had been small, there had also been Father to take care of. She chopped that line of thought off as sharply as an executioner's sword. She did not want to remember those days when she'd had to keep an eye not only on baby Lily but on her drug-addled father.

Suddenly she became aware that Lily was tugging at her sleeve—so hard that it was a wonder she hadn't torn it off. But then Mother had always made clothes to last.

"What?" Swallow frowned.

"So what's the house going to do for the Seven Seven this year?" Lily demanded. She'd set her heavy basket of leaves down while she got Swallow's attention. It was now ten feet away. Had Lily been trying all this time to get Swallow to notice her?

On the seventh day of the seventh month, everyone celebrated the festival of the Weaving Maid and her sisters. There had been no one in Heaven who could spin and weave like the Weaving Maid, but then she'd gotten married to a cowboy. She'd been so happy that she'd neglected duties, and so Heaven had separated the two with the Milky Way. But once a year, the magpies of the world formed a bridge so the pair could get together.

Every year, the inhabitants of the girls' house put on an extravaganza in honor of the Weaving Maid and her six sisters. The girls' house pooled their money together to hire carpenters to build a stage, and musicians and entertainers to amuse the crowds, and food vendors to fill their stomachs. Everyone was welcome to the party.

Swallow hadn't been able to afford the assessment she

owed for the party. Instead, she'd worked extra on the dozens of things that needed to be done for the festival, including presents for the Weaving Maid and her six sisters. Swallow was very skillful with a needle and made the loveliest cloth shoes.

And then there was the Surprise. . . .

"There's going to be music," Swallow said cautiously, not wanting to tip off Lily about the Surprise. Once her little sister knew, then everyone else would too.

Lily wrinkled her nose. "There's always music. But it won't be a real show until there are acrobats."

"What do you know about shows?" Swallow demanded. "You've never seen one in your life."

"But Aunt Piety saw one in Canton, and there were acrobats." Lily pantomimed them moving like birds through the air.

Swallow refrained from pointing out that it was physically impossible for humans to do the stunts that Lily was demonstrating. Her little sister liked to ignore such inconvenient details as gravity. Instead, she jerked her head behind her to Lily's basket.

"Now pick up your basket," Swallow said. "If the silkworms starve to death, there won't be any festival for you."

As Lily jogged back along the path, she looked over her shoulder. "Is it the silkworms you're worried about or *him*?"

Swallow tried to pretend ignorance, but she knew she

was a terrible actress. "*Him* who?"

"The songbird." Lily hefted her basket up. "The one you always see around now."

"Oh, him," Swallow said, annoyed with her little sister. "It's just coincidence."

Lily was grinning. "There've been an awful lot of them lately."

"You're imagining things again." Swallow began to walk faster so that the leaves rattled within her basket. If she went fast enough, Lily wouldn't have the breath to talk.

She hurried through the groves of trees, where stripped branches alternated with full leafy ones, and skirted along the narrow dike-paths between the ponds where fat fish swam. Once, many centuries ago, she would have been passing through fruit orchards and rice fields, but the silkworm was king now and ruled everything.

Swallow paused at the edge of the last grove to wipe the perspiration from her face and then adjust her clothes and hair so she would not appear to have rushed.

"I don't see what the rush is all about," Lily puffed as she caught up with Swallow. "*He'll* wait. I mean, all he's got to do is watch his stupid buffalo."

Realizing that she wanted Lily to look just as casual, Swallow set her basket down and smoothed Lily's hair down, then used her sleeve to dab the sweat. "We don't want strangers to call us bums."

Lily grinned impishly. "Especially if they're from another clan."

When they emerged from the grove, the boy was lying on the opposite bank of the stream. He was slender with a broad forehead. He sat up quickly when he saw them, and he nodded shyly to them. His queue, which he had coiled around his neck, flopped down his back at the sudden motion.

Swallow inclined her head slightly in return. Though they had been encountering one another like this for months, it would have been too forward to speak to a stranger from another clan.

Lily, however, thumped her basket down on the bank and then sat down. "We see your pet every day. What's his name?"

The "pet," his water buffalo, sat in the middle of the stream up to its nostrils, eyes and curved horns like a small, oddly shaped island. The muzzle twitched appreciatively when it smelled the freshly picked leaves in their baskets.

The water buffalo rose, water rilling down the broad glistening back. With a snort that sent up a spray of water, the buffalo began to plod toward Lily, who it assumed had thoughtfully brought it a snack.

Lily motioned with her hand. "Shoo! Shoo!" Even when she picked up the basket and scrambled behind Swallow, the buffalo kept coming. "Shoo! Shoo!" Lily repeated, a little more shrilly.

Swallow didn't have the slightest idea of how to stop a buffalo. "When I tell you," she instructed Lily, "drop your basket and run."

"I'm not going to lose the whole basket," Lily said. "It took too long to pick them."

"Tiny, come here!" the boy said with a clap of his hands.

The buffalo twisted its head to look at him but kept on toward Swallow and Lily.

"Here!" the boy ordered more sternly, and slapped his hands together even more loudly.

Water surged back and forth through the stream as the buffalo turned around ponderously.

Getting to his feet, the boy stretched out a hand. "That's a good fellow."

The buffalo climbed awkwardly up onto the opposite bank, lowering its head and wriggling its ears.

"You don't want to invade that island," the boy said, rubbing the buffalo's head as if it were a dog. "The clan there is ferocious."

"I'll cut him up into steaks," Lily threatened, still behind the shelter of her sister.

Swallow smiled at Lily over her shoulder. "That buffalo's way too tough. Everyone knows that clan is too stingy to feed it right."

Their two clans had been taking spouses from one

another for generations, so it was all right to trade friendly insults.

The boy slapped the buffalo's fat side. "Don't let them hurt your feelings. Everyone knows they're the underfed ones. That's also why they're always late. They're too busy searching for something to eat."

"Unlike the idlers on your island, we have chores," Swallow tossed back.

"Unlike your clan, we know how to enjoy life," the boy said, slinging an arm around Tiny's neck.

Lily wrinkled her nose. "Tiny's an awful name for a buffalo."

The boy rubbed the back of his head. "Sorry. I should've thought of a better one. My family says I don't have much imagination, so I have no idea why they let me name the family animal."

Swallow nudged Lily sharply with her elbow. "Well, I think it's a cute name."

The boy gave a grunt as his cheeks reddened. In all these months, this was the longest conversation they'd had.

Lily, though, was not done. "What's your name? And don't tell me it's Tiny too."

"Happy," the boy said. "My parents have more imagination than I have." Embarrassed, he swung his eyes toward Tiny.

Swallow had a hundred things she wanted to ask him

besides his name, but she'd already been bolder than was proper.

Happy began to hum deep in his chest, and Swallow squirmed, knowing what that presaged. A moment later, Happy lifted his head and began to sing a tune about a boy fishing underneath a blossoming cherry tree.

With a smile, Swallow listened. Up until Lily had taken matters into her own hands, this had been the extent of their communication and their relationship: He sang and she listened. At first, it had been pure accident that Swallow and Lily had paused for a rest by the stream when the boy had brought his buffalo down. After that, they met by silent agreement every day at this time—though both would have insisted it was purely coincidence.

When the boy was done, he nodded to them again and shoved at Tiny's shoulder so the buffalo swung around and began to trudge back home.

But this time as she watched them leave, the boy spun around and waved to her.

Blushing, she caught herself starting to raise her hand to wave back. Instead, she forced her arm down.

It was bad enough to chat with a strange boy so long. It was time to begin behaving again like a proper young woman.

CHAPTER 3

Lily

As Lily and Swallow continued on to their home, Lily couldn't help fretting. "You're not going to marry him and leave me, are you?"

"Don't be silly," Swallow said. "I don't know him at all. I just happen to like his voice."

"For a frog croaking," Lily said sourly.

"Don't be like that," Swallow said. Annoyed, Lily stamped her feet loudly, but Swallow appeared to be too happy to notice.

So she'll get married and then it'll be just Mother and me, Lily thought, feeling suddenly very little and very scared. Her big sister could be awfully picky sometimes, but she was also steady as a rock. Lily could depend on her more than even on Mother.

She eyed her smiling sister as they walked along. *Mother*

should know before it's too late, she decided.

When they left the last grove, they skirted their pond, where the fish darted like slim shadows. Their pig rooted around among the weeds along the sides.

Beyond the pond sat their house. Up close, Lily could see green splotches on the roof where fungus was growing on the straw. Plaster had fallen from one wall, exposing the bamboo interwoven with strips of mulberry bark. Swallow always frowned when she saw the wide hole.

Uncle Prosperity, their landlord as well as a clan elder, should have repaired the house but never did. The only way it would get fixed was if they did it themselves, but they were always too tired from chores. Growing seven generations of silkworms each year consumed eight months of intensive work. At the same time, they also had to take care of the fish in the pond for most of that time and the family pig the whole year.

Their pig was scratching at the dirt with a trotter. "Hello, Cloud. Did you miss me?" Lily asked in a high, sweet voice.

"The pig's not a pet," Swallow said. "It's going to be some family's dinner. You're just asking for pain and sorrow when we sell it."

"There's no reason why he can't be happy in the meantime," Lily said. "Isn't that right, Cloud?"

Cloud, though, was too busy trying to trace a morsel to pay attention to his sympathizer.

Lily sniffed the air. *Oh yes, it is definitely fish dumplings today. Home*, Lily reminded herself, *is still home, no matter how shabby.*

Their mother came out of the house with a bowlful of dumplings. No matter what their troubles, she always had a smile for them. "I thought we could eat outside and enjoy the sunshine."

Setting down their baskets, they sat together on a bench and began to eat. Lily said, "Swallow's seeing a boy from the next island. His name's Happy."

Swallow flushed. "We just happen to bump into one another."

"Every day," Lily supplied.

Mother scrutinized Swallow. "Does he come from a good family?"

"They own their own water buffalo," Swallow said. Only a prosperous family could afford the upkeep of one of them. "He knows a lot of songs and can really sing well." She caught herself and shrugged. "Not that I really care," she added lamely.

"Well, Lily's been there as your chaperone, so I guess it's all right." Mother smiled up at the homely mud nest clinging to the eastern side of their house. "I guess the nest is working. When swallows build their nest on a house, it's a sure sign that a girl in that house is going to become a bride."

"But I don't live here anymore," Swallow argued. "So if any girl's getting married here, it's Lily."

"I'm never getting married," Lily said stubbornly.

"You might sleep in the girls' house, Swallow," Mother said, "but you work here; you eat here. And by my book, that means you live here too."

"You're just going to encourage the pests to come back," Swallow said. "And then they'll attack us again."

Lily could remember having to shield her head with a basket while the parents had been raising their brood.

"But they also eat bugs, so they keep the mosquitoes down." Mother defended her favorite birds. "And they have pretty wings that curve like Swallow's hair." Lily's own hair had been pulled into two stubby pigtails, but the older girls in the house had helped Swallow shape her braids into a lovely design that was pinned together on the sides of her head.

Lily scowled up at the nest. "I still ought to get a stick and knock it down."

Mother nudged her. "Don't you want to be an aunt? Swallows also are a sign there'll be plenty of children."

"Who wants a lot of snotty brats around?" Lily demanded.

"Well, they also bring good luck," Mother sighed. "And we haven't had much of that lately."

Lily slumped against the wall. "That's true enough."

As they finished their meal, Mother asked, "Swallow, have you learned this one yet?" She began to hum a tune.

"The girls taught me that one," Swallow said.

In the girls' house, the older girls taught the newcomers how to read and write, but Lily loved all the stories and songs that Swallow had also learned. She couldn't wait until she was old enough to go there.

In the meantime, Swallow had borrowed one of the books, a collection of legends, from the girls' house and brought it home. Mother, who had learned to read in her former clan's girls' house, read a chapter out loud to her every night. Sometimes, if Swallow had time, she even took a turn.

Closing her eyes, Lily leaned contentedly against a wall and listened to her mother and sister harmonize, letting their words flow into her mind.

They sang about the Weaving Maid, who spun her own silk just like they did. But unlike them, she also wove it into such fine cloth that all the robes in Heaven were made from it. Then she met a cowboy and fell in such a deep love that she could only think of him. The neglected silkworms died, and her loom gathered dust. When Heaven found there was no more silk for new clothing, it separated them with the Milky Way so that they could no longer get together.

However, the magpies felt so sorry for the Weaving Maid and the Cowboy that once every year, they swarmed together, overlapping their wings and bodies to form a living bridge. And the Weaving Maid would cross, trying to step lightly so she would not hurt her friends, feeling the trembling, feathery bodies beneath her feet.

The song was over all too soon.

"I can't wait until I get to go to the girls' house," Lily sighed.

Mother put an arm around her. "Are you so eager to leave me?"

"Well, no," Lily said, fumbling for an answer. "It's just that it sounds like so much fun."

Both her mother and sister broke into a laugh. "It's not all fun," Swallow said. "There are all sorts of rules, like keeping yourself and your space clean. When you break them, you have to pay a fine."

Lily, who was always a little messy, was suddenly worried. "How much of a fine?"

Mother tugged at one of her pigtails. "Small ones. And it all goes into a kitty. Before the girls are about to get married, the money pays for a nice banquet." She swung the pigtail back and forth playfully. "My group was so bad at the rules that later we could afford not only a banquet but a blind singer. A famous one."

Lily wrinkled her forehead in puzzlement. "What's so good about a blind singer?"

"They're trained from childhood to entertain," Mother said.

"So," Lily said thoughtfully, "the messier I am, the better the fun at the end."

Swallow shook her head. "You're so sloppy that you'll

be able to hire a whole opera troupe."

Lily grinned at the possibility, but between all the work, the warm sun, and the full stomach, Lily could not help yawning. From the corner of her eye she saw that her sister's and mother's mouths were also open. They glanced at one another, and then all of them began laughing.

"When it comes to keeping you up, silkworms are worse than any baby." Mother smiled. She arched, pressing a hand against the small of her back to ease the ache there.

"Not as bad as Lily," Swallow said. "She cried all night and all day."

"I never." Lily lifted her head indignantly. "Mother said I was the best baby."

"She just didn't want to hurt your feelings and have you start bawling again," Swallow teased.

Suddenly her sister and mother stopped smiling, though. Lily saw the shadows in the dirt and turned.

It was Uncle Prosperity, whose slight stoop made him lean his head out like a vulture. With him was Father.

"I'm back," Father said.

CHAPTER | 4

Lily

Lily didn't know whether to be happy or scared. Father stood, barefoot, his exposed ankles almost as dark as the dirt he stood on. The crown of his head was shaggy and the hair at the back of his head woven so sloppily that it was a tangled black mass. His eyes were rimmed in red, and his nose was running. He stank, as if he had been wallowing with pigs.

"Are you all right?" Lily asked, starting to get up.

Mother caught her shoulder and forced her back down. "We don't have any money."

Father drew his sleeve across his face. "What kind of greeting is that?"

"What did you expect?" Swallow asked. Her face and tone were as hostile as Mother's. "The only time you come home is when you run out of cash."

"Now, now." Uncle Prosperity patted the air as if it were dough he was shaping. "He's done with the Mud."

Uncle Prosperity wore a robe and vest despite the heat, so his face was flushed and sweaty right down to his double chins. He'd bought a scholarship, which entitled him to certain official perks and tax exemptions—and, he assumed, the right to act like a busybody. He was always finding immorality everywhere, citing the Confucian Code for support, and generally making everyone's life miserable. If he had not been the richest man in the clan, folk would have chucked him into the nearest stream.

Father's head bobbed up and down eagerly. "Yes, yes." As he started to shamble forward, Mother slid backward across the dirt, drawing Lily and Swallow with her. When he saw that, he stopped, his face working in pain as if someone had kicked him in the belly. "I've changed."

Mother's tense fingers dug into Lily's shoulder. "You've said that before."

"But I mean it this time," Father said. "I haven't had any Mud in months. I'm getting stronger every week. Then I'll work day and night. I'll make things just like they used to be. You wait and see." Over the years, Father had gradually sold everything. Even though they stayed in the same house and worked the same fields, they were now tenants.

Lily thought of her father the way he had been, always with a kind word, someone everyone liked. It seemed like a distant, golden age. "Really?" she asked wistfully.

"Don't bother hoping," Swallow said angrily to her sister. "He'll just disappoint you."

"I swear that I've changed," Father said. Tears ran down his cheeks, striping the dirt on his face.

Uncle Prosperity waddled up to them. "A married woman shouldn't be handling the silkworms so much." The clan believed that a married woman might damage the silkworms at certain stages of their lives.

Mother stiffened. "I've never had any complaints about my silk."

"Even so," Uncle Prosperity said quietly, "it's not right." He clapped a hand on Father's shoulder. "Your husband admits he did wrong. So should you." His tone made it clear it was a command, not a request.

Next to Lily, Swallow was shivering with rage. Suddenly, she stooped, and her groping hand found a rock, and she lifted it menacingly over her head. "Go away!"

Uncle Prosperity jabbed a finger at Swallow. "How dare you!" He twisted his head to glare at Mother. "See how wild the girls are growing? They need a man about the house."

Swallow snorted. "You can't call this . . . this thing a man."

"Please," her father said. His knees buckled suddenly, and he sagged to the ground like a broken puppet. "I have no place to go."

Mother pressed her lips tightly together for a moment and then patted Swallow. "Put down the rock."

"But—," Swallow tried to protest.

"He's still your father," Mother said. She rose, shoving Lily into Swallow's arms, and then approached their father cautiously as if he were a dangerous animal.

He watched her with wild, red-edged eyes. "I missed you. I missed all of you."

Without turning around, Mother said to Lily and Swallow, "Girls, feed the silkworms."

Father tilted back his head as if he were noticing the silkworm shed for the first time. "Yes, it's that time of year again, isn't it?"

CHAPTER | 5

Swallow

It was just like Father to ignore the frenzy with the silkworms that was taking place all over the Three Districts. Seeing him standing there with that sloppy grin on his face brought back all the old nightmares.

Swallow had been small when the Demon Mud had first sunk its claws into Father. He had left and come back on several occasions, each time repeating the same pattern with his family of tearful promises followed by arguments, shouting, temper tantrums, and eventually the beatings. Mercifully, Lily had been too small to remember the last time he had left, but now the monster was back.

With a bump of her hip, Swallow nudged her little sister toward her basket, and when they had each picked theirs up, they entered the house. As they crossed the threshold, the coolness wrapped itself like a soothing cloth around them. It was dim inside the living room, with the one tiny window hardly shedding any light. There was very little furniture for people: a table and some bamboo stools, along with the boards and trestles that were stacked in one corner and became a bed at night.

Like their lives, the rest of the space was devoted to the silkworms. The cone-shaped spinning racks were stacked one on top of another in columns that rose to the ceiling, empty circular trays and baskets, along with baskets of leaves from previous harvests.

Swallow set down her basket of leaves they had just picked. Though they felt dry, they had to let them air to make sure the dew was all gone.

"Don't let Father fool you," she warned. "You can't trust him."

"He seems nice," Lily said stubbornly as she placed her basket beside Swallow's.

"For now." Swallow pressed her lips together into a thin line. "You were too small to remember when he came home the last time. He acted so repentant. Got very pious too. You'd have thought the Buddha and the saints were ready to come down from Heaven and testify that he was their best friend. And I wanted so hard to believe that he had changed—just like you're doing now. But then the tiger came out, and he began to . . . to beat us."

Lily looked stubborn. "I don't believe you."

"Don't or won't?" Swallow asked, exasperated.

Arguing wasn't getting the silkworms fed, so she began to inspect the leaves in the other baskets from previous harvests, selecting two of them, and they opened the door and entered the second room, where the silkworms lived. Because the tiny window was shuttered, the room was as dark and dry as the inside of a stove—the silkworms liked it that way. Broad circular trays set into bamboo frames rose from floor to ceiling on either side, leaving only a narrow aisle between the two rows. A charcoal brazier was burning at the end, heating the air for the newly hatched silkworms.

Next to it were several boards laid over trestles. Because the silkworms needed to be fed eight times through the day and evening, they took turns sleeping there.

A solitary silkworm enjoying its meal would not make enough noise to hear, but a group of silkworms munching away produced a sound like a monsoon rain pounding the dirt. Even so, Swallow and Lily were usually so exhausted they were able to sleep.

"We're back. Did you miss us?" Lily called softly to the wriggling silkworms.

Even though it was hard to believe the diners could hear anything, the girls always spoke in low, gentle voices, because loud noises upset the silkworms. But then most everything bothered the insects. Like finicky maiden aunts, their charges had to be protected against too much light, cold, heat, moistness, and bad smells as well. If Lily and Swallow didn't guard them, none of them would ever grow up big and healthy.

"They're bugs," Swallow said in a hushed voice as she rolled a leaf into a cylinder. With a knife, she cut it in two, arranging the halves next to one another before she quickly shredded them. "They don't understand you."

"How do you know?" Lily said, beginning to cut up the leaves with a second knife. "They might."

Even though Swallow knew it was silly, she didn't want even her attitude to disturb the silkworms, so she shoved the argument from her mind and tried to think calm, peaceful thoughts instead.

When they had enough pieces, Lily pulled out the tray. The new, pale silkworms were no bigger than ants as they wriggled about among the remnants of their previous meal. Wherever they crawled, they left tiny strands of silk behind them on old leaf fragments, so the tray looked as if it held the web of a crazy spider.

Swallow began to sprinkle the new leaf bits onto the tray evenly. "They're not pets." Immediately, the leaves began to stir as the worms climbed to the surface to snack.

"I know," Lily said sadly, "but that doesn't mean we can't keep them happy until the day we kill them. It works, doesn't it? Nobody gets cocoons as big and fine as ours."

"That's because we take care of them, not because we chatter at them like parrots," Swallow said, dusting the last leafy morsels from her palm onto the tray.

As Lily took in the constantly shifting patterns, her imagination took flight again. "So maybe they can't talk. Maybe they're trying to write a message to us." She pointed at the wriggling worms. "Don't they look like they're forming the strokes of words?" She spread her hands. "The tray's like a page in a book." Since Lily had not learned how to read yet—that would happen when she was old enough to move to the girls' house, where the older girls would teach her—books had always seemed half magical, so she would not have been surprised if the worms really could do that.

"So worms have their own secret language?" Swallow asked sarcastically. "Does that make you the Scholar of Worms?"

Lily watched the squirming worms change their positions as if they were forming the next lesson. "It's the language of silk."

"We shouldn't be talking so much anyway. The noise might put them off," Swallow scolded, and, putting her hands on the tray Lily was holding, shoved it back onto the rack.

When they had cut up more leaves, this time Swallow was the one who dragged the rack out and Lily who fed them. Taking turns sliding out the trays and feeding the occupants, they repeated the process with the other trays.

By the time they were done, Lily was grateful to escape the hot, smoky air. The trouble was that they could hear their mother still arguing with Father and Uncle

Prosperity, but the din created by the hungry silkworms made it impossible to hear their exact words.

When Mother saw them peeking from inside, she beckoned them to come back outside.

Father beamed at them. "Isn't it wonderful? We're going to be a family again."

Swallow shot a look of betrayal at their mother. Mother was biting her lip as if she were already having second thoughts.

"It's just day by day," Mother insisted. "One slip and he's gone."

Uncle Prosperity clasped his hands behind his back, satisfied. "Agreed."

Father spread out his arms. "How about a hug?"

The hostile Swallow backed up a step. Even Lily hesitated because of the smell.

Father waved his outstretched arms like wings. "Come on, girls," he coaxed nervously.

Lily might have gone, but Swallow wrapped her arms around her sister and held her tightly. And Lily was almost glad of the excuse.

Standing with his arms out, Father looked like an awkward bird. "I said give me a hug." Anxiety was sliding into fear. And with Father it was only a short step from fear to anger.

Mother cleared her throat. "Maybe you should wash up first."

Father glanced down at himself and then straightened.

"Yes, you're right." He gave them a timid smile. "I don't blame you, girls. I barely recognize myself."

"Get some water for your father so he can wash up," Mother ordered, her face a mask.

They went back into the house and into the kitchen.

"I think Father means it this time," Lily said, hoping to dispel some of her sister's doubts.

"Right now," Swallow said as she entered the kitchen. "Wait until the Mud starts calling to him."

"I don't think it helps when you scold him, you know," Lily said as she lifted the lid from the large jar where they stored water. "If you did that to me, I'd want to . . . to . . ."

"Run away?" Swallow used a dipper to fill a big bowl. "He's very good at making people think it's their fault that he uses Mud. But he does it because he wants to." Slinging a clean cloth across her shoulder to use as a towel, she picked up the bowl. "You keep away from him. If he senses any softness, he'll use it for his own ends."

Despite Swallow's instructions, Lily couldn't help watching from the doorway of their house. By then, Uncle Prosperity had gone, his duty done.

When Father stripped off his ragged shirt, she gave a little cry of distress. His rib bones stuck out like a series of ugly ridges, and his arms were like sticks.

Swallow shot her a dirty look and jerked her head for Lily to leave, but Lily felt as if her feet were glued to the spot. Father cleaned the dirt from his face and hands and then washed his torso. When he picked up his shirt again, he shook his head. "Was I really wearing this mess?"

"I think you still have a spare change of clothes," Mother said.

Father laughed and indicated the rope that held the pants around his emaciated waist. "They'd never fit. I'll borrow something from the neighbors." He ran a hand along the hair fringing his skull. "I have to ask someone to loan me a razor anyway . . . unless . . . ?"

Mother shook her head. "I don't keep razors in the house after that other time."

Father beat a fist against his temple. "That was so stupid. I'm sorry. I should never have threatened you."

"No, you shouldn't have," Swallow said.

Father rounded on his heel. "It's never, never going to happen again. I swear."

Bare-chested, he went out shortly after that. They could hear his voice, warm and friendly, as he greeted some passing neighbors, but they were cool toward him. No surprise there. He'd borrowed and stolen from almost everyone in the clan.

But Father was the head of the household, and tradition and custom insisted he had a right to be here. In its own way, the clan was locked into a pattern of actions as rigidly as the silkworms.

But not me. He's never going to fool me again, Swallow thought bitterly.

CHAPTER | 6

Lily

There was no sign of Father when they went back outside to feed the fish with the waste the silkworms had left on the old trays. When the trays had been cleaned and left out to dry, they chopped up the mulberry leaves. Silkworms wanted their homes clean and tidy and their meals always the same and always perfect.

Lily would be glad when the silkworms grew, because the leaves wouldn't have to be quite so fine as now. In the final stage before the worms spun their cocoons, the girls could just feed them the whole leaves.

Father came back around dinnertime, sauntering into the house in new clothes, his chin and the crown of his head freshly shaved and his hair trimmed and combed. Someone had even braided his queue properly. She would not have recognized him now as the disheveled beggar from the courtyard.

"What happened to you?" Lily asked.

Father rubbed the newly trimmed skin. "I met Aunt Piety. She used to take care of me when I was a boy." Aunt Piety was an elderly relative three houses over, and the clan said she didn't have a mean bone in her body.

When he had sat down, Swallow and Mother began to serve their simple meal of rice and vegetables. Lily could not resist hovering at his elbow. "Father, where did you go while you were away?"

Father pushed out his lips and made a puffing noise. "Oh, all over. I've been to Canton." He leaned in close to her. "I've even been so close to a foreigner that I could touch him."

"I saw one of their ships today," Lily declared proudly.

"No, you don't say," Father said. He acted as if the sighting were significant enough to be recorded in the clan gazette, which chronicled centuries of major events.

Despite Swallow's warning looks, Lily felt as easy with Father as if he had never left and began chatting with him. Mother, however, was still cautious, and Swallow openly antagonistic. And that made Father nervous.

All through dinner, Father kept trying to reassure himself and them by asking them over and over, "Isn't this nice?"

And when dinner was done, he placed his palms humbly on the table. "This is all I deserve to sleep on tonight."

"No," Mother said, "you use the bedroom. I'll sleep with Lily in the silkworm room." Because the silkworms had to be fed at steady intervals through the night, it was easier to sleep on a bed made out of boards there. "What would people say if they knew you were sleeping out here?"

Father, though, shook his head, the newly shaved skin gleaming in the candlelight. "They'd say that the table was good enough for the likes of me."

He's really sorry for what he did, Lily thought happily. She was puzzled by the weary look that Mother and Swallow exchanged.

The kind, friendly man next to her on the bench was so unlike the monster that Swallow had described. "Do you want to play a game?" she asked Father.

"I'd love to play a game," he assured her eagerly.

"Do you know how to play cat's cradle?" she asked.

"Do I know cat's cradle?" Father grinned. "You're looking at the champion of the Three Districts."

Lily jumped up. "We don't have string, but we've got some cord."

"Cord's a little thick, but that will be the challenge," Father said agreeably. His hands were shaking, though, so Lily decided that she would keep the patterns simple.

Swallow tried to pull her back. "Hey, it's our turn to clean up the dinner things."

"That's all right. I'll do it," Mother said, and stood up. "You should head back to the girls' house. I know you've got a thousand things to do."

CHAPTER | 7

Swallow

Swallow was too surprised to resist as her Mother tugged her to her feet and then dragged her toward the door.

"You're already at the girls' house? My daughter's grown up so fast," Father said. "And I missed it." He wiped a hand across his eyes, and when he lifted it away, his fingers were glistening with tears. "I can't tell you how glad I am to be back home."

Swallow dimly remembered the good old days before the Demon Mud had claimed him—of sitting by the pond in the warm twilight and watching the sun set, of him lifting her up so high that she felt taller than the mulberry trees. Suddenly Swallow yearned as fiercely as Lily to believe that he had changed, had returned to the father he had been.

No, she reminded herself, *you've seen the penitent before. He won't be able to keep it up. He's just a husk of what he was, telling you what you want to hear without meaning any of it. It won't be long before the shouting and the beatings start all over. And then the tearful apologies and honeyed words will follow. Over and over, it will go on until he deserts us again.*

Her confusion only added to her misery as her mother tugged her into the lane and then shut the door.

Swallow pulled free from her mother. "Why did you leave Lily alone with him?"

"She's safe enough for now," Mother said.

"But—," Swallow began to protest.

Mother gave a sad little shake of her head. "He's too busy playing the reformed sinner, so he'll behave for a while."

"If only it would last." Outside, Swallow drew a deep breath, but the air was so humid that it felt as if she were choking on a damp cloth. Cloud the pig grunted to her from his pen where he spent the night. "Why did you agree to let him come home?"

"Because he's my husband and the father of my children," Mother said simply.

Swallow sighed, because she could hear generations of ghosts from more than four thousand years whispering the same thing to her: that even if he was a bully, a thief, and a liar, he was also her father.

She glanced behind her at the house. "Lily's too young to remember his last visit."

"She's as hopeful now as you were back then," Mother said.

"That made it all the more confusing and scary when he got mad and started to hit us." Swallow took a deep breath and it let out raggedly. "And then . . . and then it hurt so much when he left anyway."

"Which is why we have to be strong for Lily's sake when he does," Mother said.

Overhead, the clouds edged the night sky. The monsoon rains would begin again. For now, though, the stars wheeled across the blackness.

Swallow's eyes searched for, and found, the bright star of the Weaving Maid. "Do you ever feel like running away from all this, going some place he can't follow—like up there?"

Her mother followed Swallow's gaze. "But even the Weaving Maid had to follow orders as dumb as Uncle Prosperity's."

Shining near the Weaving Maid, but more dimly, were her sisters. Smaller, younger, weaker, more vulnerable. Like Lily.

Whatever else happened to her and Mother, she would protect Lily at least.

"There has to be a way," Swallow insisted.

Her mother sighed. "It's good to be young and so hopeful." She put a hand on Swallow's arm and gave her a slight push. "Well, you won't solve everything overnight."

And so Swallow wound up leaving her mother gazing up at the sky and the Weaving Maid.

She made her way past the silent farmhouses and

mulberry groves, the water in the ponds shimmering beneath the moon, her feet following the path on their own while her mind went over the lyrics of Happy's song.

Until the moment that Father had appeared, she had been dreading this night. Now she wasn't sure which was the worse evil: home with Father or the girls' house, where humiliation waited for her.

The girls' house was lit up, as she knew it would be, and everyone was a frenetic whirlwind inside.

As soon as Swallow entered, Aster said, "You're late." She was the oldest girl in the house and had vowed never to marry. For such a solidly built girl, she moved with quick, abrupt motions like a fussy hen. "You should have been back for auditions an hour ago."

Swallow had neither the energy nor the stamina to tell Aster about her father. There would be expressions of horror from her housemates and a recounting of his past transgressions. The last thing she wanted was to sift through those awful memories.

She wanted to stop thinking about him for a little while. "I'm sorry. I had chores to handle."

"You have duties here," Aster said pointedly. "And you kept Big Sister waiting."

Big Sister was a former inhabitant of the house, Narcissus Moon, who had left to work as a seamstress at a Canton theater and had wound up marrying the owner. Though this was the first time that Swallow had met her, she had heard all about her.

In her thirties, Big Sister was a tiny woman with more makeup than Swallow had ever seen on a woman before, and though she was dressed in a blouse and trousers, they were of satin with silk piping on the cuffs. At Aster's request, she was helping them plan the entertainment for the Seven Seven.

Big Sister clapped her hands together. "All right, this is what I've come up with. First, you're going to dance for the audience." She named a folk dance that all the girls had learned as children. "And then you're going to form a tableau."

"A what?" one of the girls asked.

"You strike a pose and hold it while the songs go on," Big Sister explained. "So let's begin the audition. Form a line now."

There were ten girls in the house at the moment, including Swallow, and they arranged themselves in one row.

"All right. A-a-and dance." As she begun to hum the traditional tune, Swallow and the others started forward. However, in the small space they bumped into furniture and one another.

"Stop, stop." Big Sister clamped a hand over her eyes as she lowered her head as if in pain. "You're all as raw as turnips." She raised her head resignedly. "Well, I'll do what I can in one night." Big Sister had arranged to stay overnight before she returned to her husband and the theater. "First of all, goddesses walk daintily. They don't look like they're striding over cow patties."

Ignoring the giggles, Big Sister threw back her head with a spine straight as a staff and began to walk in short steps, looking almost as if she were floating.

Swallow began to clap in admiration, and her housemates joined in. "Oh, you should be up on the stage."

"Yes," Aster agreed. "It's a shame it's against the law."

Big Sister shrugged. "It's some fussy old bureaucrats who made that rule. They say actresses corrupt the public morals."

"You know a lot about the theater," Swallow observed.

Big Sister raised an eyebrow ironically. "For a seamstress? That's my official title, but I do a lot more at the theater."

"Then you should get the credit," Aster said sympathetically.

Big Sister laughed cheerfully. "Yes, I should, but what other job would let me boss so many men around?"

"Even your husband?" Aster teased.

"Especially him," Big Sister grinned. "Because when he listens to my suggestions, he makes money."

Swallow asked a question that had been bothering her. "Isn't what we're planning to do illegal too?"

Big Sister dismissed her worries with a wave of the hand. "That's only if you act on the stage. Women do traditional folk dances for audiences all the time. And afterward you're going to stand there in a tableau. Think of yourselves as just part of the stage. But enough talk." She nodded at Swallow. "You. You try walking for me."

Self-consciously, Swallow tried to copy what she had seen.

"Not bad," Big Sister grudged. "At least you're trying." She pressed one hand against the small of Swallow's back and the other against her stomach. "Let's start with something basic like posture."

When Big Sister shoved hard from front and back against Swallow, a little puff of air escaped from Swallow's mouth as she raised her head and stood up straighter.

"That's better," Big Sister said. She kept both hands pressing Swallow as they took several paces together. "Now try to remember to keep your back straight and head up when you dance. And remember, you're a goddess."

Trying not to slouch, Swallow minced across the floor, with the result that Big Sister covered her face a second time. "Swallow, what do you think the myth of the Weaving Maid is about?"

Swallow was offended she was being asked such an obvious question. "It's about love, of course."

Big Sister folded her arms across her stomach. "Think for a moment. First she loses her sisters. Then she loses the man she loves." When Swallow looked blank, Big Sister explained, "Whatever she loves, she loses."

"But that's so sad," Swallow objected.

"That's what it's about, though," Big Sister insisted. "Now, this is what you're doing." She rolled her eyes like a lost buffalo calf. "When you want to be doing this." She began to walk timidly, her face showing wonder and anxiety at the same time.

Then Big Sister had each of the others try walking like a goddess. When the last had tried to stroll divinely across the floor, Big Sister announced, "Thank you all for putting up with my scolding. There are plenty of actors who would have thrown tantrums over what I said to you. I wish I could select you all, but I only need seven." She motioned to six other girls and then at Swallow. "And you are our Weaving Maid."

"Me?" Swallow asked, stunned.

"I borrowed the costumes from the theater, so we can't make any alterations," Big Sister said pragmatically. "And you're the only one who will fit her outfit."

Aster and the chosen five held their robes up against themselves, while the other three who hadn't been selected hid their disappointment and admired the outfits.

Big Sister dipped her hands into the trunk and pulled out a small package wrapped in cloth. "Now, this costume is for an empress in an opera, so it should be suitable for the Weaving Maid. Swallow, you get to wear this master-piece."

With a flourish, she removed the cloth, revealing an elaborate headdress of wire and foil that glittered in the candlelight, and the metallic butterflies and flowers shivered with the slightest movement.

There was a collective "ah" from the other housemates.

Big Sister raised the headdress, and Swallow thoughtfully crouched so Big Sister could put it on her.

Big Sister made some adjustments and stepped back. "There. It fits like it was made for you."

"Look, look," Aster said. And when Swallow just stood there self-consciously, Aster grabbed her hand and led her over to the mirror.

"I'm turning into a bug," she giggled. "Look at those antennae."

"*Gold* antennae," Big Sister corrected.

And even if she knew the gold was just fake foil wrapped around metal, Swallow could not help admiring how it glittered in the candlelight.

"And this," Big Sister said, reaching into the basket, "is your robe." She lifted out the costume. The silk was a reddish purple that reminded Swallow of a ripening plum. Gold embroidered phoenixes danced above clouds, and the long delicate sleeves swayed like colorful waterfalls.

Swallow sucked in her breath. "It's beautiful."

She'd never had anything this fine. None of them had. And it was hers. At least for a little while. Timidly, she reached out a hand and touched a sleeve, petting it like a cat. As her hand luxuriated in the silk, she thought of Lily, wishing her little sister could be here now.

Aster took something else from the basket. "There are shoes to match." She pointed at the embroidery on the toes, which repeated the phoenix motif from the robe.

Swallow's excitement carried her through the rest of

the rehearsal as the select seven repeated the dance again and then took the poses and places that Big Sister showed them.

After an hour, jaws began cracking open in huge yawns. Each girl had put in a full day working at her home, and now they were forcing themselves through strenuous exercise—not only the dance but the tableau as well, for Big Sister hadn't chosen the easiest postures to hold for a long time.

Finally, Big Sister relented. "Well, this will have to do. Let's go to bed."

Swallow's excitement made her forget how tired she was. "Could we rehearse some more, Big Sister?" Some of her housemates groaned at that prospect.

Big Sister shook her head. "When you're this tired, you're liable to just stumble from one mistake to another instead of learning anything more."

"I . . . I don't want to stumble around at the performance," Swallow said. "Folks will say we might as well have dressed up a water buffalo." She glanced at the six sisters, and this time each of them nodded. Fear of humiliation was a strong motivator. Swallow turned back to Big Sister. "And anyway, would the Weaving Maid and her sisters quit now?"

Big Sister smiled approvingly. "I like your attitude. All right, another hour."

CHAPTER | 8

8th day of the 6th (intercalary) month of the era Way of Honor

August 2, 1835

Swallow

Though it was still cloudy the next morning, it hadn't rained after all. Swallow yawned all the way over to her house. As exhausted as she was, she'd been too thrilled to sleep.

Head up, back straight, she pranced in small dainty steps along the path. Mist was rising from the fishponds, so that she felt as if she were dancing through the clouds rather than along a dirt track. She couldn't remember when she'd had this much fun.

Her exhilaration lasted until she saw her home. Suddenly the spring left her legs, and she slogged on to the doorway.

Father was still on the table snoring, while Lily squatted, watching him curiously as if he were an exotic bird that had flown into the house. As he mumbled and smacked his lips, Lily made a shushing motion to Swallow. "He's like a big silkworm."

"Except we'll only get misery from him," Swallow said sourly, "not silk."

Suddenly Father gave a twitch, drawing up his knees against his chest.

Lily jumped to her feet. "What's wrong with him?"

His eyes shot open, but he seemed to be staring right through her at something else, something horrible and monstrous that made his eyebrows rise in terror.

Too scared to move, Lily stayed where she was, her voice rising louder and louder as she demanded to know what was happening.

"It's all right. Everything will be okay," Swallow assured her hastily as she ran into the kitchen.

Mother was at the stove making porridge from last night's rice. She whirled around. "Father?"

"Yes." Swallow snatched up an empty bucket and ran back outside.

Sweat beaded Father's forehead as he sat up. She barely got the bowl in front of him before he began to vomit, his body heaving long after he had emptied his stomach.

"Take care of Lily, Swallow," Mother said. She had a wet cloth in her hand. "Can you two girls handle everything alone? I'll have to nurse Father today."

"Yes." Swallow set the bowl down and then, wrapping

an arm around her little sister's shoulders, tried to pull her outside.

Lily, though, was rooted to the spot as she gazed at him. "Is Father going to die?" she asked in a small, worried voice.

"No, he's just very, very sick," Swallow said, giving her a little reassuring hug before she practically carried her into the kitchen.

In silence, they ate a quick breakfast of hot rice porridge with slices of Mother's pickled ginger. Then they cleaned up the kitchen before they went back outside.

Swallow kept a tight hold of her sister's hand, tugging as Lily dragged her feet.

"Will Father be all right?" Lily asked, worried.

"Of course," Swallow said, and thought to herself, *But will we?*

CHAPTER | 9

Swallow

She tried to keep Lily too occupied with work to brood very long about Father, but even then her little sister kept going back to check on him. And when it came time to pick the leaves, Lily didn't want to go that far away. "What if something happens to Father while I'm gone?"

Lily was as trusting and fragile as a baby chick, and Swallow just wanted to wrap her arms around her and never let her go. She judged that Mother was right: Father was in his penitent stage, so it was safe to leave Lily with him for now. "Then you stay and help Mother take care of him," Swallow said. "I'll get the leaves myself." It would mean two trips, but it was the next best thing she could do for her sister.

However, as Swallow walked with her basket along

one of the paths, folk peered at her from among the trees or looked up from the fishponds they were tending. Apparently word had spread that her father had come back, reminding everyone of the shame he had brought not only to his family but to the entire clan.

Some gave sympathetic nods to her, but others regarded her suspiciously. A cousin even spoke in a voice Swallow was meant to hear. "It won't take long for the rot to spread to the next crop," she said.

Swallow rounded on her heel. "Were you talking to me?"

The woman tapped a brown-edged leaf. "I was just talking about this mulberry tree."

From her companion's malicious laugh, though, Swallow was sure they were speaking about her. Their father's return had reminded the clan of his sins, and many would believe that he would pass on his tainted blood to his daughters. And yet, if the family had turned him away, they would be criticized instead. In the eyes of the clan, the family could do nothing right.

After that encounter, when she saw other people whispering, she was sure they were gossiping not only about him but about his children as well. Cheeks burning, she knew it would not be long before the notoriety spread to the surrounding villages.

She had barely gotten to the trees when she heard Happy singing. *He'll find out about me soon enough*, she thought to herself, *and I couldn't bear to see his face.*

So she stayed right where she was, trying to avoid the time when he found out about her father. She could bear the clan turning against her, but not him.

When he switched to a sad, plaintive song, the tears rolled down her cheeks, but she went on working.

"Hey!" the boy called. "Hey!"

But she ignored him.

She was still crying long after he had stopped shouting.

CHAPTER | 10

Swallow

Swallow made another round-trip to harvest leaves, enduring all the smirks and even hostile looks twice. By the time she returned the second time, Father had shuffled outside to a bench with Lily's help.

The two of them were sitting, their faces turned up like flowers drinking in the sunlight.

Without turning her head, Lily asked, "How are you feeling now, Father?"

Stroking her hair, Father said, "I'm even better now that I'm with my girls." He looked up when he saw Swallow's shadow and pursed his lips. "It's easy to apologize and make promises. Words are cheap. I'll show all of you how much you mean to me as soon as I'm strong enough."

This selfish man was destroying their lives, but he

didn't care. Anger choked Swallow, so she turned her back, wanting to avoid the sight of the liar. "Lily, we've got to feed the silkworms."

"I don't want to," Lily said stubbornly.

"Help your sister like a good girl," Father said. "I'll be fine for a while. I'm just going to nap."

Through the rest of the day, Lily kept checking on Father, fretting and fussing over him like a mother bird with her chick.

Lily was so full of love. But that would only make it more painful when Father showed her his heels. Those were the times that Swallow wanted to hug her. But those were also the times when she wanted to scold her little sister for not listening to Swallow's warnings.

Mother, at least, seemed to understand what was running through Swallow's mind. As soon as their simple dinner was done, Mother began to gather up the bowls. "I'll clean up, Swallow. I know you have a lot to do still, so go back to the girls' house."

Relieved, Swallow didn't try to argue. "Good-bye, Lily."

Lily, though, was engrossed in a game of cat's cradle with Father, her fingers entangled in a pattern. It was Father who waved. "Good-bye."

Too exhausted to be angry, Swallow left, walking along the paths with others returning to their homes with dirt-smudged faces and tools over their shoulders. At first, her head swiveled this way and that to see who was gossiping about her.

When she caught someone smirking, she glared at them until they dropped their eyes. And when she got back to the girls' house, there was a full-blown row going on.

"I am not going home," Aster was saying to her mother.

"You can't stay here with that girl," her mother started to argue, but she fell silent when she saw Swallow coming toward them.

"Aster, I don't want my family to cause any more trouble," Swallow said. "Maybe you should leave for a while."

Aster bore in on her mother. "You've known Swallow all her life. Has she ever done anything wrong?"

"Well . . . no," her mother admitted reluctantly.

"But there's always the possibility," Swallow said ironically, "because I have my father's blood."

Aster whirled around. "I've lived with you, Swallow. I know what you're like. You may be inconsiderate and noisy—oh, and you have the annoying habit of smacking your lips sometimes when you sleep—but you're not some crazy addict like your father."

Swallow had endured all that day's hostile looks and insults without crying, but this kindness brought tears to her eyes. "Thank you."

Ashamed, Aster's mother shifted her feet. "Humph, well, you can stay for now, Aster." She glanced at Swallow. "But I'll be keeping an eye on you."

Aster hooked her arm through Swallow's. "How was your day? No, don't tell me. I think I know what it was like. Just come inside."

The other girls were there, and as soon as Swallow stepped through the door, one of them brought her a basin of water and a towel to wash. As soon as she was done cleaning up, another brought her a cup of tea and then whisked her over to the table.

"But it's my turn to clean the house," Swallow protested.

Aster clamped both hands on her shoulders and held her down on the bench. "Not tonight."

Swallow was a little dazed. "You're making me feel like a queen."

Aster got the broom and raised it in salute. "No, you're our Weaving Maid, and we're your loyal sisters."

Yes, Swallow decided, *you're all my sisters—in spirit if not in blood.*

And she forgot her father and the ugly looks thrown at her by the clan and instead let herself snuggle in the warmth and shelter of their sisterhood.

After the floor had been swept and the dining table shoved against one wall, the mood carried over into the rehearsal with plenty of smiles and laughter.

CHAPTER | 11

Lily

That evening when Swallow had left and Father had said good-bye to her, she was rude and did not answer. He pretended to concentrate on the game of cat's cradle they were playing, but she heard his soft sigh.

Lily knew that once her sister's mind was set on something, no amount of arguing would change it. She could only hope that as time went on, Swallow might soften a little, but it wasn't going to happen immediately.

It wasn't long after Mother had gone into the silkworms' room that Father hopelessly fumbled his turn. The string wound up as tangled as Lily's hair in the morning. He grinned weakly as he pulled the mess from his fingers. "I guess I'm getting tired."

Lily hunted for something to make him feel better.

Swallow and Mother always looked so peaceful when they were reading out loud to her. So maybe it would work with Father. "I know what will make you smile," she said, and got the precious book. "Let's read one of the old legends."

He hesitated at first but took it. "Legends? Sure, why not?"

Lily snuggled against him as he opened the book and began to tell her a story. It was a good one about Yi the Archer, but there was something odd about it.

"How can you read upside down?" she asked.

Father tried to bluff. "When you get real good at reading, you can do it either way," he said, but he righted the book and went on.

When he was finished, he closed the book. "How did you like it?"

"It was okay," she said, scratching her head uncomfortably, "only . . ."

Now it was his turn to look uneasy. "Only what?"

"The words sounded like you, not the book," Lily said, trying to explain her thoughts. "It wasn't the same . . . the same . . ."

"Style?" Embarrassed, he set the book on the table. "There's no fooling you. When I was a boy, I went straight to work in the groves and ponds. And the mulberries and fish don't teach you to read like the girls' house does."

Lily tried to make him feel better. "I liked your story, though."

"Better than the other ones in the book?" he asked. When she didn't answer right away, he patted her on the arm. "Never mind. I'm just an ignorant clod of dirt and always will be. Not like you girls." He turned as Mother came out of the silkworms' room. "But I know more than one way to have fun." And he asked Mother to sew a little sack together and then fill it with dried beans.

"What for?" Mother asked curiously.

"I need some exercise," Father said.

Mother whipped the sack together in no time and presented it to him with a smile.

"Thank you," he said as he stood up. Then, dropping the sack, he kicked it with a foot so that it bounced upward. "The object of the game is to keep the sack in the air as long as you can," he puffed. He managed the trick two more times before he fell down.

"Let me try," Lily said.

The sack bounced all over, but Lily was nimble enough to get over to it as it fell and kick it into the air again. Four was her record.

He tried to demonstrate all sorts of trick kicks but rarely managed to pull them off, usually winding up sitting on the floor instead.

The evening was as precious to Lily as the biggest, shiniest pearl. The only thing that marred its perfection was the gap between Lily and her big sister now. But it was Swallow who had dug the chasm between them, not her.

In a way, Lily was even glad of it, because it meant she would get even more of Father's attention. It was to her he would tell his jokes so she would laugh, and it was to her he would talk about the things that he had seen in his wanderings.

And that was fine with her.

CHAPTER | 12

*9th to the 11th day of the 6th (intercalary) month of
the era Way of Honor
August 3 to 5, 1835*

Swallow

For the next two days, Swallow harvested the leaves in the late morning instead of in the afternoon. She missed the boy's songs, but at least she didn't cry. And the support of her housemates helped Swallow get through all the spiteful looks and words from the rest of the clan.

Then, on the third morning, she went to the spot outside their house where they piled the leaves with the silkworms' waste. But it was gone.

Lily popped out from behind a corner of the house as if she'd been waiting for this moment. "See, see, Father fed all that stuff to the fish already."

Swallow glanced toward the pond and saw her father, bare-chested, wading through the water. Silvery fish darted about around his legs.

"I'll earn my keep. After all, I don't want you feeding me to the pig like your discards," Father called. Any misshapen silkworms were removed from the trays and became tidbits for Cloud the pig. Father held up the two lotus flowers that he had uprooted from the mud. "See? I'll do my share and clean out the pond. Clean ponds mean happy fish. We're going to have the happiest, biggest, and fattest fish ever."

But a little while later, when she went back outside with the leaf basket, she found Father napping beside the water. He hadn't picked more than one more lotus before he'd grown tired.

"Shush," Lily said as she fanned him.

Swallow rolled her eyes in disgust. "Look at him. He does just enough to make you think he's working, but he's still the same lazy bum."

"Are you blind?" Lily asked in a fierce whisper. "Can't you see Father's trying? He just doesn't have the strength yet. You're making it harder for him to recover by being so mean to him."

Swallow wrapped her arms around herself as if she were suddenly feeling cold. "Have you ever wondered why we don't have a family altar and everyone else does?"

"I wondered about that," Lily admitted. "I mean, folks say it's a little patch of Heaven right in the house. Where's ours?"

"Our grandfather made a beautiful one." Swallow

nodded to Father. "But he took it with him when he ran away and sold it. It all went up in opium smoke."

Lily was shocked. "He's different this time," she whispered softly. "I'm sure he's really sorry that he did it."

Swallow gave a snort. "The trouble is that he doesn't stay sorry for very long. And then he'll let you down. He always does. Why do you keep fooling yourself?"

"Is it so bad to want a father like everyone else does?" Lily asked.

"You've made a pretty picture in your head," Swallow said. "And when Father shatters it, I'll have to be the one to pick up the pieces."

Lily looked very small and very vulnerable at that moment. "Don't you want a real family?"

"What do you think Mother and I are?" Swallow demanded. "This is a real family. And when *he's* not around, it works just fine."

Lowering her head, Lily hid her face in her hands, shoulders shaking as she started to sob. Swallow felt terrible, as if she'd been plucking the down from a baby bird. She wanted to apologize but knew that would only encourage Lily's fantasy.

The noise roused their father, who sat up groggily. "Wha's wrong?" When he saw Lily was crying, he put his arm around her. "Did you fall and hurt yourself?" When Lily just shook her head, he glanced at Swallow. "What happened?"

"I told her the truth," Swallow said. She felt tears stinging her eyes, so she whirled around and ran blindly away, stopping only when she came to the stream.

Setting down her basket, she sat down on the ground.

Yes, she thought to herself, *I would like a father. And yes, I would like a family like so many people have.*

She tried to remember the times when Father had joked with Swallow the way he did now with Lily. There must have been some occasions. Unfortunately, the many bad memories crowded out any good ones.

She drew up her legs so she could rest her head upon her knees, deciding that she had never felt more miserable.

Suddenly she heard a familiar voice singing. With a shock, she thought about getting up and retreating, but her legs felt as weak as if they were stuffed with cotton.

"Where have you been all this time?" Happy asked.

She looked up. The boy was in a small, narrow boat filled with baskets of freshly picked mulberry leaves. "What are you doing here?"

"Maybe I'm a scout for our invading horde." The "invader" guided the boat over to the bank, where it gently bumped.

Swallow sniffed skeptically. "Don't be ridiculous."

"There's no fooling you." The boy grinned. "So excuse me while I finish drawing a map of your defenses."

Swallow dropped her chin back on her knees. "Go ahead."

"Do you mind answering some questions first, like how many are in your militia?" the boy asked playfully.

She gazed at the water rippling by. "I've got more important things on my mind than this silly talk."

He cleared his throat. "Do you want to tell me about it?"

Even if he had been one of her own clan, Swallow would usually have kept her thoughts locked up tight inside her. And Happy was a stranger from another clan. Yet his concern was so plain in his voice and face that Swallow suddenly felt an overwhelming need to talk to someone about the frustrations and misery of the last few days. "Will you promise not to repeat any of this to anyone?"

"May I eat a thousand needles if I do," he said fervently, in an oath that children used.

It was a relief to pour out all the misery and the frustrations of the last few days. She finished with, "So it's hopeless. I'm trapped." Her eyes searched his face for the same malicious expressions people had been giving her lately.

She waited anxiously now while he pursed his lips in thought. Then he blew out his breath explosively. "You're wrong, you know. There's one way out."

She stared at him, bewildered. "What's that?"

"Get married." He studied a bare, muddy toe. "I'd be willing to."

Swallow frowned. "Don't joke like that."

"I mean, I want to," he said, the words rushing out of him as he grew flustered. "I could ask my parents to get a matchmaker and everything."

She gave a shiver. "My mother never met my father before their marriage. It was a matchmaker who set it all up."

"A matchmaker got my parents together," the boy argued, "and they seem happy enough. So it works out some of the time."

The conversation was getting too wild and reckless for Swallow's taste. She stood up uncomfortably. "I have to go."

He hung his head. "I'm sorry if I offended you."

She'd hurt his feelings. "It's my mother and little sister. I can't leave them alone with my father."

He seized on her last words. "But maybe there'll be a time when you can?"

She felt a faint spark of hope. "He won't stay. And when he's gone, I . . . well . . . I could at least think about other things then."

He kept the boat against the bank with easy motions of the oar. "I'll wait."

She arched an eyebrow and repeated the vow. "And you'll swallow a thousand needles if you're lying?"

He arched his head to expose his neck. "A million right down the gullet."

Swallow thought she heard voices coming toward them. "You should go."

He sighed. "All right. I have to deliver our spare leaves to a farmer who's lost a couple of trees to pests."

"That's why you're out so early," she said, finally understanding.

"Lucky for me," the boy said. "Will you be here at the regular time tomorrow?"

Heart thumping, she said, "Yes."

With a nod, he swung the bow away from the bank and then out into the stream, resuming his song.

She thought about the boy's promise on the walk to the grove and all the time she picked the leaves.

And then, on the way back home, her conversation with Happy delighted her so much that dull, boring, sensible Swallow even gave a skip, heavy basket and all.

CHAPTER | 13

Lily

Lily had distracted her father by getting him to tell her stories about his travels while they played cat's cradle by the pond.

When Swallow came back with the first basket of leaves, she was humming a new tune that Lily had never heard before, so she wondered if her sister had heard it from that boy, Happy.

Swallow looked so smug that Lily almost asked her, but she knew what would happen if she did. Mother would get upset. And Father . . . well, if he lost his temper about that, Lily might not be able to stop him. Besides, the boy might be a bit silly, but he seemed harmless enough. So she kept quiet.

One fuss a day was more than enough.

CHAPTER | 14

*12th day of the 6th (intercalary) month of the era
Way of Honor
August 6th, 1835*

Swallow

The next morning Swallow still felt like skipping despite what had had happened the previous day and the exhausting rehearsals that evening. However, when she entered her home, Father was standing in front of the door to the silkworms' room, while Mother held him back. "You can't come in here," she said frantically.

He spread his arms. "How can I show you that I've changed if you won't let me?"

Looking frightened but determined, Mother shoved him back. "The silkworms pay for everything. We can't afford to lose any of them."

"They're my silkworms too, you know," he said, tapping his chest. "You have to obey me."

That was true enough. As his wife, she owed him

absolute obedience. She dropped her eyes submissively but still stubbornly blocked his way. "Yes, I'd have to, but I have to think of the family first."

"I'm the father," he insisted. "Don't you think I'm part of that family too?"

"Not yet," Mother said.

He began to sulk. "You don't trust me."

Mother relented, and her voice softened. "Not yet."

"At least admit that I'm the head of the household," he pleaded.

Mother still held her head down. "Not yet."

The muscles in his jaws twitched as if he were holding back his anger. Swallow glanced at his hands, wondering when he was going to strike Mother. Her shoulders clenched in anticipation.

Suddenly he let out his breath in one explosive rush. "All the way here, I planned how I'd start over. Why isn't anything going right? I'm just trying to make things up to you."

Mother lifted her head again. "Do what you want outside, but please stay out of this room."

Father took several long, ragged breaths. "Very well. I can see that the very notion of having me near the silkworms scares you, and that's the last thing I want to do anymore." Pivoting, he stalked out of the house.

Lily glared at Mother. "I think you're being horrible to Father." Spinning around, Lily darted past Swallow and after Father. "Wait for me," she called to him.

Mother slumped against the doorway. "I knew that once he got comfortable, he'd stop playing the penitent and become the emperor again."

Swallow tried to find some straw of hope. "But he stopped."

Mother massaged her forehead with her fingertips as if she had a headache. "This time. But it's only going to get worse and worse."

"Maybe this time it'll be different," Swallow said, hoping for all their sakes that she was right.

CHAPTER | 15

Lily

Father was sitting by the pond, his shoulders hunched. Lily plopped down beside him. "Why won't they let you help with the silkworms?"

Father sat on his hands to control the quivering in his fingers. "I don't blame them. If our places were changed, I wouldn't either."

Lily crossed her arms as she muttered, "Well, I hate Mother."

He shook his head. "Don't ever say that again. She's done more for you than I have. I've been a miserable excuse for a father."

Lily began to tear up. "But she'll drive you away again."

Father pulled his hands from underneath him so he could wrap his arms around Lily. "Shh, shh, I'm not going anywhere." He looked over his shoulder at the house. "I need to do something right now that shows your mother I've changed." Suddenly his eyes widened with excitement. "That's it." He tried to shove himself to his feet but fell back.

Lily put a hand under his arm for support. "What is?"

"Mother said I could do what I wanted outside," Father said as he straightened clumsily. "So I'll keep one promise I made to her a long time ago."

Uncle Prosperity lived on a little rise in a house not much different from their own, except it had been kept up, so it wasn't a wreck like theirs, and there was a gnarled old pine that shaded it in the afternoons.

Lily sat beneath it and watched Uncle Prosperity's fat pig root about in the dirt while her father went inside. When he stayed in there a long time, Lily started to get antsy and was just about to check on him when he came back outside.

He was bending backward as he carried a large, tightly woven basket. "Thank you, Uncle," he called to the interior.

Lily ran over to him. "Let me take that."

"No, no, carrying stuff is my work," Father said, but he hadn't gone more than twenty steps before he was puffing heavily.

"What's in it?" Lily asked, trailing him.

"A new home," Father said.

They wound up carrying the heavy basket between them, and when they reached their house, they set it down by the hole in the wall. "Say good-bye to this eyesore," Father said.

When Lily had fetched a large old pan at his request, Father opened the basket's lid, revealing the powder inside. "What's that?" she asked.

"Plaster," Father grinned, one cheek already pale with the stuff.

Using the hoe, he mixed it with water, and then with broken boards they began to trowel it on the wall. When they had filled the hole with plaster, they tried to smooth it with the board, but the patch still came out a little too lumpy.

When they stepped back a few paces to survey their work, she saw that the plugged-up hole glistened a bright white against the old wall.

"You've got plaster in your hair," Father said.

She looked at the white patches on his clothes. "And you've got as much plaster on you as on the wall."

And they both laughed, tired but happy over a job well done.

CHAPTER | 16

Swallow

Swallow was just coming out of the silkworms' room with Mother when Lily came inside with all the energy of a waist-high typhoon. "Come and see! Come and see!" she cried eagerly.

"See what?" Swallow asked. At that moment, all she wanted was a cup of tea and a brief rest.

Lily was too excited to explain, though. Instead, she seized Swallow's hand and then their mother's. "Look, look!" Backing across the floor, she tugged them along.

Outside, Father stood with his arms folded, looking as smug and satisfied as if he'd built the Great Wall. "What do you think?"

"It's wonderful," Mother said. Even Swallow looked pleased.

"I'm sorry. The last few years are sort of hazy," Father

said, rubbing his forehead and leaving white stripes behind. "But I finally remembered that I promised to fix the hole. It's a little late, but at least I did it."

Yes, Swallow thought, *maybe Father really has changed this time.* Like Lily, she also wanted a regular family.

"I'm going to fix up this wreck until we have the best home ever," Father said with a lordly flourish of his arm.

Suddenly Swallow drew her eyebrows together, because the replastered wall seemed to be bulging a bit. She was just going to mention it when the new plaster began to sag outward like the belly of a pregnant pig.

Lily had noticed it too. Grabbing up the board, she raced toward the house. Father joined her a moment later with a board of his own. Using the boards as trowels, they scraped and patted furiously.

"You've got it," Swallow encouraged.

However, the plaster kept oozing around their fingers as if it were determined to escape from the wall. Swallow had just taken a step forward to help them when a large patch of plaster plopped on the ground. Then another and another, too many for them to stop.

Father stepped back as he tossed the board aside. "I must have mixed in too much water." He smiled apologetically at Swallow. "I'll go right back to Uncle Prosperity's so I can mix up another batch. This time I'll get it right."

Mother was instantly cautious. "How did you pay him for the last batch?"

"It looks like we're going to have a fine silkworm crop this year," Father laughed. "Don't worry."

"But we're counting on every cash," Mother protested. "We don't have any extra to waste on making the house pretty."

Swallow put a hand to her mouth, realizing the real cost of Father's scheme.

Mother gestured toward the silkworms' room. "I'm sorry, but you can't mortgage any more of the crop."

Father spread his arms in frustration. "But without more plaster, I can't seal up the holes."

"No," Mother pleaded. "We can't afford it."

"But it was a good try," Swallow said sympathetically. "Thank you."

Father's eyes darted about desperately. "I'm not going to let you down, Swallow. I'll fix something else." He gaze fastened on the roof. "All right, all right. I'll repair the roof."

This time it was Lily who said, "No!"

Father rounded on his heel angrily. "You're siding with them now?"

"That's not it," Lily said, taking his hand and clinging to it. "You're too shaky to be up on a ladder yet."

"You still have trouble staying on your feet sometimes," Mother added.

"But I want to show you that I've changed!" Father shouted.

"Not by breaking your neck," Swallow pointed out.

It took their combined efforts before Father sullenly agreed to give up on the roof for now, but he maintained a surly silence for the rest of the day.

Swallow wished she could say something that would cheer him up, but she could come up with nothing.

And she felt another trickle of fear. The nightmare of Father's last visit was still repeating itself all over again.

CHAPTER | 17

Lily

To Lily's relief, Father was his cheerful self again by the next morning. Outside, the misshapen lumps of plaster on the ground had hardened. They really should have cleaned up the mess while it was still damp, but after the argument, everyone had wanted to forget the drying mounds.

Father's head swiveled as he gazed at the debris for a moment. "You know, rich folk bring weird rocks from thousands of kilometers away just to plop them down in their garden."

She loved the way he tried to make everything special. "And they're not half as strange as ours," Lily giggled.

He looked at her gratefully. "At least I'm good at making you laugh."

Sitting beside the pond, he sharpened the hoe blade.

"If your mother and sister won't let me make this shack into the best house, I'll have to be useful in another way." He examined the blade and then used it as a support to stand up. "So instead *I* will take on all the mean, nasty, dirty jobs."

"And I'll help you," Lily promised.

They went to one of the groves, where Father examined the tree trunks for pests, enlisting Lily's help because her eyes were sharper. When they found some, he used the hoe to scrape them off. However, they had barely finished the first mulberry when the tremors overtook him and the hoe slipped from his clumsy fingers.

"Ai!" he yelled in pain, and fell to the ground.

Lily saw the long, ugly red gash along his calf. As she watched in alarm, the bloody area began to widen.

"Make a tourniquet," Father said, and started to tear off a sleeve.

Fighting down her panic, Lily tied the sleeve around his leg above the wound. Then she used the hoe shaft to tighten the sleeve, cutting off the blood.

He leaned against the tree, using both hands to hold the shaft steady while Lily ran back home.

There was quite a fuss after that, for the front door had to be taken off the house and neighbors had to be rounded up to use it to carry Father back home.

Aunt Piety was a healer of sorts, so she clucked and fussed over Father as she examined the injury. "It looks a lot worse than it is," she said as she bandaged it. "But I don't want you overdoing things for a while."

After she had left, Father sighed. "I just have no luck."

Lily tried to cheer him up. "Let's sit down by the pond and watch the fish."

"That might be just the tonic I need," Father said. He started to get up with her help to leave the house, when they heard the tapping of rain on the straw roof. The sound grew louder until it was the like the rapping of knuckles, and outside, the pond was hidden behind a silvery curtain. The next moment several ribbons of water began to fall from above.

Mother and Swallow hurried in from the silkworm room and began to put out pots and bowls to catch the leaks.

Father tilted his head up toward Heaven. "So you won't even let me have that much," he grumbled. "Yes, sir. I got no luck at all."

CHAPTER | 18

*14th day of the 6th (intercalary) month of the era
Way of Honor
August 8, 1835*

Lily

Despite Aunt Piety's warning not to exert himself too much, Father was still determined to impress his family the next morning. With the heavens dropping rain, Father turned a shaky hand to fixing the house inside, even with one bad leg.

However, either through accident, ignorance, impatience, or clumsiness, he botched every attempt. Trying to hammer out a dent in a wok, he put a hole in it instead. Trying to repair a basket, he wove a straw patch over the hole, but it fell apart in no time.

As his shoulders started to sag, Lily hurriedly challenged him to a game of cat's cradle.

Father took the game seriously, so as they played, he was too busy concentrating to brood. However, as she held out her sixth pattern for him to take between his fingers, he just stared at it instead.

"You know," he said thoughtfully, "I once got some work at this real fancy place over in Nam-hoi District. They raised silkworms there, see. And they had these nets." His mind was racing so fast now that he could not express his thoughts in words. "And they did this. And that." His hands worked in quick, jerky motions. "That's it! Your mother doesn't know everything. Go get some cord. Lots of it. As much as you can."

Puzzled, Lily got the ball of cord, and when she brought it back, Father was staring through the rain outside the open doorway. "What are you going to do with this?" she asked.

"A net," Father said.

Lily glanced in the direction of the pond. "Why? We've already got plenty of fish here."

"Anyone can catch fish," he scoffed. "I'm going to catch money."

"How?" Lily asked.

"You'll see," he laughed. "You all will."

Lily watched anxiously as Father cut the cord into various lengths with a knife from the kitchen. There was just enough.

He fumbled with the strands as he began to tie them together into a knot. He was still at it when Swallow fetched one of the spare baskets of leaves.

"What are you making?" Swallow asked.

Lily spoke up before Father could. "A net," she pro-claimed.

Father grinned up at Swallow. "Your mother doesn't know everything about silkworms. I do too. And I'm going to show her. This net is going to help us raise the best silkworms ever!"

Swallow grunted skeptically and went back into the silkworm room.

Father watched Swallow leave. "There was a time she loved me." He began to work on the incomplete net, but his hands had begun trembling so much that he began to botch the knots. "Come on, come on, you useless things," he said to his fingers.

Lily seized them. When she felt the tremors passing through his hands, she squeezed them tighter. "Let me be your hands, Father. Show me what to do."

She kept encouraging him with all the hope she could put into them, and after a while the sunshine and her company seemed to soothe him, so his hands were steady once more.

"When Swallow was your age, we used to sit by the pond and watch the fish all the time." Father looked sad. "And now she doesn't want anything to do with me."

Lily hated to see him hurt. "When you finish your net, she'll see how special you are. Here. It'll go faster if we both work on it."

Father freed his hands and picked up the half-finished

net from where it lay on his lap. "Space the knots about this much," he said, showing her. "And tie them this way."

Lily nodded her understanding and then slid the string through her fingers, estimating the distance until she was halfway, where she began tying knots. She went slowly at first, but with repetition her rhythm increased.

CHAPTER | 19

Lily

Father did not even want to stop for lunch, and though her tummy was growling, Lily kept him company. This was one scheme that was going to succeed.

They were finished in time for the next silkworm feeding, but again Mother wouldn't let him enter the room.

Father held up the crude net. "But Lily and I want to demonstrate what we made."

"We don't have time to waste like this," Swallow said.

Lily was so mad that she could have spit. "Why won't you give Father a chance? You're just being mean."

The net began to shake in Father's hands as new tremors seized them. "Don't pick on your sister."

"Well, she's picking on you," Lily said.

"Shush, shush," Mother said, frantically flapping her

hands. "No fighting. Or you'll upset the silkworms." Mother reluctantly stepped aside so Father and Lily could enter. "Show us your contraption and then leave."

When they were in the midst of the tray racks, Father told Mother, "Slide out one of the trays."

When she had taken it out, he put a net over the tray. It fit exactly. "And now will you put leaves on top of the net, Lily?"

By now, the silkworms were in the final stage before spinning their cocoons, so all Lily had to do was spread mulberry leaves over the net. She had barely covered the net when, smelling fresh leaves, the hungry silkworms started to crawl through the spaces between the net's strings. Soon the broad green leaves began to heave as the large silkworms emerged on top to begin feeding. In no time, the tray was hidden by the wriggling worms.

"Well," Father hinted hopefully, "what do you think?"

"That's very clever," Swallow said grudgingly.

Father was grinning from ear to ear. "Using nets is cleaner and less likely to spread disease, because you're not having to pick up the silkworms by the handful. Healthier silkworms mean better silk, and better silk means more money."

At Father's direction, Mother and Lily lifted the net by the corners and set it on a clean tray. When the worms had eaten enough of their meal, they would fall through the net's interstices onto the clean tray itself, and they could take the net away.

"Isn't Father amazing?" Lily beamed at her mother and sister.

Father was as eager as a small boy waiting for a piece of candy for a good deed. "See?" he hinted. "I've found out a few tricks. We'll have the best silkworms ever."

Just as he started to smile, Mother said, "I'm sorry, but we don't have enough cord to make more nets. And we can't afford to buy any more."

Father began to rub his forehead agitatedly. "I didn't think about that."

Lily glared at her mother. Why couldn't she see what a good idea the net was? More importantly, why couldn't she realize Father was trying to make up for what he'd done in the past?

"Then we'll weave our own cord out of grass," Lily shot back, "and make our own nets in time for next year. Because Father's going to be here a good long time."

Father dropped his hand, relieved. "That's right."

CHAPTER | 20

15th day of the 6th (intercalary) month of the era
Way of Honor
August 9, 1835

Lily

They had planned to wander about the island, harvesting whatever grasses they could find so they could begin weaving their cord, but it rained all the next day.

Father sat at the table, looking gloomily through the open doorway at the rain thundering against the sky and splattering the muddy ground. Inside their home, water trickled through various leaks in the roof to patter into pots and jars laid on the floor. In front of him was a cup of tea that had grown cold.

Swallow set a fresh cup of tea in front of him. "I thought you might like something warmer in this weather."

Father twisted his head in surprise. "Thank you."

Swallow took the old cup. "I thought you and Lily

were just playing another silly game when you were making the net. But it could actually be useful."

Father wrapped his hands around the new cup. Steam rose from the surface. "I really am trying to help."

Swallow opened her mouth to say something, but then closed it right away and gave him a quick nod instead.

As she disappeared into the kitchen, Lily nudged him. "See? Swallow's coming around. Just wait until next year. Mother will see what a good idea it was when she has all those fine, fat silkworms."

"I'd like that," Father said wistfully.

Seeing how happy it made him, she began to elaborate. "And then we'll show the whole clan."

Father slapped the table excitedly. "Yes, yes. That'd be even better."

Lily had never had such a receptive audience for her daydreams. By this point, Mother or Swallow would have dragged her back down to earth by telling her to get on with her chores instead of chattering on.

"Then they couldn't say anything bad about you," Lily said confidently. "They'll brag about you instead." She gestured and imitated Uncle Prosperity's voice. "There goes the smartest man in the village. He's traveled all around and learned all these new things."

Father rested his chin on a hand. "Wouldn't that be grand?"

Lily's imagination began to soar. "And then . . . and

then"—she thrust out her arms—"the whole province will find out."

"The governor too?" Father asked shyly.

"Of course," Lily said, rapping a knuckle on the table for emphasis. "He'll probably want to see you."

"All we need is the nets." Father looked at the dark clouds scuttling overhead. "Come on. Clear up. Give me a chance."

CHAPTER | 21

Lily

Despite Father's prayer, Heaven sent rain for the next four days. Lily found the best way to keep up Father's flagging spirits was to embellish the fantasy, the two of them even enacting various scenes in which different people would be amazed—from Uncle Prosperity on up to the governor.

"Why," Lily said in a low, pompous voice, "in all my days as a governor, I've never seen silkworms so fat and content."

Father pretended to bow several times humbly. "Your Honor is too kind to this humble servant."

Lily put a hand over a fist. "I beg you to teach this miracle to others."

Father squared his shoulders, and his chest swelled. "Sir, for the sake of the Empire, I accept."

Between Lily and her father, the fantasy took on a life of its own during that rainy, homebound period.

The skies finally cleared on the fifth morning, so they would have gone out to find the raw stuff for nets, but Mother announced that the silkworms had grown so fat and huge that they should set out the spinning racks. They could have done it inside if it had been raining, but it was easier to begin outside.

Lily, of course, was expected to help, and Father wanted to. "Please put my muscles to use," he begged. A corner of his mouth twisted up. "At least, what's left of them."

"But you're still limping," Mother said.

"Let me do my share," Father said.

Mother smiled. "All right, but promise me that you'll stop as soon as your leg starts bothering you."

He looked so grateful. "I won't let it."

Eagerly he hobbled outside with the racks, stacking them into a large pile. "You see? It's just like the old days." He caught himself. "I mean before . . ."

"Yes, we know what you mean," Mother said gently.

He was disappointed, though, when Mother wouldn't allow him to help with the next step because it involved handling the silkworms.

"I . . . I thought you'd changed your mind," he said, slapping his hands helplessly against his sides.

It was actually Swallow who headed off trouble by

suggesting, "You're the foreman, Father. Tell us when we miss a spot."

"Right, right," he said, reluctantly accepting the compromise. As the rest of his family sprinkled the silkworms over the racks, he limped around, telling them where they needed more silkworms.

The sides of each rack were dotted with loops of thin bamboo that were just the right size for a cocoon. And soon the worms had wriggled into the spaces and begun weaving snug little homes for themselves of fine thread.

After a short while, Father set the racks against a shady wall, reversing them after an hour so that the cocoons would distribute evenly across the racks.

By the afternoon, the silkworms had finished creating their new homes, filling the racks with fat little cream-colored ovals. And in the evening, Father brought the racks inside, stacking them in rows on top of one another around a small charcoal stove, which would keep the temperature high and yet even, so the silkworms would use up all their silk and the cocoons would be their thickest.

This was the hardest and most exhausting stage. For three days and nights, someone would have to keep an eye on the silkworms, for they were now at their most vulnerable to diseases and other bugs. As well as checking on the cocoons, they would have to keep the fire in the stove at a steady temperature.

Of course, Father wanted to take a shift. "Let me make things easier on you."

Even as Mother was reluctantly shaking her head, Lily jumped in. "You can help me keep watch, Father."

So, later that evening, he helped Lily tend the fire in the stove and then inspect the cocoons. "Everything's fine on this side," he said.

Lily checked the racks on her side carefully and then came around to thank him—at the same time examining the racks he had just looked at. It was her excuse to make sure Father had done a good job.

He gave a snort. "Did I miss something?"

"I'm sorry," Lily said, coloring.

"It's all right. I know this is probably your mother's idea," Father said as he sank down on a bench and motioned for her to join him. When Lily did, he took her hand. "Did you ever wonder why I started to take opium?"

Lily was not sure she wanted to know, but curiosity got the better of her. "No, why?"

"Because I thought it would make me happy, but it was all a lie." He smiled sadly. "But I did learn the secret to real happiness."

"What's that?" Lily asked.

"Family." He laughed harshly. "I already had it and didn't know it. And it was only when I threw it away that I realized what I'd lost."

Lily squeezed his fingers. "You've got your family again."

"No," Father corrected her, and tapped on his knee to emphasize each of his next words, "but I *will*."

CHAPTER | 22

Lily

Despite the hard work and the lack of sleep, Lily preferred watching the cocoons to the next step of killing the pupae in the cocoons.

First, though, Mother selected a few of the cocoons from the racks and put them back into the silkworms' room. These would be allowed to finish their life cycle and become the parents of the next generation.

They rearranged the racks with the rest of the cocoons around a charcoal stove and then covered them with blankets with vent holes. The smoke would smother the remaining silkworms within their cocoons, but the fire would have to be tended all night so it did not grow too hot or too smoky.

Lily dragged her feet, not wanting any part of this, and it wasn't long before Father noticed Lily's uneasiness. "I'll take care of this," he said.

Mother shook her head. "No, it's Lily's turn. Everyone has to help."

"Sure, except me," Father laughed. "What's the worst that I can do? Kill them? We're going to do that anyway."

"We don't want to damage the cocoons," Mother said. Her jaw worked as she tried to fight back a yawn and lost.

"You and Lily can barely keep your eyes open, and Swallow's exhausted from handling both the silkworms and the festival," Father wheedled. "Let me take over for Lily, then."

That embarrassed Lily, because it made her sound as if she were trying to avoid work. "No, really. I'll be all right."

"She can do it," Mother insisted.

He patted Lily's shoulder affectionately. "You've had to grow up way too fast, haven't you?" He looked back at Mother. "I can't change what happened. All I can do is try to make up for it now."

Lily had an idea for a compromise. "How about letting Father share my shift again?" she suggested to Mother.

Mother gave in. "Yes, all right."

"And when Father and I make more nets," Lily boasted, "you're going to be glad he came home." By now the pair had spent so much time with their fantasy that they regarded it as a given fact.

"That's right," Father declared. "Once I've got my nets, the whole clan's going to be happy I did. Just you wait."

CHAPTER | 23

Lily

The next day, they set up the reeling machine outside, next to their squat little stove. Some folk sold their dead silkworms to the small reeling workshops, where about a dozen men would turn out the silk. But many were like Mother and still preferred to do it themselves.

On the stove, they put a pan and filled it with water, bringing it to a gentle boil. Near it, Mother sat on a stool with a pair of long cooking chopsticks in her hands.

Desperate to prove himself, Father volunteered, "I'll tend the stove."

"No," Mother said firmly. "One of the girls will." At the moment, it was Lily's turn, while Swallow took care of the surviving silkworms who were still maturing in their cocoons. "But you can bring water when we need it."

Father clasped one hand over the other as he begged

again, "Please. Let me help you."

Mother relented. "Thank you for offering, but you haven't done this in a while."

"Sure." Father's shoulders sagged as he smiled sadly. "And the Demon Mud's muddled up my memory pretty bad too."

"You could watch," Lily suggested. "And maybe you'd remember."

"I'd just distract you," he said, and limped inside.

Lily started to get up and go after him, but Mother snapped, "Silkworms."

Lily turned back to the pan and dumped in enough cocoons to cover the roiling surface.

Mother alertly watched the cocoons bob up and down on the restless water, waiting for the gum that held the threads together to dissolve, the layers to separate, and the cocoons to loosen. Then her chopsticks began to dart about among the cocoons, first helping peel off the outer layer of fibers, which would be good only for wadding in clothes. It was the middle layer she wanted, as it unraveled in one long, continuous filament.

Suddenly, her chopsticks darted down like kingfishers pouncing on tasty little fish. With deft motions of her hand and fingers, she gathered filaments until she had six of them, and then, with a twist of her wrist, she teased them into the beginnings of a thread, which she lifted dripping from the water and fed onto a reeling machine.

Lily turned the crank so that the silk thread began to

wind onto the reel. Her arms and shoulders were already aching—and yet she had been allowed to take a rest when she had traded places with Swallow, one of them helping Mother, the other tending the next crop of silkworms. Lily could only imagine how sore Mother must feel, for there was no one to replace her.

Mother had to stay by the pan, continuing to coax the strands onto the reels until the cocoons had completely unwound. Then she would begin the process all over again with more cocoons.

No one else in the village was as skilled as Mother. No matter how deft the fingers and how many helpers there were, it was hard to manage all the necessary parts of the process. The water had to be kept at the right temperature, the strands had to be caught and wound into a thread in an even flow. Worse, sometimes the breeze changed direction, and the smoke might damage the silk fibers. Then Lily had to snatch up a fan and frantically blow it away.

Mother's thread came out fine and even and fetched the highest price. And she could sense when the breeze was about to change, and before it changed, she would tell Lily to pick up the fan and keep the smoke away from their silk, so they were always ready when it happened.

"How do you know what's exactly the right thing to do, Mother?" Lily marveled.

Mother laughed. "Silk's in our blood. You'll learn soon enough."

CHAPTER | 24

*24th to 29th day of the 6th (intercalary) month of
the era Way of Honor
August 18 to 23, 1835*

Swallow

It started to rain again the next day, so they had to reel
inside the house.

Ever since the demonstration with the net, Swallow
had tried to be more pleasant to Father. At first, she had
considered the net just another way for Lily to amuse their
father—just like all their games of cat's cradle. So she'd
been as surprised as Mother when their project turned out
to be both clever and useful. And she had been pleased
and impressed when Father had helped with the spinning
racks and the rest of the process.

Now, with the heavens dumping buckets of water
outside, they had to set the stove just inside the doorway,
and while one of the girls tended the fire and put cocoons
into the boiling water, the other had to fan the smoke out
of the house. Otherwise, it would collect within the room,
damaging the silk. But they also still had to keep an eye

on the remaining cocoons to see when the moths emerged.

"Mother," Swallow suggested, "maybe Father could take over fanning?"

Mother looked over at Father, who was sitting on a bench by the table. "Are you feeling strong enough?"

He got up eagerly. "Just try me."

So he was set to waving the fan, which he did with enough enthusiasm to create his own gale of wind, under the watchful eye of one of the girls.

When it was Lily's turn to help Mother, she saw how Father was puffing and swinging his arms clumsily. "You should stop for a bit," she said.

"I'm fine," Father said.

Mother didn't look up from the pan. "Sit down," she said. "You won't be any help to us if you collapse suddenly."

His arm dropped as if it had turned to lead. "All right. Just a little rest. But I'm not going to let you down this time."

And he was true as his word, returning shortly to fan the smoke away vigorously.

The sky was still pouring four days later when the moths they had reserved broke out of their cocoons, so Swallow had to leave the reeling to Mother, Lily, and Father while she stayed with the insects.

Moist and weak, each moth crawled away from its ruined home on six spindly legs. Over the centuries, they had been bred so that they had neither wings nor mouths when they were born—Swallow always felt a little bad about that.

As the newborn moths stumbled about on the trays, Swallow picked up the split cocoons and set them aside to be sold later for an inferior brand of silk. The family could let nothing go to waste, because every cash counted.

The next morning, the moths began to carry out their last goal in life: to mate and then lay their eggs all in the space of that day. It was evening when Swallow set aside the last of the eggs. These would provide the final crop of silkworms this year.

Father hobbled to the doorway. "Want me to feed the carcasses to the fish?" Even dead, the moths served a purpose.

Swallow had not been looking forward to going out in the downpour. "Thank you," she said.

When he returned for a second load, he was so soaked and muddy that Swallow said, "Maybe you should rest."

He limped to the basket she had filled with more expired moths. "I can't whine about getting wet when the moths only get to live a day."

He didn't complain about the trips back and forth through the rain. Tired as she was, Swallow had a cup of hot tea and a towel waiting for him when he was done.

He accepted both gratefully. "This is feeling like the old days, isn't it?"

She wanted to say yes, but she glanced at Mother, who was listening to them as she sat working at the reeler.

Mother shook her head. It was still too soon.

Swallow didn't want to disappoint Father, though, after all his hard work, so she smiled.

He could interpret that any way he wanted.

CHAPTER | 25

Lily

I t didn't stop raining until five days later, when Mother reeled the last strand of silk.

Mother set her chopsticks down and then stood up, pressing her hands into the small of her back.

Skeins of silk hung on hooks on every available bit of wall space. Lily went over to one of them, but when she reached out a hand, Swallow grabbed her wrist. "Are your hands clean?"

Lily held up her palms. "See?"

"Wash them again," Mother ordered. "We don't want to mar anything."

Grumbling about the fuss, Lily went into the kitchen, barely wetting her hands, but somehow she still managed to pass inspection when she returned.

She raised her fingers to the pale silk thread and

stroked it gently, her fingertips tingling to the softness and the coolness.

Father hooked a thumb into the waistband of his pants. "Just think. A couple of hundred years ago, your mother would have woven it into cloth just like the Weaving Maid."

"No, thank you." Mother stretched, working out the kinks in her muscles. "I'd rather sell the silk to the weavers." There were small workshops of weavers, all of them male, organized into a guild.

"I bet we'll sell the silk for a lot of money this year," Lily said, surveying the skeins.

"Of course." Father swept his arm in a grand arc to include all the skeins. "The silkworms were the best I've seen, and since your mother is the best reeler, her silk will fetch the best price ever. I bet there'll even be extra money beyond the budget." He spun around excitedly. "Don't you think she deserves a treat? Something special for dinner. Let's buy some beef."

"Beef!" Lily started to drool at that rarest of possibilities.

Father put his hands on Lily's arms in a sign of unity. The two were dangerous together, because they egged one another on. "Let's have the best banquet ever."

Swallow sighed. "Why does everything have to be the best with you? You've always got to have the best house, the best silkworms, the best pig, and now it's the best meal."

Father hunched his shoulders defensively. "What's

wrong with wanting the best for my family?"

"Because it's impossible to have the best all the time," Mother explained gently. "And then you get frustrated. And then . . ." Mother hesitated until she had worked up enough nerve to finish. "And then the Demon Mud starts to call."

Father shook his head vigorously. "I'm finished with the Mud. I did my share of the work, and I would have done more if you had let me. So I ought to have some say in how we spend that extra money."

Mother smiled apologetically. "I wouldn't count on that surplus, but if we did, we should save it for something we really need. We have to be careful with our money and put it to the best possible use."

Lily balled her left hand into a fist and then clapped her left hand over it. "We need to celebrate being a family again," she begged.

"I could make sticky cakes," Mother offered.

"I love those," Swallow said, and tried to urge her sister into accepting a smaller celebration. "So do you, Lily." Lily's eyes, though, were on Father, who had squatted down so that he was eye-level with her. "You know. Your mother's right. We do have to spend that surplus carefully. And I think the best way to do that is to get cord for nets right away."

"I thought we were going to weave our own cord," Lily said.

Father wagged his head from side to side. "Well, yes,

but that would take so long; we wouldn't have nets until next year's crops." He jerked his head toward the silkworm room. "But if we can buy cord ready-made, we could have nets for this year's crops. And then I could demonstrate them to everyone right away."

Lily began to grow excited. "It'll make the plan happen even faster."

Father grinned from ear to ear. "Exactly."

Mother smiled patiently. "Wait, wait, you two. We don't have that extra money yet. And even if there was, I wouldn't get cord."

Father rose. "You said we'd use the surplus for something we need. Well, we need this."

"That's not what I had in mind." Mother folded her arms. "Every year we struggle to make ends meet. It'd be nice to have a little reserve set aside. Maybe if we have another good year, we might take a risk on this scheme."

Father could see the dream fading away in the distance. "But you saw how useful those nets were," he begged desperately. "Please! The clan treats me like I have the plague. I need those nets to impress everyone."

He and Mother went back and forth for a while, but though Mother always spoke softly and respectfully, as was his due, she wouldn't budge.

Finally, in a voice raw with frustration, he asked, "Why do we always have to do it your way?"

Mother lowered her head submissively. "I'm sorry, but

we've only survived by staying cautious."

Father slapped his legs in frustration. "I'm beginning to think I'll never satisfy you. You just want to punish me for the rest of my life and make me feel like trash."

Mother's head bobbed up and down. "I'm sorry. I'm sorry, but we just can't take the chance."

"How dare you defy me." Father curled his hands into fists. "I'm your husband! I'm the father!"

Swallow threw herself between her parents. "Don't you dare hit Mother!" She stretched out her arms as if she were a protective wall.

Father's breathing came in ragged gusts as if he were climbing up a mountain rather than fighting to control his temper. "I wasn't . . . I mean . . ." His words died away.

Mother stared and then held out an arm. "Come here, Lily."

Lily, though, stayed right by Father's side. "Why do you keep insulting Father like that?"

Mother kept her arm stretched out as she couched her voice in a low, calm tone. "Yes, I shouldn't do that, should I?" She wriggled her fingers at Lily. "So please come here and whisper to me what I'm doing wrong."

Lily wrinkled her forehead, as if suspecting Mother was trying to trick her into leaving Father. So, keeping a wary eye on Father's fists, Swallow darted in and snatched Lily away from him.

"Let me go!" Lily screamed.

Her sister ignored her, dragging Lily into their mother's arms. Mother clamped her arms tightly around Lily as if there were a tiger about to pounce upon them.

Father stammered indignantly, "I-I'd never hit Lily."

Defiantly, Swallow stationed herself again in front of her father. "You beat me when I was her age."

Father glanced down at his fists and guiltily opened them. "I guess I didn't know my own strength. I didn't mean to hurt you."

Swallow bore in recklessly, the fury making her voice quiver. "The pain was still there. But you know what I hated most about the beatings? Afterward, you'd make up excuses so I wouldn't blame you—just like you're doing now."

All the confidence, all the hope, all the optimism sagged and dropped just like the plaster he had mixed. "I've changed. I really have. But will you ever see that?" Pivoting, he staggered out of the house.

Lily wriggled free from her mother's grasp. "I hate you both."

"We're doing this for your own good," Swallow tried to explain.

But Lily was already running through the doorway after Father.

She found him where she knew he would be—sitting by the pond. But today his shoulders sagged, and he rocked back and forth, looking like a lost and lonely child.

"I try and I try and I try," he was muttering as Lily walked quietly up to him. She intertwined her fingers with his, but he didn't even seem to notice. Mother and Swallow were standing anxiously outside the house, ready to race down to rescue Lily from him.

"Please be patient a little longer," Lily coaxed. "They'll come around."

"What's the use?" he mumbled sadly. "They're never going to forgive me. I see that now."

And no matter what Lily said or did, he kept wallowing in misery like a pig in mud.

CHAPTER | 26

Swallow

Shaking with fear and anger, Swallow sagged onto a bench. They had finally arrived at the part of the family pattern that she had been dreading. She had wanted to cringe and hide, but instead she had forced her legs to run so she could put herself bodily in front of her mother.

All the terrifying memories flooded into her mind— the shouting, her mother's painful cries, and worst of all, her father's face, as grotesque as some mask of a monster. And she wanted to crawl under the table, where she had always tried to hide when she was small.

Then she remembered her little sister. "Lily!" She tried to jump to her feet, but it was as if they had turned to sand, so she took a wobbly step toward the door.

Mother was kneeling, unable to move from her spot. "It's all right for now. This is only a squall, quick to arrive and quick to blow away."

However, Swallow knew just as her mother did that the frustration would build in their father until he became a destructive storm. "What do we do?"

Mother shoved herself up from the floor. "For now, you go to the girls' house and stay there."

"I can't leave you and Lily," Swallow said.

"You have to prepare for the Seven Seven." Mother tottered toward the doorway, peering out. "It'll take a few days for his anger to build again. Until then, I should be able to handle him." She beckoned to Swallow. "He's at the pond with his back to the house, so he won't see you if you go around behind it."

Swallow gave her mother a hug when she joined her. "What do we do after the festival?"

Her mother pressed her lips together thinly. "We survive whatever Heaven sends us."

"I don't think Heaven is behind this," Swallow said bitterly.

Her mother shrugged. "Whoever is the instigator, it's been this way for women for thousands of years."

Swallow could see why Aster never wanted to get married. "It's not fair."

"Things rarely are," Mother said. "That's why we count on one another."

"The family," she agreed—meaning herself, Lily, and Mother.

Her mother smiled. "That's right. And don't come

back until after the festival. For now, just think about the Seven Seven."

Swallow shook her head. "I can't leave you alone with him."

"You know how he is," Mother assured her. "He'll sulk and grumble like a small boy, but he'll do what he's told as long as we ask nicely."

That was true enough. In the past, it had always taken a while for anger to fill up his reservoir to the bursting point again.

Mother was trying to give Swallow the only gift she could—a momentary respite from her father. And Swallow gladly took it.

Giving her mother a quick squeeze, Swallow slipped outside, holding her breath as she glanced at her father. He was all hunched up, so she quickly went around the house and along another route to the girls' house, away from him.

CHAPTER | 27

6th to 7th day of the 7th month of the era
Way of Honor, or the Seven Seven festival
August 29 to 30, 1835

Lily

Father sulked all the next day, the eve of the festival, and no matter what Lily said or did, she could not cheer him up. She hoped that the Seven Seven would lift his spirits, but it had started to rain again. If it was still pouring the following day, the celebration would be canceled.

Mother and Swallow weren't any help with Father either. Swallow stayed at the girls' house, and Mother served him his meals but spoke to him only when necessary. Instead, she eyed him warily, as if he were a river about to burst his banks and destroy everything.

To Lily's relief, the morning of the festival was bright and cloudless and the air cleansed by the previous storms.

But then she had a new worry. Who would take her? Up until now, Swallow had been the one to escort Lily, but this year, as a member of the sponsoring girls' house, she would be busy with the festivities themselves.

"I asked Aunt Piety to escort you," Mother said.

Father looked at her, hurt. "Why not me? Do you think I'd lose my own daughter?"

"I just thought you'd be bored," Mother said tactfully. "After all, it's mainly a festival that celebrates women's crafts and things."

"But it's open to everyone," Lily urged. "So you should come too, Father."

Father scratched the back of his neck. "No, maybe your mother's right. I would be bored."

Before Father's spirits could sink any deeper, Lily tugged at his sleeve. "If you don't go, you'll miss the acrobats. You'll really like them."

Father glanced at her sideways. "Hmm, I haven't seen acrobats in a long time."

"This year the girls' house is going to have the best celebration ever," Lily said. "They're planning something special, and I think Swallow's going to be part of that."

Father pursed his lips. "I missed so much of her growing up. I'd like to see that." He swung his gaze toward his wife. "Unless you need me." When she hesitated, he grinned ruefully. "No, of course you don't."

Aunt Piety showed up around sunset. She beamed when she saw Father—she was one of the few who did in the clan. To her, he was still the same little boy she had babysat.

"Now, don't go wiping your nose on your sleeve," Aunt Piety admonished him. "And if you're a good boy, Auntie will have a nice treat for you."

Father grinned for the first time in days. "I will, Auntie."

The festival was magical. Colored lanterns had been hung around the courtyard of the ancestral hall. "Will you look at that," Father said, gazing around.

"It's like a fairyland," Lily said, clapping her hands in delight.

"The girls've done the clan proud this year," Aunt Piety said, as proudly as if she had decorated the hall herself.

There was already a crowd in the courtyard when they got there, and they joined the people in front of the altar to the Seven Sisters. Fat red candles cast a soft light over bowls of fruit and flowers, while incense sticks stuck into cups of sand sent up thin ribbons of sweet fragrance. Scattered among the bowls of offerings were bowls of young green rice shoots, like miniature rice patches. Tiny lamps had been cunningly hidden among the shoots so that they gleamed like fireflies.

With Father trailing along behind, Lily and Auntie paid their respects to the Seven Sisters, and then Auntie pulled two threaded needles from her sleeve. "Here. You're old enough now."

Lily took one of them and watched while Auntie laid

the other on the altar beside a dozen more needles and even some small bits of cloth with embroidery.

"The Weaving Maid's one of us, do you see?" Auntie said. "Her magic comes from her needle, not a sword or a staff."

Don't forget us, Lily said silently to the Weaving Maid, and added her needle to the rest. *Or Father. He means well, but he just doesn't have any luck.*

Bowing their heads three times again, they went on to the tables of the gifts.

The first one had a set of wooden furniture in miniature and decorated with intricate designs of sesame seeds glued to the wood, jars of cosmetics, a tiny sedan chair so the sister could be carried from one heavenly palace to another, lovely dresses, and a pair of shoes with embroidery. Lily recognized her sister's handiwork in the shoes.

She and Auntie stood admiring the presents—so much care, so much ingenuity and hard work, so much love. When they finally moved on, Lily gasped, because connecting the first table to the next was a miniature bridge fashioned out of almonds, rice grains, and flowers.

There were seven tables in all, each with an equal number of presents so none of the sisters would feel slighted.

Father surveyed everything wryly. "This really isn't a place for a man. Everywhere else in China the festival's about the love between the Weaving Maid and the Cowboy, but here it's all about the Weaving Maid and her sisters. Look, the Cowboy's just an afterthought."

He jerked his head to the side at a smaller altar on which a tiny man's robe lay—something for the Weaving Maid's husband, the Cowboy. There were a few women there asking the Cowboy to watch over their sons, but most people stayed with the Seven Sisters, asking them for help.

"Now, now, don't work yourself into a tizzy. Everyone's welcome." Auntie would have patted him on his head as she had when he was a boy, but now that he was an adult, Auntie could not reach that high, so she satisfied herself with patting him on the arm. "I know what'll make you feel better. How about that treat I promised?"

Vendors were selling all sorts of treats, and the smell of grilling meat made Lily's mouth water. Auntie splurged and bought them a stick of beef. "There, we'll share this," she said, holding it out to Father.

He smiled shyly. "No, let Lily go first."

The beef had been marinated in some sauce, and Lily had never tasted anything so good.

"And later," Aunt Piety teased, "we'll get some water from the well and put it in a basin so you see your future husband." People said that if an unmarried girl did that, then the Weaving Maid would reveal whom she was going to marry.

"I'm never getting married," Lily said as she licked her fingers.

"Now, now. I want grandchildren," Father said as Lily handed the stick to him. Holding it like a sword, he bowed to Aunt Piety. "Thank you, my lady."

Behind them a woman murmured, "*He's* got his nerve strolling around grand as a lord."

Lily twisted around to glare at two women, but they were too busy giving Father hostile stares.

He handed the stick over to Auntie, appetite all gone. "You're wrong, Auntie. I'm not welcome here."

"Never mind them," Auntie soothed. "All those two biddies do is gossip." And then, in a much louder voice, she said to the pair, "A festival is no place to sling mud."

Father shifted his feet as he glanced around uneasily. "I don't belong here."

Up until then, Lily had been too busy seeing all the attractions to pay attention to the folk around her. Now she noticed other women of the clan glowering at Father.

"What's a wife beater doing here?" a third woman said to another in a loud voice that they were meant to hear.

Father pivoted slowly, aware that there were scowling faces on all sides. "I'm beginning to know just how those silkworms feel inside their cocoons with the smoke coming in." He began rubbing his arms vigorously, as if there were something sticking to him. "We want to live. We want to escape. But we can't. We're trapped in what we wove."

"You leave him alone," Lily hollered defiantly. "You're wrong about him."

The women shook their heads knowingly at one another.

Father flung his arm out. "That's right. I'm going to wipe those smug looks right off your faces. Pretty soon you'll be bragging that we're in the same clan."

All around them, women smirked. Several even started to laugh.

"You stupid cows!" Father spun as he flailed his arm through the air. "I'll show you. I'll show everyone."

"That's right. Next year, you'll be singing another tune," Lily said.

Father glanced down at her. "No, not next year. Next month."

Lily scratched her head. "But Mother already said no. So we have to weave the cord first."

Father's hands had started to tremble again. "I don't think we can wait until next year. We need to get it now."

"I have some cord," Aunt Piety said.

"Not in the quantity we need," Father said. "I'm going home to make Mother see reason."

Lily seized his hand. "Please stay," she begged.

"We really need those nets." Father tugged free from her grip. "Besides, if I'm here, the crowd will be too busy insulting me to pay attention to the stage. It's only kinder to Swallow if I leave."

And he slipped away, quickly disappearing into the crowd.

CHAPTER | 28

Lily

Lily stood, wondering if she should go back with him, but Aunt Piety stroked her back. "He'll be all right, dearie. He's always telling me how glad he is to be back home, so he's not going to do anything to ruin that. He'll rant a little until he cools down, just like he did as a little boy."

"I've been looking all over for you," Aster said. If she had noticed Father, she gave no sign, nodding a greeting to Aunt Piety instead. Then Aster took Lily's hand. "Swallow wanted you to get good places."

Lily was torn between following Father and disappointing Swallow. But after all, Aunt Piety had known Father even longer than Lily had, and she had said Father would be all right. So she let Aster lead her and Aunt Piety to the front of the stage, a large wooden platform painted red with a curtain set up in back of it.

"This is the best spot to see everything," Aster assured them. "So be sure not to move. Tonight's entertainment is really special, so you don't want to miss any of it." Then, excusing herself, she wriggled through the mob as she headed toward the rear of the stage.

As they waited, Lily asked Aunt Piety what Father had been like as a boy. "He was always walking in the clouds, that one," she reminisced.

"Swallow says that's what I do," Lily said.

She tugged at one of Lily's braids. "Then find a husband who's got his feet firmly on the ground."

"He's got to be someone I can trust," Lily said.

Auntie tapped the tip of Lily's nose. "While you're wishing for the impossible, ask for one who's rich too."

After a while, the group around the stage began to grow, so Auntie planted herself behind Lily. Though she was elderly, her elbows were still as sharp as ever, so she kept everyone from crowding them.

The show was everything that Swallow had promised. There was a clown who had everyone in stitches imitating a farmer trying to catch a pig; a magician who performed miracles with eggs, huge metal rings, and an inexhaustible bag; and acrobats who tumbled about on the stage and juggled as the musicians set a breakneck pace with the crash of cymbals and the thump of drums.

When the acrobats somersaulted off the stage, the musicians stirred, readying their instruments. Then plaintive notes began to rise from a lute, and the singer stepped onto the stage in elegant yellow and a scholar's cap.

He zigged and zagged back and forth over the boards as if he were wandering far and wide.

"What's the matter with him? Can't he see us?" Lily wondered out loud. "We're standing right in front of him."

"Shh," Aunt Piety whispered. "This is how they do it on the Canton stage. I think all the actors have bad eyesight."

All during the other performances, people had been chatting and moving about, but now everyone fell silent and still as they watched excitedly.

Finally the boards creaked as the singer stood right in front of them, glancing down to wink at Lily. Then his shoulders heaved up and his chest swelled beneath his robe as he drew a deep breath and began to sing in a voice so beautiful that it made Lily ache inside.

She stared up at him raptly, listening to a song about loneliness. *Someone needs to give him a good hug,* she thought to herself.

Then the curtain at the back of the stage stirred, and a goddess stepped out in an elegant robe of silk. It was hard to tell through the makeup, but the shape of the face reminded Lily of Aster. However, instead of moving with her usual stride, she drifted over the boards in small, gentle steps, so that she seemed to float along like a cloud and so quietly that there was only the faint whispering of her shoes. She took up a position to the far left and struck a pose.

There was also something familiar about the next five girls as, one by one, they wafted across the stage as lightly as silk floss in a breeze. It was as if the magic of the festival had transformed plodding, cotton-clad farm girls into airy sylphs of the sky whose feet barely brushed the earth. Eventually, all six of them formed a line, leaving a gap in the center.

"Scandalous!" Uncle Prosperity suddenly spoke up. "Decent girls shouldn't be up there on display!"

"Oh, shut up, you old goat," a boy shouted back. "Why can't you just let us enjoy something for a change?"

"Who said that?" Uncle Prosperity demanded. "I see you!"

There was a stir in the crowd and the patter of running steps as the boy ran off and Uncle set off in pursuit.

A real professional, the singer kept right on performing during the disturbance, as if he were used to such things. He turned sideways with his arms extended as the Weaving Maid herself emerged.

Lily couldn't help giving a cry of delight as Swallow shuffled softly across the boards, as weightless and graceful as the others. She was dressed in an embroidered robe, and her hair seemed to float about her head like streamers.

Different pins had been thrust through her hair, and adorning the pins' tops were butterflies that seemed to flutter as she walked.

"Is that Swallow?" Aunt Piety gasped.

"No," Lily corrected her in a hushed voice, "that's the Weaving Maid."

She stood, drinking up every moment so she could tell Mother what she had missed.

As Swallow assumed her station in the center of the line, the singer began a sweet romantic tune of courtship to her, and then a rapturous song when the Weaving Maid said she would be his.

The girls remained as frozen as statues while the singer clasped his hands together and sang sadly of how Heaven had separated them.

The singer was so talented that he could switch to a falsetto and sing as the Weaving Maid herself as she lamented to her sisters:

"Oh, sisters, where are you?
All day I work; all day I cry.
Silk is lovely but silk is tears."

It was the same song that Swallow and her mother had sung the day Father had returned, but this time when she heard it, Lily felt as if her insides were crumbling. Tears streamed down her cheeks as she wrapped her arms

around herself, and she heard Aunt Piety and others begin
to sob.

As the last notes faded away, the cymbals suddenly
crashed and the horns began to tootle a lively tune.
Suddenly the singer was all smiles as he switched to a
comic song, pretending to be the sisters as they debated
on how best to help the Weaving Maid. Some of the solu-
tions were as far-fetched as Father's notions, including
gluing the pair together so that it would be impossible for
Heaven to separate them again.

And then one sister had the idea of appealing to the
magpies.

> "Magpies, magpies, don't you also weep?
> Don't you also wish to help?"

Lily hopped up and down, clapping with everyone else
as the acrobats returned to the stage, dressed as magpies,
and flung themselves through the air as if they had wings
of their own.

The acrobat-magpies danced about and then formed
the bridge across which the singer stepped, moving toward
his love on stage just as the Cowboy would travel over the
feathery bridge to the Weaving Maid tonight in the sky.

All too soon, it was over, and with it the night's festival.

CHAPTER | 29

Lily

Lily lingered by the empty stage, reluctant for the magical evening to end.

"Did you like it?" Swallow asked.

Lily turned to see the Weaving Maid coming toward her, still in full costume and makeup but walking like a normal girl instead of a goddess.

"Why are you crying?" she asked Lily. "Didn't you like it?"

Aunt Piety was squatting beside Lily with her arm over Lily's shoulders, because Lily had been weeping so hard that she'd gotten the hiccups. "I think it was too much excitement for her."

More emotions swirled around Lily's mind than she could identify. "I just feel . . ." Lily said between hiccups, "so sorry for her. She loves him so much, but she loses him."

"Not forever. And she still has her sisters," Swallow reminded her, gently brushing away a tear from Lily's cheek. "That has to count for something."

"I suppose so," Lily said, and wiped the tears from her face with her sleeve. "Even if it . . . was sad . . . it was . . . the best one ever."

Swallow tapped her nose. "Don't go saying that or you won't have anything to look forward to in the future."

"Well . . ." Lily scratched her head, annoyed as she tried to find an argument. "I mean . . . all right . . . it's the best one *so far.*"

Swallow patted her affectionately. "Yes, when it's your turn in the girls' house, you'll put on one even better."

"You were lovely," Aunt Piety said. "How did it feel to play the Weaving Maid?"

"Wonderful," Swallow said, and began to hum the Weaving Maid's song, moving her hands as the singer had.

Lily had never seen her sister so lively. It was as if her costume were still enchanting her.

Chuckling, Lily copied her for a moment, trying to prolong the magic of the evening. All too soon, the tune ended.

"I wish it was Seven Seven every night," Lily sighed.

"Let's stretch it out a little longer," Swallow suggested, and took Lily's hand. "Come back to the girls' house with me. You can sleep over."

Lily rubbed her hand against her trousers to try and clean it before she touched the robe. It felt even more tingly than the silk skeins had. "Can I really?" she asked as she fingered the material.

"I've already gotten the others' permission," Swallow said.

"You planned this." Aunt Piety laughed. "Well, tonight was your special night. Enjoy it."

Swallow entwined her fingers through her little sister's. "I want her to stay happy as long as she can."

Lily was tempted, but she thought about Mother. She had to be a dutiful daughter. "I should go home and tell Mother all about this evening."

Swallow stiffened at the thought of Father also being there. "I guess I should go too."

"Tonight's your special night. You should enjoy yourself." Aunt Piety patted her on the shoulder. "Don't worry about a thing. Your father's fine. He even was here."

Swallow's voice became tense. "He saw me?"

"No, he left before the performance. He'll be sorry he missed it." She frowned. "All those mean women drove him away."

"Did he leave mad?" Swallow asked anxiously.

"Oh, no," Aunt Piety soothed. "Just the opposite. He was as excited as someone with a burr in his shoe. Something about some nets."

"Nets!" Swallow gasped. Her head twisted in the direction of her home. "Mother's all alone."

Aunt Piety misunderstood. "Well, she had the silk-worms to take care of."

Swallow, though, was already running, holding up her costume so it wouldn't impede her stride.

"Swallow, where are you going?" Aster called. "You've got to take off your makeup and return the costume."

But Swallow had disappeared into the night with Lily close behind her.

CHAPTER | 30

Swallow

Branches tore at Swallow's robe and hair as she plunged down a path through a grove. By the time she reached its far side, her headdress was tilting drunkenly, and her locks dangled like broken ropes on a ship's mast.

For most of the evening, Swallow had felt as if she were living under some enchantment. Long before the show, there'd been the thrill of Big Sister applying her makeup with brushstrokes as light and gentle and sure as a mother cat's tongue licking its kittens.

And then there had been the miracle of putting on the robe—of feeling the silken material envelop her in luxury and make her feel special and set apart from the Swallow she had been.

As each of her six sisters prepared in turn, their

excitement added to hers—as if the exhilaration were added to a bowl that they all shared. And the emotion had only increased until they had set foot on stage.

The gasps of awe and wonder had been like little puffs of air that sent her floating higher and higher across the stage.

Like Lily, she had not wanted the evening to end, and she had planned to give her sister one evening away from Father. Like Mother, she had thought he was calm enough for now. She realized now that she had only been fooling herself. He had changed just as he'd been insisting, but the transformation wasn't for the better. There was a new desperation that had edged his last tantrum. At the time, she hadn't wanted to admit it, but she realized it now. If anything happened to Mother, it would be her fault.

So she ran on, trying to hold up the hem of her robe but knowing that it was dragging in the dirt despite her best efforts. Twice, as she ran along narrow dike-paths, the dirt crumbled beneath her shoes and she nearly fell into a fishpond. Somehow she managed to keep her balance and drive on.

"Wait for me," Lily puffed from behind her.

Swallow was afraid of any delay, though, and kept on, slowing only when she reached their house.

It was dark inside, and there was only the chirping of insects to mar the night's stillness.

"Mother?" she called.

Panting, Lily caught up with her. Leaning forward so she could rest her hands on her knees, she said, "You missed a wonderful show, Father."

"Stay here, Lily," Swallow said. She pulled one of the pins from her hair. Perhaps she could use the sharp tip as a weapon. Holding it like a dagger, she walked cautiously toward the house.

"What's wrong?" Lily asked. She had ignored Swallow's command and was padding at her heels.

"Shh," Swallow said, and tiptoed ahead cautiously. As she neared the door, she stumbled over something. When she looked down, she saw in the moonlight that it was the swallow's nest.

"Oh, it's broken," Lily said.

"It was getting old and crumbly," Swallow tried to reassure her, "so it's no wonder it fell off."

When she entered the house, she almost slipped on something wet on the floor and had to put a hand on the wall to support herself. "Stay there, Lily. And I really mean it this time," she said, praying that Lily would listen at least this once.

She shuffled through the blackness, hands groping through the air toward where the candle usually stood on the table. She found the cylinder and then the flint and the steel. Sparks flew as she struck them and lit the wick. Picking up the candle, she turned.

"Mother!" Lily wailed.

Mother was lying on the floor near an overturned stool. Blood covered her face and pooled around her head. Swallow had slipped on the edge of the puddle, and her bloody footprints now led from the doorway to the table.

As she went toward Mother, Swallow ordered sharply, "Don't move, Lily."

Lily, though, was too petrified even to breathe.

Swallow knelt beside their mother, relieved to see she was still breathing. The blood was coming from a gash on her forehead. "Lily, tear off a sleeve. I need a bandage."

Lily stood still as a statue, so Swallow got up. Her sister said nothing as Swallow ripped off the sleeve and then pressed it against the wound.

"Find Aunt Piety," Swallow said.

Lily blinked, then spun around and darted off.

"Wh-what . . . ?" Mother's eyes fluttered open.

"Shh, don't try to get up," Swallow said.

Mother's eyes widened. "Who are you? What are you?"

Swallow realized she was still in her makeup and it had probably been smeared. With her hair hanging askew, she must have looked more like a goblin than a goddess.

"It's me, Swallow," she said. "This was my costume." She added, "What's left of it."

Mother gestured. "Your father."

"I think he left already," Swallow said. It was as if the old pattern had compressed itself into one tantrum and then one sudden violent fit.

"He came back talking about the nets," Mother said. "He wouldn't stop telling me how much he needed them. And he just kept getting madder when I would tell him no."

"So he finally lost his temper and struck you," Swallow said.

"I must have fallen and hit my head on the stool," Mother said. "I don't know what happened after that."

Swallow had thought that something was odd when she had touched the wall. Suddenly she knew what it was. She should have felt silk, not bare plaster. She looked near the doorway. The hook was empty.

She twisted her head this way and that.

All the hooks were empty.

The silk was gone.

CHAPTER 31

8th day of the 7th month of the era Way of Honor
August 31, 1835

Swallow

The men of the clan searched for Father, and they found that one of the clan's boats was missing. With the women gone to the festival and the men tending the silkworms that evening, he'd been able to make several trips to load up a boat and leave. With so many waterways crisscrossing the district, he could be anywhere.

Mother's cut, Aunt Piety said, was messy but not deep. Though she was still a little weak from the loss of blood, she would recover. The same, though, couldn't be said of their finances.

Swallow and Lily sat on a bench outside with Mother.

"Father wouldn't do that," Lily said. "I bet it was bandits."

"Face the truth. It was Father. He even fooled me for

a while," Swallow said.

She looked at the sky, wishing she truly were a goddess who could escape up there. But the robe was gone, along with the elaborate hairdo and the cosmetics, the music and lights, the stage. And she was back to plain, sensible Swallow in her usual dark cotton blouse and trousers and the hairstyle for an unmarried girl. It was as if the fairy of last night had vanished, leaving an ordinary girl stuck in the mud now.

As a mere human, she would have to do the best she could. Her stomach twisted with fear as she began to suspect what that might be.

What about Happy? she asked herself with a pang of sadness. No, he was as good as dead to her now. Just like that life. And inside her memories she shut a door firmly and locked it.

Lily shook her head, still refusing to believe. "But Father said—"

"You can't trust everyone," Swallow said, feeling tired. She'd made the same mistake that Lily had.

"Father was trying so hard," Lily said.

"The Demon Mud tried harder," Mother said sadly.

CHAPTER 32

9th day of the 7th month of the era Way of Honor
September 1, 1835

Lily

Even now, Lily hoped that Father would come back with the silk and the boat. But he hadn't yet by the time Mother and Aunt Piety had gone to see Uncle Prosperity.

Mother looked upset when she got back, and Aunt Piety was cursing him. "That mean, old, spiteful man. He just wants to make someone else more miserable than him."

As Mother slumped onto a bench, Swallow sat down on one side of her while Lily sat on the other. "What happened?" Swallow asked.

"He's not going to give us an extension on our debt or our rent," Mother said in a dull voice, as if she were already dead. "Worse, he wants to be compensated for the boat that Father stole."

"He's the one who forced us to take Father in," Swallow protested.

"We pointed that out to him, but he said he'd only been doing his doo-tee back then." Aunt Piety grimaced as if the words tasted foul. "And he's only doing his doo-tee now."

"Never mind, Auntie," Mother said, trying to cut her off.

However, once Aunt Piety had started, she couldn't stop. Instead, she looked directly at Swallow.

"He said that show was so scandalous that he's going to set an example for the rest of the clan by punishing your family for letting you go onstage. But that spiteful old miser just wants to get his paws on even more money."

Lowering her head into her hands, Swallow began to weep. "Then it's all my fault."

Mother looked accusingly at Aunt Piety and then put her arm around Swallow. "Even if we could have sold all the silk, we would have been in trouble. We had already missed our rent quite a lot."

Lily blinked. "So there wouldn't have been any surplus anyway." She felt the sadness twisting her insides. "Why didn't you tell us?"

"I should have." Mother sagged against the wall. "But I didn't want you girls worrying more. You already worry enough."

"The clan won't stand for this," Aunt Piety said.

"Most of the clan owe him money too," Mother said. "They may not like it, but they won't object."

"Then I'll take up a subscription," Aunt Piety said. "We'll settle up your account."

"They have their own debts, so I doubt if they can give very much," Mother said. "We really have only one thing of value."

Swallow brushed the tears from her cheeks with swipes of her hand. "Us."

"You can't leave your children," Aunt Piety protested to Mother.

Swallow squeezed her mother's fingers. "No, Lily still needs you. And you can do more for her than I can."

Lily burst into tears. "No, sell me. It's all my fault. I never should have talked so much about those stupid old nets."

Mother put her free arm around Lily. Turning, Lily buried her face against her mother's shoulder. "Shhh," Mother said. "If it hadn't been the nets, then he would have wanted money for some other scheme. That's just the way your father is."

Lily's voice came muffled as Mother's blouse soaked up Lily's tears. "Well, I'm never going to talk wild again. From now on, I'm going to plant my feet firmly on the ground."

Swallow massaged her sister's back. "Good. Because you'll be the only one able to help Mother from now on."

Lily felt numb inside, but she knew Swallow was right. She sat back up, tears streaking her face, eyes already getting puffy. "I will."

Swallow rose so she could wrap her arms about both her mother and sister, tightening her embrace so that their heads were together and they seemed like one person.

As they rocked back and forth, Swallow whispered into Lily's ear, "Just remember. The family always comes first."

Lily felt a strength, an energy flowing into her from Swallow. The magic of last night was there, had always been there in her sister. The fairy of last night had only been a costume. The power in her sister was a power as solid as the earth, a power she was trying to share with Lily now.

Lily pressed her forehead against Swallow's. "One day I'm going to have my own family," she swore. "And I'm going to keep everyone safe and happy. I won't trust that to anyone else but me." She hugged Mother and Swallow with a fierce love. "And I promise you one more thing."

"I think you already took a big enough oath." Swallow laughed softly.

"I won't forget you," Lily insisted, "and neither will my children or their children's children."

"You're my tigers, my tigers," Mother murmured. And they stayed like that a long time, laughing and crying together.

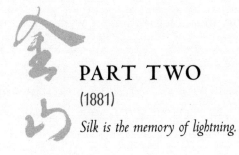

PART TWO

(1881)

Silk is the memory of lightning.

*F*rom 1839 to 1842, China fought a war to stop Britain from selling opium. When China lost, it was forced to lease land to Britain that became Hong Kong. Worse, the war created chaos in southern China, where the war took place. Clans revived old feuds, and bandits became common. Natural disasters like floods also added to the misery.

Things became so desperate that in 1849, when gold was discovered in California, these southern Chinese were willing to risk the deadly voyage to the Land of the Golden Mountain, which is what they called America.

China subsequently fought a second war to halt the drug traffic from 1856 to 1860, and again lost.

At the same time, in 1858, the French began taking over territory in what is now Vietnam, Laos, and Cambodia. There, they began to create large factories to make silk thread.

By 1881, silk was still a major industry in the Three Districts, but another major source of money was the remittances from the men who worked in America and who called themselves Guests of the Golden Mountain.

CHAPTER | 33

5th day of the 8th month of the era Honor's Bond
September 27, 1881
Heaven's Blessing, Nam-hoi District (next to
Shun-te District), Kwangtung Province, China

Little Swallow

The brush thumped against the back of Little Swallow's head.

"Do you have to be so noisy?" Peony grumbled sleepily and rolled over onto her other side. "The sun's not even up yet."

Angrily, Little Swallow found the brush on the floor and pitched it back at her housemate. "Grandmama expects me to start the cooking fire."

From the other side of the room, Jade said, "Tell her you can't do it anymore. It makes you too tired at work. That's how I got out of it." Like Little Swallow and Peony, Jade came from the village, and though they slept at the girls' house, they were expected to help their families before and after their jobs at the factory.

"You try telling that to my grandmama," Little

Swallow griped. She stood on one leg like a crane as she pulled a cloth shoe onto her other foot.

Jade pulled her quilt over her head in mock terror. "I'd sooner put my head in a tiger's mouth."

Little Swallow finished dressing and then braiding her hair. There was just enough moonlight left, so she picked up a mirror. A face with high cheekbones and small, high-set eyes gazed back at her. It was not the prettiest face, but it was hers, so it would have to do. She tucked in a few last strands and inspected her handiwork carefully. The house fined sloppy hairdos, and Peony was especially vigilant when she was awake.

Then Little Swallow tiptoed past the other house-mates who were still asleep. Even though they had held the Seven Seven festival only a little while ago, they were already preparing for the next one—though it would be hard to top what they and the other houses had just done. With the wages from their factory jobs, they could hire the very best performers. And even if it was still a matter of pride to show off their craft, and all the gifts had been made by hand, they had used costly materials worthy of an empress.

Half-finished miniature chairs littered the table, and the house reeked of paint and glue and varnish. Little Swallow's own eyes ached from sewing a miniature dress last night by candlelight. And that was her grandmother's fault. She'd taught Little Swallow to sew so well that the other girls had left the clothing to her.

Grandmama had often told her that silk was in their blood, but remembering how many times the needle had stuck her during lessons, she knew her blood was also in the silk.

As she closed the front door behind her, Little Swallow resented the fact that she had to still do chores in the morning before work and then do more of them in the evening afterward. Peony, whose father was rich, took meals at home, but outside of helping with the cleanup, her time was her own.

Grandmama, though, insisted that idleness was a formula for disaster. As Little Swallow closed the front door behind her quietly, she wondered if the pattern to her life was ever going to change.

Little Swallow had lived in the village all her life, so she could travel its lanes with her eyes shut. She had no problem now walking through the cool darkness. She found herself looking up at the autumn sky, searching for the Weaving Maid and her six sisters, wondering if they had as much work as she did. However, when she heard the first rooster crow, she broke into a run. She needed to have the water boiled for Grandmama's tea before Grandmama got up.

Her heart sank when she smelled the smoke coming from her family's home. She was already too late. Steeling herself for the lecture, she let herself into the house. In the living room on a mat and wrapped up in blankets, her little brother, Doggy, looked like a giant silkworm in his cocoon. Just as she'd feared, her grandmother had already left the mat she shared with Little Swallow's sister, Wisteria, the youngest of the three children.

Guiltily, Little Swallow slipped past him into the kitchen and found her grandmother already in front of the stove. The kitchen was toasty warm, and there was a delicious aroma in the air. Her grandmother was dressed for the day in a clean blouse and pants and vest. Her hair was done up, her face and hands scrubbed with Cousin Fortune's gift—soap brought back from the Land of the Golden Mountain, which was what the clan called America. With a rueful smile, Little Swallow admitted to herself that Grandmama could have passed even Peony's rigorous inspections.

For such a tiny woman, Grandmama packed more energy than Little Swallow and all her housemates combined. In her fifties, Grandmama tended the house and family with the devotion of a dozen servants.

Little Swallow's father was a clerk for the reeling factory and had met her mother when he'd ventured into Shun-te District on a buying trip. However, her mother had died giving birth to Wisteria, and Grandmama had moved in to take care of them. The village half-jokingly referred to it as the Shun-te Invasion—but only if her formidable grandmother couldn't overhear them.

Little Swallow tried to remember her mother and felt guilty when she could not. It seemed now as if Grandmama had always been here, filling up their days and nights.

"Your great-aunt Swallow was always the first one to wake up. You have to live up to your name," Grandmama said without turning around.

Little Swallow was not her formal name recorded in the clan books but her nickname—given to her by her grandmother after a favorite sister who had sold herself into slavery for the sake of the family.

Ears burning, Little Swallow resisted the impulse to hang her head penitently like a six-year-old. "I'm sorry, but it's hard to match her." Little Swallow wished she could have taken another nickname. She knew she would never have the courage to sell herself to save her family.

Grandmama relented. "Well, I know how I felt when I was being compared to your great-aunt all the time." Her rough hand touched Little Swallow's cheek. "And you look so much like her that sometimes I forget you're not her."

"I really do try to work as much as she did, you know," Little Swallow insisted.

Grandmama chuckled. "And I suppose it's hard to get up before me. I never can sleep for very long. It's all those years of raising silkworms." She put something on a plate and turned around. "So here." And she handed it to Little Swallow.

When Little Swallow saw the sticky cakes on it, she felt herself starting to salivate. "I love those."

Grandmama beamed. "Grandparents are supposed to spoil their grandchildren." When Little Swallow made a choking sound, her grandmother added defensively, "Well, I do."

Little Swallow had to admit that there was some truth to that. Though Grandmama was strict with her grandchildren, she had never struck them—which the village considered another of her quirky habits. But then Grandmama had never needed physical threats. One look was usually enough—not only for her grandchildren, but for stray dogs, idling delinquents, and pushy peddlers—to make them behave.

"Whatever happened to your sister after . . . after she went away?" Little Swallow asked as she sat down on a bench next to the table. Having cleaned it to Grandmama's rigorous standards, Little Swallow thought she knew every nick, dent, and whorl in the grain pattern.

Grandmama poured some tea and shuffled over toward her. "I heard some merchant bought her, but I was never able to discover his name or where he lived. Even so, I tried and tried to find her, but I never could. Today would have been . . ."—she corrected herself hopefully—"is her birthday."

Little Swallow suspected the truth. "Is that the real reason you couldn't sleep? Were you thinking about her?"

"It might be," Grandmama admitted, and set the cup in front of her. "The sticky cakes are her favorite too."

Little Swallow lost her appetite for a moment. She was herself and not that other girl. The last thing she wanted to do was copy her great-aunt's tastes too—it was a shame she had liked the sticky cakes, because that ruined the flavor for Little Swallow.

However, when she saw how sad her grandmother had become, Little Swallow forgot to sulk. After a moment's thought, she said cunningly, "Perhaps she's sitting under some tree on the Golden Mountain right now and thinking of you too."

As Little Swallow had hoped, her grandmother's face softened. "Maybe with golden nuggets shining all around," she said. "And so bright you have to shut your eyes." And she went on.

As disciplined and pragmatic as her grandmother could be, she also had an inventive streak she usually kept hidden like a jewel wrapped in layers of dark cloth. But when she let her fancy roam free, her mind would take the wildest flights, especially when it came to the Land of the Golden Mountain. And listening to her grandmother describe that strange, faraway land, Little Swallow felt as if she had grown wings and flown there.

As happened too often, though, in the very midst of the fantasy, Grandmama's happy expression changed to a guilty one. It was as if her conscience had pulled at her mental reins and brought her to an abrupt halt. "We've got so much to do today. Why did you make me waste time like that? Shame on you."

"I like your tales," Little Swallow said, nibbling at another of the slender, rod-like cakes. "You make up ones better than the traveling storytellers." Though Little Swallow was grateful for the conscientious way that her grandmother took care of her family, Little Swallow loved Grandmama's imagination the best.

Brusquely, Grandmama began to fill up a bowl with treats. "No, no, that's a bad habit of mine. I can't give in to it," she said, more to herself than to Little Swallow.

Hoping to entice her into telling another story, Little Swallow said, "The stars were so pretty as I walked here."

Grandmama refused to take the bait, bustling around the kitchen instead. "Maybe you wouldn't have been late if you hadn't gazed at the stars."

"Remember when I was small?" Little Swallow coaxed. "We'd be in the kitchen just like this morning. And you'd take me on your lap and you'd tell me stories about the stars."

Grandmama stubbornly kept on working. "You're too big for that now, and I'm too busy."

Little Swallow just as persistently continued to try to tempt her grandmother. "Sometimes you used to sing that song to me." She began to hum the tune.

Grandmama finally paused. "Yes, the Weaver's song."

Her face took on a faraway look as she began to sing it.

Little Swallow joined in, her strong voice supporting her grandmother's frail one.

"That brings back old memories," Papa said. He stood in the doorway, bringing his palms almost together as, not wanting to wake his other children, he simply panto-mimed applause.

Little Swallow jumped up to get him some tea. "You're up early."

"I have to take a little stroll this morning." Papa was wearing his new robe and vest that Grandmama had sewn for him. "The weavers' guild is trying to bully the farmers into selling their cocoons to them instead of to the fac-tory. So I'm going to escort some sellers here personally."

Suddenly worried, Little Swallow paused as she got a cup. "They say a lot of the weavers are martial artists, and they're even organized into a regiment."

Papa threw back his head and laughed as if Little Swallow had told the funniest joke. "The weavers? They're just all bluster. And if it comes to fighting, I can handle myself." It was Papa who had taught her what she knew of Tai Chi and still exercised when he had time in the morning.

Grandmama gave a grunt. "I don't know. I hear the weavers are desperate. It's been an awful year for silk-worms, and the reeling factories like yours are buying up the few cocoons that are around. If the weavers can't get cocoons, they won't be able to reel their own silk. And without silk, their looms will just gather dust."

"Then they should pay more for the cocoons," Papa shot back.

The weavers' guild and the reeling factories both competed for cocoons. The weavers reeled the cocoons into silk, which they then wove into cloth, but the reeling factories sent their skeins of silk to weaving factories all over the world. Little Swallow had heard that some of the foreign factories were bigger than their village. But the money the foreigners paid for silk allowed the reeling factories in China to pay a higher price for the cocoons.

"You know they can't pay as much as your factory," Grandmama argued. "The largest weavers here don't have more than a dozen looms in their workshops. It was better in the old days before everything got so specialized and so much bigger. When I was Little Swallow's age, we raised our own silkworms and reeled our own silk at home."

"Times change, and we have to change with them." Little Swallow felt she should defend her livelihood. "The foreigners like the factory silk better. They say our machines make the thread finer and more even."

Grandmama bristled. "I'd put up my mother's thread against machine-made any day."

Papa raised his palms as if trying to hold back a charging buffalo. "And I'm sure the foreigners would buy her skeins in an instant. We don't get the quality of cocoons like in the old days."

"That's because farmers don't reel their own silk, so they don't care," Grandmama sniffed. "But maybe you should take some of the clan militia along too. You can't steal a person's livelihood without them getting mad and scared. The weavers are likely to do anything."

"I'll have Cousin Beanpole," Papa said, sitting down on the opposite bench.

Grandmama snorted as she put more cakes on a plate. "He's usually so addled with Demon Mud that he's more of a danger to himself with a spear than he is to the weavers."

Little Swallow felt a chill. Their cousin was just another victim of the foreign drug that had destroyed so many others.

"I know"—Papa spread his hands in resignation— "but he was the only one willing to go. Anyway, he's only for show. Those farmers are scared of their own shadow. All I'm doing is making them feel safe enough to come here in their boats and sell their stuff. I'll be a regular admiral with my little flotilla."

Reassured, Little Swallow poured tea into her father's cup. "Well, if any weaver gives you trouble, you threaten them with Grandmama. That'd make anyone behave."

"Ha," Grandmama said, and nudged the plate of treats toward her son-in-law.

Papa's eyes lit up when he saw the sticky cakes.

"What's the occasion?" He suddenly became nervous. "Did I forget someone's birthday?" He swiveled his head so he could glance guiltily first at Grandmama and then at Little Swallow.

She was about to tell her father that it was her great-aunt's birthday, but Grandmama gave a slight shake of her head. The celebration was their private secret.

"I just felt like it today," Grandmama said, and motioned to the two small baskets on one end of the table. "I even made lunch for you and Little Swallow."

Through the narrow window high up on the kitchen wall, Little Swallow saw the sky lightening. "I have to go," she said, tossing back the rest of her tea. She got up and took her lunch.

Grandmama wriggled her fingers toward the neglected treat. "Don't forget a sticky cake." She watched thoughtfully as her granddaughter snatched up the treat.

Little Swallow opened her basket. It was an omelet and vegetables over rice. Simple but filling fare. Setting the cake on top of it, she said, "Thank you, Grandmama. Be careful, Papa."

And she hurried out of the house. There wasn't time to do her Tai Chi, and she was already feeling stiff.

But there was no choice. She couldn't be late for work.

CHAPTER | 34

Little Swallow

The sky was fast growing lighter in the east, and Little Swallow should have picked up her pace, but when she saw all the lights burning in the mansion, curiosity got the better of her. Like the factory, the mansion had foreign lanterns that used a liquid— something called kerosene—that had to be brought in special from overseas. She wondered why Peony's father, Cousin Fortune, was being so extravagant this morning.

Thirty-two years ago, Cousin Fortune had risked the dangerous voyage to the Land of the Golden Mountain. When he'd retired and come back to China, he'd wanted his home to be just like the houses of prosperous Americans, so he'd built it with high walls perforated with tall windows of glass rather than presenting a solid, safe shield against the world. He also had the nerve to build it fifteen feet higher than the other houses—the more superstitious in the village grumbled that he was stealing more than his share of the luck being sent down by Heaven. Now his home dominated the village, as his story dominated their lives.

Even before his return, he'd sent so much money home that his family was magically impervious to the perils that everyone else faced: the bandit raids, the crushing taxes, the plagues, the floods and droughts, which any year threatened to reduce honest people to wandering beggars. (Peony was the only one in the girls' house who didn't have to work—though to her credit she didn't put on airs about her wealth—and unfortunately, that gave her far too much time to enforce the rules.)

Though Cousin Fortune's letters home had diligently listed the many dangers of the Golden Mountain, other men and boys had tried to imitate him and become Guests in America. Though many of them had died during the voyage or during their stay there in that lawless country, others still kept leaving. (Just the other day, another cousin in the girls' house had heard her brother had been killed by a drunken American.) The mansion had become a monument to Cousin Fortune's past and the clan's future.

Fed by the clan's gossip and her grandmother's imaginings, Little Swallow had always wanted to see the Golden Mountain. Since Cousin Fortune had filled his mansion with artifacts from there, his home would have to do. After all, even if she couldn't find out the reason why the lights were burning, she wouldn't mind seeing the foreign furnishings.

Standing on tiptoe, Little Swallow searched for a gap in the heavy velvet drapes that covered the windows so she could peek inside.

She had just enough time to glimpse odd padded chairs covered in a plush, deep green velvet when the curtains jerked apart and a stranger gazed back at her.

He was in Western-style clothes, and his queue had been braided tight against his head. The Manchus, who ruled the Middle Kingdom—or China, as the Americans called it—had ordered all Chinese males to wear their hair in one long braid down their backs to represent the horses that the Manchus had ridden in their conquest. So the Chinese rebels, who wanted to drive them out, cut off theirs. By pinning the queue against the back of his head, the stranger complied with the law, and yet his short hair suggested he sided with the rebels.

Little Swallow stood petrified as he left the window.

Too late, she heard the front door open. "Can I help you?" The stranger stood there. He had an odd accent that Little Swallow could not place, and in his hand was the most outlandish hat with a wide felt brim curled along the side edges like a leaf shriveling in a fire. There was also a dimple tucked into the top of the crown, so that it looked like a small mountain with a dell instead of a rounded peak. A narrow belt of bright red and blue beads ran around the base of the crown, and there was a feather tucked into it.

"Uh, no, no," Little Swallow said, backing up. "I was just, you know, waiting for somebody."

At that moment, Pearl rounded the corner. She lived in one of the other girls' houses in the village and was the sole support of her grandparents, mother, and little sisters and brothers. "Little Swallow, ready for that steamy jail?"

"And here she is." Little Swallow hooked her arm through Pearl's and dragged her startled friend along.

"Who's that?" Pearl asked, twisting her head to stare at the stranger.

"Shh, I don't know," Little Swallow said as she tugged her friend away, "but he's scary."

Pearl freed herself. "Cousin Fortune's whole place frightens me."

Nervous, Little Swallow looked over her shoulder, but the stranger had disappeared back into the mansion. The drapes were closed again.

She thought of the alien things she had seen inside. "At least it's not boring."

Playfully, they matched steps together. "All we've ever known is this village. It'd be nice to have a real adventure and go there." Little Swallow hardly believed her own daring. Neither she nor Pearl had ever been beyond the clan's territory.

Pearl shook her head. "They say it's even more danger-ous for girls than for boys."

"I know," Little Swallow sighed. "Sometimes I even wish I were a man so I could go."

"It's still too risky. Besides, what does the Gold Mountain have that we don't have?" She pointed to the general store that had been constructed against the village wall. Next to it was a rice store and a butcher shop—all owned by the company and all selling everything cheaper than anywhere else. "We've even got our own doctor. How many other places can say that? I'm staying right here."

"With the other cabbages," Little Swallow teased.

"And proud of it." Pearl giggled. "Hey, do you think that fellow came to ask Cousin Fortune for Peony? A lot of the clan would say it's high time."

Peony was the oldest in the girls' house by several years and had often said she was never getting married. So far Cousin Fortune had humored her, but it was widely held that he had spoiled her too much and she should already have started a family of her own.

Little Swallow made a face. "Well, she won't have him. Who'd want a husband who dresses so weird?"

Pearl and Little Swallow called out their greetings to the other girls heading toward the factory. They were all about the same youthful age, because operating the machines required nimble hands and good eyesight—though those things would not last forever. When that day came, Little Swallow would have to find some other way to help the family.

More workers trickled out of other lanes, merging into a wide, long river of several hundred young women from the ages of thirteen to twenty-five. After years of straining her eyes in the dimness, a factory girl usually had to leave at twenty-six.

However, this morning, twenty-six seemed a long way off for the two friends. Chatting with one another, they left the village, skirting along a fishpond on a dike that had been newly repaired thanks to their employer. The clan's fishponds spread out before them like the bronze scales of a fish. Fruit orchards rose like tufted fins.

More females were streaming in from the neighboring villages on the island. Others were even arriving in small boats rowed by male relatives, climbing up the bank to the factory where mulberry orchards had once stood.

Little Swallow thought it was a little ironic to replace the trees that fed the silkworms with the machines that would process them. Idly, she wondered if one day the factory would grow so large that it would replace all the orchards and ponds. Even if it was her livelihood, she hoped that day would never come.

A tall brick wall had been constructed around the factory to protect it against the annual river floods, which could be quite high. The factory peered over the wall now like a dark alien monster. Columns of brick stood at the corners and were spaced along the sides, providing the main support for the tiled roof. Wooden walls filled in the spaces between the brick columns. Gray smoke rose from the chimney, the steam engine's boiler having been fired up hours before.

Everything about the factory had been controversial. Again, some of the clan had complained that the tall building would steal Heaven's blessings before they could reach the lower houses. And the tall chimney was all wrong by the rules of wind and water, or geomancy, as they were also called. It threw off the lines of energy that ran through the earth. Some of the clan had even complained about having men and women working side by side.

If Uncle had not given some shares to the clan elders and small doles to widows and elderly folk, the factory might never have been built. Since then, any opposition had been silenced, not only because so many families depended upon the workers' wages but because of the many services Uncle had provided and his generosity to public works. If more factory owners were like Uncle, there would be fewer complaints.

Even so, Uncle's workers paid a personal price. Pearl sighed, inspecting the back of her free hand. The skin was chafed and red from the hot water she had to handle. "You know what my brother called me the other day?" She didn't wait for an answer. "Crab claws."

Little Swallow held up her own hand. Her slender fingers were rough enough to show she had a hard job, but were still much smoother than Pearl's. "My grandmother has an ointment. I'll get you some."

They passed through the gates of the brick walls and into the courtyard, where row after row of buckets had been set near the well. Little Swallow and Pearl got in line, waiting their turn until they could each fill a bucket with water. Then, bucket in one hand and lunch basket in the other, Little Swallow trudged behind Pearl toward the factory.

Uncle was standing by the doorway, greeting the workers as they entered. He wore an elegant robe woven and embroidered with his very own silk.

There was a chorus of "Good morning, Uncle" from the workers. Even if they weren't part of his clan, he liked everyone to call him Uncle.

Years ago, Uncle had been a schoolteacher in this very village but had left to make his fortune as a merchant in what had once been Chinese territory in the south, but which the French had seized and now called Indochina. There, he'd become fascinated by the factories the French were constructing and studied everything. When he'd made his fortune, he'd returned and constructed the factory in his home village rather than in one of the cities, because, as he liked to joke, he'd rather be skinned by his own kin than by strangers.

He'd even avoided bad feelings with the rival clans by openly sharing information with anyone who wanted to start a factory. When his own clan objected, he argued that if he kept his knowledge secret, envious clans would use their connections in the government to close him down. However, if those clans were also in the silk business, they would use those same connections to encourage the industry instead.

He wasn't afraid of competition, arguing that the rest of the world hungered for Chinese silk, so there would be plenty of customers to go around.

Next to him, his son wore a Western-style suit and shoes—of better quality than the stranger's—but Uncle's one affectation was the French-style cane with the gold handle and tip, which he used as a pointer.

Uncle beamed as if Little Swallow were his own granddaughter. "Little Swallow, how've you been eating?" He swept his cane up in a salute.

Little Swallow ducked the swinging stick easily. When Uncle became excited, he got careless, so she'd been prepared.

Since she was already bent, she simply gave her head a polite little bob. "Fine, Uncle. Grandmama made some sticky cakes this morning."

Uncle patted the tummy that bulged beneath his robe. "No one makes them better than she does."

Little Swallow straightened cautiously, one eye on the

still-upraised cane. "I'll ask her to make some for you," she promised—*even*, she thought, *if I have to fight off my greedy brother and sister to get them to you.*

Uncle lowered the cane to his shoulder. "Your father's going to bring me some good cocoons today, right?" Though his pose was nonchalant, there was a hint of anxiety.

"He's taking along an armed guard," Little Swallow said, deciding it would only make Uncle worry more if he knew it was Cousin Beanpole who was supposed to protect the precious supplies.

Uncle patted her on the shoulder guiltily. "I'm sorry it's come to this, but we really need the cocoons for all those orders of ours."

Little Swallow managed a smile. "I think it would have been better to take along Grandmama instead."

"A formidable woman," Uncle agreed. "Oops. I'm so sorry." In taking the cane from his shoulder, he'd tapped a girl behind Little Swallow.

As he apologized and fussed over his victim, Little Swallow and Pearl stepped inside onto the floor of red, unglazed tiles, which were so good at absorbing all the day's moisture.

The windows were shuttered, but some light fell from the sliding skylights overhead. The skylights' panes were shell polished to paper thinness, so they shone with a silvery light like slices of the moon. The air inside was still humid from yesterday's steam, and the bricks were dark with dampness and smelled of mildew.

A main aisle divided the large, long room into two halves. In each half were row after row of long tables. There was a shallow, dark gray porcelain basin at each reeling station, which fit into a hole on top of the table. A steam pipe would heat the water in the basin so the cocoon strands could be separated.

Just a little behind each station was the reeling machine. Pulleys and belts ran to the steam engine at one end of the factory in an intricate but dangerous web. Grandmama had brought her mother's hand reeler with her. It seemed like a child's toy compared to the factory's great mechanisms.

Some of the girls headed to the left to the large room to sort cocoons, but Little Swallow and Pearl walked down the main aisle. Each table had a name and each station a number. When they reached the table of the moon, they sidled into the narrow space between table and reeling machines, easing around the other chattering girls already at their stations until Little Swallow and Pearl reached eight and nine respectively.

Her basin was just as she had left it yesterday, tilted to one side. Fitting the basin into the hole, she filled it with water from the bucket and then set the pail on the floor. The steam was rattling in the pipe as it heated the water.

As the other girls quickly took their places, the steam

engine at one end of the factory began huffing and chuffing as if working itself up to the day's labor.

As they waited for their shift to start, Little Swallow pumped her arms to loosen her muscles. "I'm still aching from yesterday. Oh, sorry." In the confined space, she had struck Pearl. There was just over a third of a meter separating each basin, so she would be bumping elbows all day with Pearl and her neighbor at station seven.

Pearl was pressing the small of her back. "It's not your fault. I wish Uncle'd give us more room to work."

"It's hard here, but my father says it's like paradise compared to other factories he's seen," Little Swallow said. "Some places are so awful that the girls have all sorts of health problems and they don't get their full growth."

With her hands on her hips, Pearl twisted back and forth. "He couldn't treat his own kinswomen too bad— especially with your grandmama keeping an eye on you."

Little Swallow chuckled in agreement. "Yes, especially my grandmama." When she'd been growing up, Grandmama had never let her get away with the slightest risk such as swimming in a rain-swollen stream. It had been exasperating to have to sit on the bank while the other children played in the water and teased her. And yet there had never been one moment in her childhood when Little Swallow had not felt safe.

Just as the water in her basin began to roil, the steam engine hissed like some monstrous snake, and the factory whistle blasted its shrill call. As many times as she had heard it, it always made Little Swallow jump.

And then their foreman, Cousin Piggy, strutted past like a little rooster as he slapped the table periodically. "Party time's over, girls," he said, and told them the size of the thread they were to reel that day.

Little Swallow and Pearl repeated the thread size so Cousin Piggy could be sure they'd gotten the order right.

Men had all the jobs with authority, from acting as foremen to servicing the engine, and unlike the girls, the men were of all ages, like Cousin Piggy, who was in his midforties.

In front of the basin was a basket full of cocoons like trapped tiny clouds. Stretching out a hand, she grabbed a handful of cocoons and dropped them into the basin until it was full.

Then she tugged at the lever engaging the reeling machine. The next moment, the belts overhead began to rumble, and gears and wheels began to creak and turn. As each girl did the same, the volume of noise quickly swelled, until the only way to make oneself heard was to shout. Since most of the girls could read, it was often easier to communicate by writing out a word with the water on the table.

When she had first come to the factory, the racket had scared her, as well as the fast-moving mechanisms. And the fear had not left her entirely, which was probably just as well, because it helped keep her alert. If clothing or hair got caught in the machinery, a girl could be maimed if not killed. She'd taken care to pin her own hair up for safety's sake.

Picking up a pair of long chopsticks, Little Swallow stared intently at the bobbing cocoons. Next to her Pearl did the same, waiting for the gum that bound the fibers together to soften.

Sweat from the heat and the humidity was already beading her face. In an hour, the factory would feel as hot as a wok cooking human dumplings. The steamy air was good for the thread, keeping it more flexible and less likely to snap, but it wasn't good for the humans who reeled it.

Taking a twig brush, Little Swallow began to pat the cocoons. After several minutes, she could feel the cocoons were softening. The best silk was on the middle and inner layers, but first she had to remove the floss on the outer layer. She went on deftly ensnaring more of it on the brush. When she finally lifted the brush, a tangled mass of dripping fibers came with it. While she kept drawing the brush away in her right hand, her left hand grabbed the middle of the waste filaments.

She always felt a shock every morning when she first felt the strands heated by the boiling water. Her hand became a bright red, but her mind had learned to wall off the pain so she could focus on splitting the snarled bunch in two.

Hooking the upper half onto a nail on the side of the

reeling machine, she freed the brush and put it down on the table, picking up her chopsticks again and using them to shove the cocoons under the water as her left hand kept drawing the rest of the waste away.

Then she balled the two halves of waste material and threw it down beside the basin with a plop. Even this stuff could be used for something, and she would turn it in at the end of the day along with her reels of good silk.

She replaced the chopsticks in her right hand with the brush once more, but this time she gently stroked the cocoons. Soon. It would be soon.

Squinting in the dimness, she barely saw the first white tendrils of good silk snag on the twig tips. They were as fine as spider whiskers. Switching the brush to her left hand, she used the chopsticks to pick a tendril. Then two. Three. With her chopsticks, she gathered them together. Four. Five.

Different thread sizes required a different number of strands. With a deft twist of her wrist, she wound them loosely together and connected them to the part of the reeling machine that would wind the strands tight and squeeze out the excess water before feeding them to the reeling machine's reel.

As the thread whipped by like lightning, her eyes searched for any tangle or knots. If she saw one, she had to stop her machine, snap off the problem, and then rewind the filaments together and feed them again into the reeler. She also had to be ready to add a new cocoon before one got used up. The idea was to get one continuous silk thread of uniform width on the reel.

No one was as good as Little Swallow. She hardly ever got fined because her thread was too thick or too thin or too dirty or the dozens of other things that had to be done for perfect silk.

Cousin Piggy said she succeeded because she had an affinity with the reeling machine, but she knew it was with the silk itself. And as hard as this was, it would be even harder with the next crop of silkworms—the one that her father was buying—because the cocoons from cooler weather were never as good as the summer crops.

Gradually the damp air began to fill with loose fragments of silk. Little Swallow couldn't help coughing. Everyone did. But they went right on working.

Grandmama said silk was in her blood. No wonder, she ate enough of it.

If she let herself think about how long her day was, she would scream. Instead, all her attention was on the threads and nothing else.

She was concentrating so hard that she did not notice Uncle's son, her cousin Virtue, until he banged his hand on the table for her attention.

"Little Swallow," he yelled over the mechanical racket. "Stop your machine and come with me. Your father's hurt."

CHAPTER | 35

Little Swallow

Little Swallow's head shot up to look at him. "Where is he?" she hollered, suddenly panicked.

Cousin Virtue waved a hand at the storage room. "Back there."

Little Swallow stood in a daze, refusing to believe her ears. It was Pearl who shut off her machine. "Go on," she shouted, giving Little Swallow a small push.

"Thank you," Little Swallow murmured numbly, hoping as she rushed off that Pearl had heard her somehow despite the noise. She hurried with Cousin Virtue past row after row of rumbling, rattling machinery and through the doorway into the side of a large room.

From the very beginning, Uncle had bought his cocoons directly from the farmers, and though the newer factories found it easier to purchase their supply through middlemen called cocoon markets, Uncle had kept on with his old ways, trusting to the relationships he had built with the farmers.

Against one wall, shelves held spare wide leather machine belts, wooden reels, and other replacements for the machinery, while silk skeins lay waiting to be packed and shipped around the world. Despite her worry, Little Swallow had to thread her way through the baskets of cocoons covering the floor.

The light shining from the outside reduced her father to a silhouette against the bright landscape, but he seemed to be sitting on a stool while one of the other clerks bandaged his head.

Cousin Beanpole stood next to him, leaning on his spear and trembling—though whether from fear or withdrawal from the Demon Mud Little Swallow couldn't say.

"What happened?" she demanded when she finally reached him.

"The weavers attacked us," Cousin Beanpole said in a daze, his drug-ravaged mind unable to understand why anyone would want to pick on him.

"I'm afraid your grandmother will finish the job the weavers started," Papa sighed, indicating the rip on his sleeve. "Look what happened to my new robe."

Little Swallow examined the bruises on his right cheek and the bandage now wrapping his head like a turban. "She'll take one look at you and make one of her ointments for you."

Papa made a face. "I'd sooner face the weavers again."

She inspected the sleeve's gash carefully. The edges were so even that it had to have been made by a sharp blade. Fortunately, it hadn't touched Papa's arm. "I can mend this," she promised.

"That's a relief," Papa said, and then slapped his knees triumphantly. "So mission accomplished. We got the cocoons through."

There were a dozen farmers huddled just within the doorway, peering behind them occasionally as if they expected hordes of weavers to pour over the wall. Huge baskets of cocoons had been dumped to the left of the doorway. Male factory workers were bringing in more from the farmers' boats, a basket hanging on either end of a bamboo pole that rested on their shoulders.

"What happened?" she asked her father.

"We'd just gotten the boats loaded when they came at us," Father said.

"They even tried to take my weapon," Cousin Beanpole boasted as he held up his spear by the shaft. "But I got the boat away in time."

Contemptuously, Little Swallow noticed that neither the supposed bodyguard nor the farmers had a mark on them. "So you held them off all by yourself?" she asked her father.

"Just until everyone left," Father said modestly. "And then I hitched up my robe, took a running start, and sprang for the boat."

Cousin Beanpole scratched the tip of his nose. "I didn't think anyone could jump that far."

"Apparently, not far enough," Little Swallow said, indicated the muddy hem of Papa's robe. "When I mend your clothes, I'll wash them too."

Papa looked about at the shed floor, satisfied. "At least, between this load and what we've got, we should have enough cocoons for a while. That should tide you over, sir, until the magistrate can send troops to keep order."

Uncle shook his head. "The weavers hired a scholar to help them with the paperwork. And he's friends with the magistrate, so the magistrate will look the other way."

Papa rubbed his thumb and index finger together. "You mean tea money?" *Tea money* was a polite term for a bribe.

"Whatever the reason, we can't expect any help from the government," Uncle sighed. "We're on our own. I've tried and tried to set up a meeting with the guild so we can reach some sort of accommodation together, but so far . . ." He shrugged.

Papa tried to smile and winced. "Right now, I'd say that they're more interested in reasoning with their fists than with words."

"At any rate, well done." Uncle clapped a hand on Papa's shoulder, and then he looked at Little Swallow. "Take our brave warrior home and tend his wounds."

True to Little Swallow's predictions, Grandmama had put Papa to bed as soon as they got home and then concocted her medicines so foul-smelling that the family had opened all the windows and doors despite the cool weather.

As usual when she left the factory, Little Swallow's ears were still slightly deafened from the noise there. She sat down with her brother and sister in Papa's bedroom.

He pinched his nose. "Phew, well at least there's one benefit from the beating: That stench will fumigate all the bugs in the house."

"I'll have you know I keep a clean house." Grandmama frowned from the doorway. She had a small bowl balanced in each hand. From the odor rising from both, it was amazing that the medicines hadn't eaten away the porcelain.

Papa shrank visibly. "Of course. I was just joking."

"Well, I wasn't when I told you to be careful," Grandmama scolded. Little Swallow and the others edged away from her, but there was no escaping the fumes. She extended the bowl in her left hand. "This ointment will take care of your outside." She thrust out the bowl in her right hand. "And this will heal your insides. So drink."

Papa started to get up. "Really, I'm feeling much better now."

"Eh!" Grandmama said sharply, and arched an eyebrow.

Papa reluctantly sank back under the "look." "But I guess it would be good to rest a little bit."

"That's right," Grandmama said, handing him the bowl. "The factory will just have to manage without you."

As Papa raised the bowl, he fought to keep from wrinkling his nostrils and failed. As a result, his nose wriggled so much that he looked like a dog sampling the air. After a sip, he tried to lower the bowl. "Wonderful! Your elixir has me feeling better already."

"All of it" was all Grandmama said. Little Swallow and her family could sympathize with Papa's situation, each of them having suffered their grandmother's remedies, but that didn't mean they were about to intervene.

Showing as much courage as when he had faced the weavers, Papa drank it to the dregs, the bump in Papa's throat bobbing up and down in a rapid beat. When he was finished, he turned the bowl upside down to show that not a drop remained.

"Good," Grandmama said, and took it from him, nodding to Little Swallow's sister, Wisteria. "Fetch my good hat." Then she beckoned Little Swallow's brother, Doggy, over. "Put the salve on your father's bruises."

"Do I have to?" he asked, reluctant to touch the stuff.

"I have to see Uncle," Grandmama said.

Little Swallow had a premonition of impending doom. "Why?"

"To make sure that worse doesn't happen," Grandmama said.

CHAPTER | 36

Little Swallow

Grandmama adjusted her good hat with one hand as she stepped outside the house. The straw of the hat had been woven in a pretty pattern and had cost all of five cash, so she wore it only on important occasions.

Little Swallow adjusted her stride to her tiny grandmother's legs as she marched down the lane. "Grandmama, you can't tell Uncle what to do."

"Just watch me," Grandmama said, holding her basket tight against her hip.

Little Swallow turned, backpedaling so she could face her grandmother directly. "But Papa works for Uncle. And so do I."

Grandmama marched on resolutely. "When I was young, I used to trust people to take care of me. But then

I realized that sometimes they wouldn't. And when they didn't, bad things could happen to me and the ones I loved."

"Oh, like my great-aunt," Lily said in a small voice as she understood. Before this, Grandmama had never elaborated on why her sister had been sold into slavery.

Even now, Grandmama didn't want to explain any further. "Yes. So I swore back then that when I had a family, I was going to keep them safe. And that's what I'm doing now."

Little Swallow pivoted back so she was walking normally. Grandmama was as fierce as a tigress when it came to protecting them, so she knew there was no use arguing.

Word had spread fast through the village, so they kept having to answer solicitous questions as they walked on. Even when they left the village, a cousin tending a fishpond called to them to ask about Papa.

"Hey, it's the nosy girl," a voice said.

She turned to see the stranger. He waved a hand to her as he spoke to Cousin Fortune. "This is the little birdie I told you about that was peeking through your window." The wide-brimmed, high-crowned hat with the dent was perched on his head now, so that he resembled a mountain with a halo cloud encircling its peak.

Grandmama clapped her hand on Little Swallow's shoulder the way she had done when Little Swallow was young and had done something naughty. From experience,

Little Swallow knew she couldn't run away.

"What did you do now?" Grandmama demanded.

"I got curious and peeked into Cousin Fortune's house," Little Swallow mumbled, and in a louder voice said, "I apologize, Cousin Fortune."

Grandmama's fingers tightened on her shoulder, not enough to be painful but just enough to warn her that there was punishment waiting for her in the near future. "I'm sorry, Cousin Fortune. I'll see to it that she won't do it again, but this is partly your fault, you know."

Grandmama was heading off a tirade from Cousin Fortune by taking the offensive.

Cousin Fortune set his hands on his chest indignantly. "Me? I didn't peek through *your* window."

"As long as your house remains a secret, people will want to see," Grandmama reasoned. "My granddaughter isn't the first. Throw your house open one day. Invite everyone inside. Maybe once they've satisfied their curiosity, they'll stop peeking."

"I am not running a theater, Lily," Cousin Fortune spluttered.

"Why not?" the stranger said. "You could charge admission and get even richer."

"I'll leave that to you," Cousin Fortune said. "You're the one with funny notions." He tilted his head back to gaze at Little Swallow. "You're Little Swallow, Peony's friend, aren't you?"

It was news to Little Swallow that she was Peony's friend. If anything, she would probably be the cause of Peony's future stomach ulcer. However, she said, "Yes, sir."

"I'm Ching Heavenly Fortune," the stranger said. "But most people call me Lucky." He lifted the odd hat up for a moment and then set it back down his head.

"Why are you wearing that absurd hat? Are you a clown?" Grandmama had all the delicacy of a water buffalo.

He tapped the brim. "This is what folk wear on the Golden Mountain."

"Only the cowboys," Cousin Fortune said.

Grandmama tapped her fingers against the basket as she studied him. "Have you even seen a cow, young man?"

"Not until I got to China," Lucky admitted sheepishly. "They're bigger than I thought."

"Anyway"—Little Swallow frowned—"you're Chinese, so you should wear a Chinese hat."

Lucky hooked a thumb under his belt and slouched. "You'll never get me to wear a coolie hat, if that's what you mean."

Little Swallow resisted the impulse to grab his collar and pull him up straight. His sloppy posture annoyed her as much as his casual attitude. "And what's wrong with a nice straw hat? Everyone wears them, including me sometimes."

"But they make my head itch," Lucky joked as he

extended his hand toward her.

Little Swallow stared at it, wondering what he wanted her to give him.

Cousin Fortune forced Lucky's arm down. "You're not on the Golden Mountain anymore. People here don't shake hands."

"Especially well-brought-up girls," Grandmama sniffed, stepping between her and Lucky.

Lucky raised his ridiculous hat again. "You have my deepest apologies, Auntie Lily. This is my first time in China." He called the Middle Kingdom by its American name.

Grandmama tilted her head to the side. "The first time? You weren't born here?"

Cousin Fortune leaned over and pretended to whisper conspiratorially. "He was born on the Golden Mountain. They can be very . . . um . . . forward there."

Grandmama eyed Lucky curiously, as if he had grown a second head. "Your poor mother. Not many women go there from here."

"My father was a merchant," Lucky explained, "who saw a new market. And he wanted my mother with him."

"Well, women aren't going to leave China for America anymore," Cousin Fortune said. "I hear the Americans are going to bar all women soon."

"No, there are going to be exemptions for merchants and scholars," Lucky corrected him politely. "I know all about the new immigration laws that the Americans are drafting, because my family contributes to the legal fund fighting them. So"—he winked at Little Swallow—"there's still a way for you to leave here."

Grandmama planted herself between him and Little Swallow, as firm as the Great Wall. "I don't know how they talk to young ladies on the Golden Mountain, sir, but *that* is definitely not how proper young gentlemen do it here."

"It's not even how they speak in Sunning," Cousin Fortune said to his visitor, "so don't be so familiar with a girl when you meet one there either."

Sunning was one of the Four Districts to the southwest of Canton.

Lucky clasped his hands together and bowed. Even when he was trying to be politely formal, there seemed something mocking about it. Perhaps it was his perpetual smile. "Yes, please forgive this humble person's ignorance," he said. "Not only was I born in America, but my family comes from Sunning."

"Sunning?" Grandmama sniffed. "That explains a lot."

Cousin Fortune nodded his head politely. "Now, if you excuse us. We have business with Uncle."

"What a coincidence. So do we," Grandmama said.

Cousin Fortune looked like he was going to object, but Lucky spoke before he could. "Then we can go together.

It'll be so much nicer to have such pretty company on our stroll."

"Thank you, that's most kind," Grandmama said, and smiled at Cousin Fortune. "It will help make up for your discourtesy."

Cousin Fortune's irritation at the intrusion changed to confusion. "What discourtesy did I do?"

"Keeping your mansion so secret, of course," Grandmama said. "Now, please, gentlemen. Let's not keep Uncle waiting."

As they set off, Little Swallow noticed that Grandmama was careful to remain between her and Cousin Fortune's visitor. Glancing at her blouse and slacks, she saw that she had forgotten to clean off the bits of silk that had landed on the dark cloth during work. She looked now as if she had rolled through the dust. Surreptitiously, whenever Lucky was looking the other way, she brushed her clothes.

Lucky was mistaken, though, if he thought it was going to be a pleasant jaunt through the countryside, because Grandmama interrogated him as thoroughly as a magistrate with a suspected murderer.

Except for his habit of ambushing overly curious girls, he seemed more than respectable. Cousin Fortune had met him overseas, where Lucky worked in his father's store. In his early twenties, Lucky had stopped by to deliver a parcel to Cousin Fortune before he continued on to his father's town in Sunning.

As they neared the factory, she could see the farmers setting off on the stream in a flotilla of empty boats.

"So you came back to get married?" Grandmama asked shrewdly. It was a common enough practice for Guests to follow. They would marry a girl here, and while the wife remained in China, the Guests would return to the Golden Mountain to work another five years before returning for a visit to their family. Often, their children only saw their fathers every few years.

"I think that's what my parents are hoping," Lucky said. "But they know better than to order me to do something."

Grandmama looked scandalized by his rebelliousness, but Cousin Fortune shrugged. "The ones born on the Golden Mountain are all a peculiar lot."

"The main reason I came to China was to set up contracts for our company," Lucky explained to Grandmama.

"And what do you think of your homeland?" Little Swallow asked.

"America's my homeland," Lucky insisted.

"Even if they're making it tough on all the Guests?" Cousin Fortune asked.

"I don't run away from fights," Lucky said.

CHAPTER | 37

Little Swallow

Uncle received them cordially in his office. He must have been surprised to see Grandmama and Little Swallow follow his visitors inside, but since Lucky and Cousin Fortune seemed to accept their company, he said nothing.

None of the factory girls, including Little Swallow, had ever been in the room. Trying not to be obvious, she looked around. His teak desk was covered with invoices and correspondence, some in American writing, and there were samples of silk thread of all widths and types on the shelves. There were odd narrow cabinets with big drawers that turned out to have more papers filed in them. It was full of odd foreign contraptions about which Little Swallow didn't have a clue.

After assuring himself that Little Swallow's father was

all right, Uncle motioned for them to take seats. Then he turned to his visitor from Sunning. "Cousin Fortune has told me you're a forward-looking young man."

Little Swallow noticed that Uncle was the one to extend his hand and shake Lucky's after the Western fashion.

When Lucky had sat down, he took off his hat and set it on his knee. "I have some ideas about the future that might benefit the both of us, sir."

Grandmama cleared her throat. "There won't be a future if we don't do something about the weavers. They all practice martial arts, so they can field thousands of fighters."

Uncle sat back down in his big wooden chair and leaned his cane against the wall. "Don't worry, Lily. I'm drafting a letter to the magistrate. A very strong one."

Grandmama lifted her head heavenward and rolled her eyes in exasperation. "That toad will just use it to light a candle."

Uncle tapped his fingertips together. "And I've already sent a letter to the weavers offering to negotiate."

"It's going to take more than words to stop the weavers," Grandmama snorted. "They raised quite a fuss in the city thirty years ago, and they sound ready to do the same here. It's not just the factory that's in danger. The whole village is. You need to call out the militia now."

Uncle was as smooth as plum paste. "Lily, if we call out

the militia, who's going to tend the fishponds and everything else? It would be a terrible economic disruption."

"The women of this clan will take over the men's work in an emergency like they always have." Grandmama tapped the desk with stiff fingers to emphasize her words. "The time to muster the militia is now, not when the weavers are at the gate with knives, spears, and torches."

Uncle tried to dismiss them by saying, "Let's discuss this later." He bent his head toward Lucky. "This gentleman didn't make an appointment to discuss the clan's affairs."

Lucky cleared his throat. "Excuse me, sir, but it does affect me, because our store needs reliable sources of supply."

"In fact," Grandmama said, "considering that some of our militia will be as useless as Cousin Beanpole, you ought to hire some mercenaries."

"That's going too far," Uncle said, and he appealed to Cousin Fortune for support. "You own stock in the company. The more guards I get, the less our profits will be."

Cousin Fortune shook his head. "I've seen what an angry mob can do. I was working in a small Chinatown over on the Golden Mountain until a bunch of Americans came in and burned it to the ground. I barely got out alive. A lot of my neighbors didn't. So I say you can never have too much protection. We need the militia *and* the mercenaries."

"And let's say the weavers burn this factory." Lucky looked about as if he could already see flames around them. "Sparks could carry into the village. A lot of the clan could lose their homes."

Cousin Fortune pressed his fingertips together and thought for a moment. "The clan leaders have shares too. They won't want to lose either their factory or their houses, so they'll call out the militia." When he leaned forward, his chair creaked. "I'd be willing to contribute to the mercenaries' pay too. And there are plenty of families whose men are Guesting on the Golden Mountain. They'll have some money, and I'll bet they've heard from their menfolk about the danger of mobs. I'm sure they'll also chip in to hire a few mercenaries."

"All right, all right. I give in." His usual charm worn away, Uncle glowered at Grandmama. "I think I'll sic *you* on the weavers first. That'd serve them right."

"Unfortunately, I'm too busy keeping my grandchildren from terrorizing the village to bother with hooligans from outside." Smiling sweetly, Grandmama set the basket on the desk. "But I know an empty belly makes even big boys grumpy. So have an afternoon snack."

When Uncle lifted the lid and saw the sticky cakes inside, he sighed. "If you'd given me these in the first place, you could have convinced me without all that badgering."

CHAPTER 38

*6th to 7th day of the 8th month of the era
Honor's Bond
September 28 to 29, 1881*

Little Swallow

The next morning when Little Swallow left the
girls' house, the lanes were crowded with clans-
men carrying spears, halberds, swords, sickles,
and a few flintlock muskets. The militia was mustering.
To the rest of the world, it was no great military threat,
but the militia would keep the weavers away from the
village.

As she passed Cousin Fortune's house, she couldn't
help glancing at it. Cousin Fortune was just shutting his
front door behind him. In his hand, he had a sleek foreign rifle. "If you're trying to snoop inside my house, it's
shut up tight. And if you're looking for Lucky, he left last
night."

For some strange reason, Little Swallow felt a little
disappointed, but she said politely, "It's a good idea to

escape while he can and get to Sunning."

"No, he'll be back. He just went to the city with Uncle's boy to hire help," Cousin Fortune said. "I have an acquaintance up there who . . . um . . . acts as a contractor in such matters."

"Why?" Little Swallow wondered. "Lucky's not part of our clan."

Cousin Fortune shouldered his gun. "You'll have to ask him."

There had been disturbing reports of clerks from the cocoon markets and silk farmers beaten up. Threats had been painted on the sides of the reeling factories all through the area. It seemed like there was a new rumor every hour. She started to worry about Uncle's son—and Lucky too, of course—because they might meet some of the angry weavers.

The next day, though, Uncle's son and Lucky returned with a dozen mercenaries. Little Swallow had grown up on stories of wandering heroes who went about righting wrongs, and the girls' house had a fine collection of such novels, so she had been expecting noble-looking warriors. The hard-bitten veterans who arrived scared her as much as the weavers did.

One of them was gray-haired and had fought the British in the last war that had tried to keep the foreigners from selling opium here. He called himself the Rain Man, which was the nickname of the hero who had led the noble outlaw band in the novel *Water Margin*. She had read the much-thumbed copy of it in the girls' house, so she knew the character had been named that because he had helped people when they needed him most. She hoped that the old, shabby fighter was up to his nickname.

The other mercenaries had fought against bandits and pirates—though from their scruffy appearance and rough manners Little Swallow wondered what side they had actually been on. However, they seemed to defer to the natural authority of the Rain Man.

Uncle had nearly choked at all the mercenaries until Lucky had told him that he was paying the other ten out of his own purse. The Rain Man, it seemed, had convinced him that they would need no less than that number.

Though the girls usually tried to preserve their precious rest time by taking lunch in the factory, as one they left the factory because they had heard the mercenaries were drilling the militia in the courtyard, the largest open space in the village. Feet stomped, blades flashed in the sun, and men chanted in unison.

Little Swallow was surprised to see Lucky's outlandish hat bobbing up and down as he trained with one squad.

After a short while, they took a break, and he came over when he saw her. "I thought you'd be on your way to Sunning now," she said to him.

"I don't like to leave a job half finished, so I borrowed this." He held his spear awkwardly.

"Have you ever touched one of those before?" Little Swallow asked.

He grinned up at the blade. "They had to tell me which end to use for poking. I've seen you doing Tai Chi in the morning. I think you'd do a lot better with this than me."

"Were you peeking at me?" she teased.

"Turnabout's fair play, and it's hard to miss you when you're exercising in the street," he replied.

"My housemates complain if I do it inside." Impulsively, she held out her lunch. "Have you eaten yet?"

He stared at the wall as he tried to remember and then looked back at her. "As a matter of fact, no. I've been too busy becoming a soldier."

"Then here." She held out her rice bowl to him. As he began to gobble it down, she couldn't help warning him. "The risk is real, you know. Why would you die for strangers?"

He paused, rice grains around his mouth. "Ah, but you're not strangers. I know Fortune and Uncle and your grandmother." He paused. "And also a certain little birdie who likes to peek in people's houses."

"Well, I think it's stupid to stay here," she said. "Go home."

He arched an eyebrow. "Worried about me?" he teased.

"Not in the least," she snapped.

He tried to talk about something else, but though it was a wonderful opportunity to satisfy her curiosity about the Golden Mountain, she was so miffed with him that she kept silent instead.

He looked sorry when the factory whistle blew. "Time to go back to work," she said, and took the bowl and chopsticks back.

"Thank you," he said.

With a polite nod, she turned.

Pearl was by her side in the next instant. "Well?"

"Well, nothing," Little Swallow sniffed. "He's . . . he's a friend of my grandmother's." Her empty stomach was already grumbling. But what could she do? She couldn't let a guest of the clan starve, could she?

CHAPTER | 39

*8th to 14th day of the 8th month of the era
Honor's Bond
September 30 to October 6, 1881*

Little Swallow

O ver the next six days, the weavers made more trouble for factories in other villages. At any moment, Little Swallow expected the magistrate to send troops to keep order, and though Uncle had Papa, who had gone back to work, write the magistrate again, nothing happened—just as Grandmama had predicted.

Despite everyone's growing sense of danger, the factory's boilers went on rumbling and the machines clanking and rattling, and the thread went on being reeled. Looms around the world were hungry for Chinese silk.

Then came that terrible morning. Little Swallow left her family's house as usual; she had begun bringing a larger lunch so that, when Lucky happened to be drilling during her mealtime, she could share it with him.

As she joined the other girls heading toward the

factory, she felt something warm brush her cheek. Thinking it was an insect, she tried to brush it away, but she felt it smear in an odd way. In the twilight, she barely made out the black smudges on her fingers. By narrowing her eyes, she could just make out more dark flakes swirling through the air.

Other girls had noticed them and stopped. All of them glanced around in alarm, looking for the house that had caught on fire. However, except for the ash, everything seemed normal.

"There," Pearl said, pointing.

In the northwest, a column of smoke rose like a pillar against the sky. Something very big was burning.

"Well, the fire's not here," Little Swallow said. "Let's go to work."

As they trudged on, the ash thickened, whirling around them like a dark snowstorm. A gong in the watchtower began to boom through the village, summoning the militia to the factory.

Girls and armed men jammed the road, so progress was slow, but eventually Little Swallow made it into the factory courtyard, where she found the previous arrivals milling around in confusion. By then, ash smeared everyone's clothes and faces.

Suddenly a man forced his way through the gateway. A big bruise covered one side of his head, and his clothes were torn. "They're coming!" He coughed as if ash were choking his throat, and Lucky took his arm.

"Militia, to me," the Rain Man bellowed. The militiamen began forcing their way through the factory girls toward him.

"What happened?" Lucky asked.

The disheveled man moaned. "The weavers had their annual guild banquet last afternoon and got all liquored up until they had enough courage to attack. They chased out the reeling girls at the Golden Sun and beat up all the men there." The Golden Sun was a reeling factory two villages over. "When I fell down, I pretended to be unconscious. I had to lie still while they spent the whole night looting the factory. I couldn't sneak away until they started to burn it down. But before I got away, I heard them say that they were coming here next."

The Rain Man had made his way over. "How many were there?"

The man sagged. "At least a thousand."

"A thousand," gasped Pearl. She was standing next to Little Swallow.

Little Swallow stood there, numb, hearing the word *thousand* repeated all around her. She had thought the weavers might send as many as a hundred or so, never a thousand. Their own militia only topped a couple of hundred.

All that morning, the weavers' army was on people's minds. The girls were so distracted, Little Swallow included, that it was a wonder no one got maimed.

By some miracle, though, everyone made it safe and intact to lunchtime. Little Swallow tried to see her father, but he was busy meeting with Uncle and the others.

Normally, most of the girls ate inside the factory, but today they congregated in the courtyard. There was no column of smoke anymore, but the light was hazy and the afternoon sun had turned a blood red.

Lucky and about twenty other militiamen were stacking crates and baskets by the factory walls. The village wall had a ledge inside for defenders to stand on, but the factory had lacked that—up until now.

With Pearl sticking close to her as if for protection, Little Swallow went over to Lucky to see what he knew.

"Maybe you should go on to Sunning now," Little Swallow suggested.

Lucky looked grim. "I think you're going to need every defender you can. Two of the mercenaries left. They said they'd never signed on for a suicide mission."

Next to her, Pearl gave a gasp. Little Swallow fought to keep her own voice calm. "What do we do?"

Lucky nodded to the factory office. "They're trying to figure out something now."

They were still outside a short while later when Grandmama shouted from beyond the factory walls, "Let me in!"

Cousin Beanpole happened to be keeping watch at the factory gates. Because of the emergency, he hadn't been able to get any opium to smoke for several days, so he was even more shaky than usual. "I've got orders not to let anyone in."

"Open those gates. Or I'll spank you just like I used to do when you were small," Grandmama threatened.

Cousin Beanpole immediately jumped down from the crate on which he had been standing. More frightened of Grandmama than he was of the weavers, he began to draw the wooden bar back.

Instantly, one of the mercenaries barked, "Hey! What do you think you're doing?"

"Saving his skin," laughed another militiaman.

Little Swallow wanted to hide as soon as she caught sight of her grandmother in her outrageous outfit. Her grandmother had put up her hair and then wound a turban around her head. In her hand she was holding a broom shaft onto which she had tied her biggest kitchen knife.

"Have you come to join the militia, Grandmother?" Lucky called.

"In a way," Grandmama said, and beckoned to him. "You seem to have the gift of gab. Come with me. I might need you to talk to help convince them."

Little Swallow stepped in front of her grandmother, trying to save her and the family from further embarrassment. "Grandmama, leave the fighting to the militia."

Grandmama stamped the shaft against the ground.

"I can stand behind a village wall just as well as inside a house. High up on the wall, I might pass for one of the militia."

"Yes," Lucky said slowly, "if every woman and old man has a weapon, wears a hat or turban, and slouches down a bit. And if it's twilight and the weavers are half blind, we might trick them."

"Have you got a better idea?" Grandmama challenged.

"Unfortunately, no," Lucky admitted.

"Then come on," Grandmama said. Her fingers prodding Lucky ahead of her, they went inside, and Little Swallow felt herself drawn along in their wake.

Papa's eyes widened when he opened the door and saw Grandmama. "Now's not a good time."

"When would be? When the factory's ashes?" Grandmama demanded, and pushed past him. "I heard the news about the Golden Sun. How are you going to defend against that horde? It's big enough to attack the factory and the village at the same time."

Uncle sat at his desk with his son, Cousin Virtue, next to him. The leader of the mercenaries, the Rain Man, sat in a chair with his back to a wall, as if he were making sure no one could sneak up on him.

"There's only enough militia to protect one but not the other," Uncle sighed.

Grandmama struck the floor with her improvised spear. The knife, hastily tied to the shaft, wobbled a bit.

"But the weavers don't know that. So fool them."

The mercenaries' leader, the Rain Man, scratched his cheek. "How?"

"Put women on the village wall," Grandmama said. "We'll wrap turbans around our heads and tie kitchen knives to poles. Just leave a few militia to stiffen the defense and put most of them on the factory walls."

The Rain Man lowered his hand thoughtfully. "We could add the old men to the village force too."

"But what if they attack the village instead of the factory?" Uncle wondered.

Grandmama smiled. "If we use the right bait, they'll head for the factory."

"And what bait is so appealing to a weaver?" Uncle asked.

Grandmama waved a hand in a grand flourish toward him. "You, of course."

Cousin Virtue shook his head. "Even if my father would agree, the elders would never accept a plan as crazy as that."

Uncle slammed a fist on top of his desk. "Then we'll make them. And the sooner the better."

CHAPTER | 40

Little Swallow

That was how Little Swallow wound up on the village wall the next morning with her housemates and Pearl. In her hand Little Swallow had a rusty sickle, and she'd piled her hair on top of her head and then wound a turban around it. All the girls and women had done that, because that way their hair wasn't likely to fall down and give them away. And the old men who were manning the village walls had done the same so everyone's headgear would be identical.

Pearl bit her lip as she stared up at the knife that she had tied to a broom handle. "I don't think we're going to fool anyone."

"Let's hope they're very drunk, then," Peony said.

"Maybe they'll be so drunk they'll be seeing double," Pearl giggled.

"Now, now, don't go making those weavers into monsters," Grandmama said as she came up to them along the ledge behind the parapet. "They're just men."

Though she had no official position, Grandmama had taken it upon herself to inspect the wall's defenders.

"But there's a lot of them," one of Little Swallow's housemates, Jade, said as she chewed a fingernail.

"And they'll be out there in the open." Grandmama gestured first to the ponds and orchards and then to the wall. "And we'll be up here. So that will even out the numbers."

Another of Little Swallow's housemates stepped over to her. "Do you really think so?"

"I know so," said Grandmama with a firm nod of her head. "We're fighting for our homes and families."

"Well, aren't they, in a way?" Peony asked.

Grandmama had made the same point when she'd been arguing with Papa that other morning. "But the difference is that we're not invading their land. They're coming into ours—which puts them in the wrong, and they know it in their hearts."

Little Swallow watched as the girls clustered around her grandmother for reassurance like chicks around a mother hen. She couldn't have been prouder of her grandmother than at that moment. Grandmama was keeping everyone safe just as she had promised to do.

"They're coming, they're coming!" One of their scouts

was pelting along the dike-paths.

"Back to the walls, girls," Grandmama said, making shooing motions. "Even spaces now."

Little Swallow had never seen a thousand people together before, and she hoped she never would again—especially since they carried spears and swords. Their torches gleamed off the wicked-looking blades—an endless river of them flowing toward them.

Grandmama paced along the ledge behind the parapet. "Now let's make those weavers think the village is too tough a nut to crack. So shout as loud as you can, girls. But don't forget to keep your voices as deep as you can." She kept her voice low and gruff as an example. "And be sure to brandish your weapons. Look fierce. You're tigers." Then she passed on, giving the same advice to the other women on the wall.

Little Swallow stared at the army advancing up the road. "They've got carts." She lowered her voice for practice until it was husky. "They had to carry away all the cocoons and silk from that other factory on their backs. This time they mean to make it easier to carry away their loot." The weavers were that confident of victory, but given their overwhelming numbers she couldn't blame them.

The village had only one platoon of militiamen, led by one of the mercenaries—about thirty men in all, who acted as a reserve. If the weavers attacked the village, the platoon would go to any trouble spot. It was hoped there would never be more than one.

Inside the factory, across from her, were the rest of the militia and mercenaries. Smoke rose defiantly from the chimney like a long black banner. As a precaution, the girls from the other villages had been told to stay home—some of them had shown up anyway to defend their liveli-hood, but they had been sent back to their villages instead.

As the weavers drew closer, the defenders' roar spread across the wall. Little Swallow began hollering in a low voice as she waved her sickle over her head. Next to her she could hear Pearl doing the same.

At that crucial moment, the factory whistle blew a long, imperious note, cutting through bedlam, and all eyes shifted in time to see Uncle mounting to the top of the wall, his feet balancing on the uppermost layer of bricks while militiamen supported his legs.

Uncle spread out his arms. Dimly his voice carried to the village. "You want me?" he said defiantly. "Then come and get me."

Shaking their weapons and fists and bellowing insults, the weavers turned as one and rolled toward the factory. For a moment she felt relieved to see them all heading away from the village . . . until she remembered that her father was at the factory as well as the quirky Sunning dialect. Lucky might be annoying, but he didn't deserve to die just for that.

In their eagerness, the weavers in the rear began to stream across the pond dikes, so that the land seemed covered with moving ribbons of humans. The dirt on the dikes began to crumble under the weight of so many feet, and weavers tumbled into the ponds, rising and wading across the shallower ones.

The burning factory had left a coating of ash on the pond surfaces yesterday, and though the women had done their best to skim it off, they couldn't get it all. Folk were already wondering how that would affect the fish. The weavers' stomping would only add to their worries. Since the ponds were packed with fish, Little Swallow wondered if the fish would be able to escape trampling. And the dikes would all have to be repaired—that is, if any of the clan survived.

An orchard in the distance began to tremble as if a terrible wind were shaking the mulberry trees. "Those vandals are chopping my trees down," an old man yelled angrily.

Little Swallow could hear him weeping and shouting curses as one by one his trees disappeared. This was bad enough. She wondered what the final bill would be when this day was finished.

An angry sea of weavers formed around the factory. Some of the bolder militiamen answered back, but the majority of them stood pale and desperate.

In the end, there weren't enough militia to match the weavers in a shouting match, so eventually the factory fell silent. None of the militia answered as the weavers carried an improvised battering ram to the front—one of the recently cut-down mulberry trees, because it still had some of the branches along its trunk. There were no ladders, though. They hadn't been expecting to have to scale the factory walls.

Uncle gestured behind him, and the whistle blew again. In the sudden silence, Little Swallow heard him ask to speak to the leaders of the weavers and try to head off the coming fight.

Several men pushed through the crowd and stepped a few paces toward the factory. Little Swallow watched hopefully as Uncle tried to bargain with them. However, hope quickly changed to despair, because the weavers' leaders had confidence in their numbers. Arrogantly, their only offer was to let Uncle and the defenders leave, but everything in the factory belonged to the weavers to take or destroy as they pleased.

Uncle threw up his hands in resignation. "Then the blood is on your heads," he said. Even as he climbed down with help from some militiamen, a musket boomed from the factory wall. And Little Swallow gave a startled jump. More clan muskets thundered.

As gun smoke streamed upward, the factory gates swung open, and out charged the Rain Man and a half-dozen mercenaries along with a platoon of militiamen.

Pearl squinted. "Why are they attacking? They're just inviting the weavers in."

Little Swallow pointed her sickle. "They're going after the leaders."

There was the clash of blades and screaming from the midst of the desperate struggle. From the factory came another volley of muskets. And then came the *crack-crack-crack* of a different type of gun.

Little Swallow tried to peer through the ribbons of smoke that had begun to wreathe the defenders. "What's firing so quickly?"

"That's Father's American gun," Peony explained proudly. "It shoots several times without reloading."

The weaver army seemed just as surprised as Little Swallow, and they milled about in confusion. Only a few of them continued to fight, following the militia as they retreated slowly toward the factory.

Another militia platoon rushed out and threw themselves at the pursuing weavers. For a moment, the fighting grew fierce as the Rain Man and his prisoners withdrew into the factory. Then the rest of the militia broke away from the battle and followed them into the factory.

The remaining weavers stood stunned as the gates shut. Bodies littered the ground between them and the factory. Then, with a roar, the weavers in front surged toward the factory, and the rest of them followed in an irresistible tidal wave.

There seemed so few militiamen scattered along the

wall. Even as the raiders climbed up to their posts, there still didn't seem enough to stop the weavers. There were more puffs of smoke from the wall and the crack of Cousin Fortune's gun. When the battering ram slowed, Little Swallow realized they were picking off the men carrying it. But not fast enough.

The sound of the battering ram thudding against the gates carried all the way to the village. Even though Little Swallow knew the gates of the factory and the village had been reinforced, she was not sure how long they would hold out.

In the midst of the gun smoke, she could just make out big kettles being hoisted on top of the wall. When they were tipped over, boiling water flooded down. Thanks to the factory well and boiler, the defenders would have all they needed.

Weavers shrieked, and the battering ram fell to the wet ground—only to be picked up by a new group. At the same time, some impatient weavers by the gates stood upon one another's shoulders to form living ladders, but just as quickly tumbled down as more boiling water poured down on them.

The weavers in the front ranks began to hesitate. The problem was that they couldn't tell the ones in the rear to wait. The rear ranks kept advancing, shoving the ones ahead until the only way for the vanguard to escape being crushed against the bricks was to climb the wall itself.

The battle grew desperate then. Despite the boiling water pouring down the walls like waterfalls, some of the weavers in the center made it up the human ladders.

That was when the mercenaries unleashed their secret weapon. Some of the musketeers' precious gunpowder had been put into small ceramic jars and pots along with nails and bits of metal to make a device they called a grenade. The top of each one had then been sealed with wax into which a long rope had been stuck as a fuse.

At this distance the jars were hardly more than dots with sparkling tops falling into the densely packed attackers, and she gave a jump when the grenades detonated. Within the rolling cloud of dust and black smoke, she could hear the weavers screaming in pain.

The weavers in the rear would not have been able to see what was happening, but they could hear the explosions, and they stopped moving, ending the pressure forward.

The most aggressive weavers would have been in the vanguard, but the majority of the weavers were more cautious and would have followed behind. These were men more comfortable with looms rather than weapons.

More than likely, these men had practiced the martial arts for an evening's exercise and companionship, not because they expected to use the skills in combat. They wanted revenge, but not if it required much effort nor much risk to themselves.

As the smoke began to rise and the dust to settle, she

could see the weavers staggering about, stunned by the flashes and the noise. Dozens lay twitching and moaning on the ground.

When the defenders threw the second batch of grenades, there was more smoke, more shrieks, and as the cloud cleared, the weavers on either flank of the front began to stream away, stumbling through ponds and orchards, desperate to get away.

Gradually, the empty space widened around the factory. When the remaining weavers saw the panicked expressions of those who were retreating, they broke too. Throwing away their weapons, they whirled around and ran back along the road, elbowing one another in their haste to escape.

Others gave up on the clogged route and simply streamed across the dikes or waded through the pools, feet struggling in the muddy bottoms like flies trapped in honey—the whole army dissolving like a wax candle melting on a stove.

Pearl pounded the wall. "We won. We actually won."

There were shouts and whoops of joy all around them.

But all Little Swallow could think about was the cost of this victory.

CHAPTER | 41

Little Swallow

When Grandmama called for volunteers to help the wounded in the factory, Little Swallow was one of the first to volunteer.

Pearl, though, declined. "I can't stand the sight of blood."

"What do you do when you have to kill a chicken?" Little Swallow asked.

"It's never come up," Pearl said. "My family can't afford one."

"I'm sorry," Little Swallow said, embarrassed.

Pearl lounged with her back against the wall. "Don't be. It's the one advantage of being poor."

When she was on the ground, Little Swallow was surprised to see the finicky Peony in the group of nurses.

About fifteen women and girls gathered around her

grandmother and the doctor at the village gates. When they were opened and the volunteers could step outside, they looked at the ruined ponds and orchards. Everywhere trees had been hacked down, and the ponds looked as if buffalo had stampeded through them. The ground around the ponds had been turned to mud, with dead fish scattered here and there.

"My pond, my pond," a woman wailed. She turned and threw a curse in the direction of the weavers' retreat.

Peony went over and put an arm around her. "It's all right. My father will understand about the rent." Little Swallow was relieved to see that the weavers had taken their dead and injured with them. After seeing the destruction, she wasn't sure how she would feel about tending a weaver, no matter how badly hurt he was.

When the factory saw them coming, the gates opened. She saw her father was alive and well—and also irate. "Go home, Little Swallow," he yelled, waving her back to the village. "This is no place for you."

Little Swallow pointed to her turban. "I'm a soldier too," she shouted back, "so a battlefield is exactly where I *do* belong." And she kept right on walking.

She'd expected some of her kinsmen to holler and tease her, and in peaceful times, they would have. But they were too exhausted and too overcome by the day's events to do more than watch.

Standing with her father was Cousin Fortune.

Gunpowder smoke streaked his face. As they entered, he wagged a finger at Peony. "Young lady, we are going to have a good long discussion about this."

"And that goes double for you," Papa said to Little Swallow.

Grandmama patted her son-in-law soothingly on the shoulder. "Quite right. This wicked girl deserves a good scolding. But later. For now there are patients for her to tend. Where are they?"

"We moved them into the storage room," Father said.

Little Swallow thought it was a bad sign that Lucky hadn't greeted her. She tried very hard not to be obvious as she glanced around the defenders, looking for him. When she saw the factory wall, she sucked in her breath. What were obviously three corpses had been laid there under cloths.

She had to fight the urge to go over and lift them, instead following her grandmother into the storage room. There were twenty-three injured, some of them very severely.

The doctor went right to work, suggesting tasks for his volunteer nurses. There were already buckets of water, so Little Swallow went about offering it to the groaning patients. She almost gave a cry when she saw Lucky lying pale with a bloody bandage on his leg and his hat covering his face. The brim was torn and the crown battered into a shapeless mass.

She sank to her knees. "Are you all right?" When he didn't answer, her fears rose. She poked him cautiously with her finger. "Can you hear me?"

He raised his hat to stare at her. "Haven't you ever heard the saying that sleep is the best healer? I was just starting to drift off."

Little Swallow grumbled to herself; *He can be so aggravating.* "I thought you might be thirsty." She held the full dipper up.

"No thanks," he said.

She leaned over to peer at his mouth. "Your lips are all cracked. You definitely need water."

His face started to flush, as if he were embarrassed. "I said no thank you."

She put a hand beneath his head and started to raise him toward the dipper. Water sloshed over the rim and onto his chest. "You're going to drink this if I have to drown you."

He looked away. "If I drink, I'll have to go. And I can't walk to the privy. All right? Now you know."

"Oh," she said in a small voice, cheeks reddening. "Well, um, I'll find something you can use for a chamber pot." She was so mortified that she felt like leaving, but she reminded herself that these were not normal times. He needed a nurse, not a modest maiden, so she copied a certain tone her grandmother used when she expected to be obeyed. "Now drink."

He raised a hand to take the dipper. "Okay, okay." He ignored the water that sloshed onto his chest.

She watched him gulp the water down as if he'd been in a desert. When he asked for a second, she gave it to him. "I was watching from the village. It looked bad here."

When he'd finished the second dipperful, he confessed, "I've never been more scared in my life."

She put the dipper back into the bucket. "Then why didn't you leave when you had the chance? I don't understand you."

The water seemed to have restored his spirits, which was good—but also bad, because he was back to his infuriating habits. "That's funny. My father often says the same thing."

She lowered his head back to the ground but kept her hand beneath him. "Why did you stay? Why did you fight?"

He gazed up at her. "Because I saw something here that was worth saving."

Her forehead furrowed in puzzlement. "What could possibly be that valuable in this village?"

"Someone I'd like to take back to the Golden Mountain," Lucky replied.

Understanding suddenly dawned, and Little Swallow glanced at Peony, who was changing a bandage. Jealousy pinched her insides. "I thought it was going to be hard to bring a woman over."

"I'm a merchant's son, so my wife would get in under the law's exemption," Lucky said. "Of course, the voyage can still be hard. And it won't be any picnic over there. So I need the right girl."

"Is that so?" She fought to keep her voice neutral.

"One that wants a real adventure." He grinned.

Peony had never struck Little Swallow as very daring. She seemed happiest when she was enforcing some obscure rule in the house's code of conduct. And then something else occurred to her. "Do you mean me? But you'd already gone inside, so how could you hear what I said to Pearl?"

"Voices carry in cold, still air," he said with his usual impudent grin.

"I talk in a perfectly normal tone," she said, and sniffed. "But anyway, I thought you'd prefer some simpering little mouse who doesn't even squeak."

"She'd be quieter," he agreed, "but not nearly as much fun. You scare me, you know? There's a core to you that's harder than steel, but that's what it takes to live on the Golden Mountain."

Her heart began thumping. It was one thing to be curious about the Golden Mountain and quite another to go there in person.

In their brief encounters, she'd come to like him, and in China, where a matchmaker often paired off complete strangers, that knowledge would put her one step ahead of most brides.

No, *he* wasn't the problem. It was where he wanted to take her afterward: The Golden Mountain was so dangerous.

Of course, they could follow the usual pattern of most Guest marriages, in which she would stay in China while he worked overseas. But she wouldn't be satisfied with that either, because part of her had also wanted to see the Golden Mountain for herself.

"Little Swallow, over here." Grandmama's voice cut through her granddaughter's whirling thoughts. "Cousin Beanpole needs water."

She was glad to be reminded of her duty. Confused, she rose again. "Yes, coming."

"Think about it, will you?" Lucky said. "And then give me your decision."

"When . . . when I have time," she said.

CHAPTER | 42

28th day of the 8th month of the era Honor's Bond
October 20, 1881

Little Swallow

For the next twelve days, there were skirmishes on the borders of the village but no full-scale attack, and then word came from the lookouts that imperial soldiers were marching toward the village. Even the magistrate couldn't ignore open warfare in his district.

The mercenaries slipped away, the Rain Man saying that they had not always seen eye to eye with the government. And it might be awkward for the clan if official troops found them in the village.

Like everyone else, Little Swallow blessed their saviors. Without them, the factory would have been lost and perhaps the village as well.

Little Swallow had climbed back up to the wall with Papa and Grandmama, waiting for the troops to arrive. Below them, Uncle, Cousin Fortune, and the other leaders of the clan stood in their best robes by the village gates.

Beyond the walls, men were repairing the dikes around the ponds and planting saplings to replace the trees cut down by the weavers. It would be quite a while, though, before the saplings grew big enough to bear fruit. The clan's land still looked like a battlefield. But as long as the clan had the factory, they'd be able to rebuild.

Suddenly, racing down the road came a dozen or so boys—her brother, Doggy, among them. "The army's coming," they announced self-importantly.

She felt like ants were crawling beneath her skin as excitement warred with dread. She'd devoured all the novels in the girls' house about noble warriors, but her head was also stuffed with the atrocities that the Manchus had committed when they conquered the kingdom. Which would they be?

Straining her eyes, she made out about twenty men plodding along with the same resigned weariness as a buffalo pulling a cart. Their shirts and pants hung on their bony frames, and some of them were even barefoot. Strutting in front of them was a young man in an outfit that would have made a peacock jealous.

"I see a clown and some laborers," she said, "but where are the soldiers?"

Papa folded his arms. "The scruffy ones, my dear, are the mighty defenders of the Manchus, and the 'clown' is their commander."

As the soldiers drew nearer, Little Swallow realized that their uniforms were so dirty that she had taken them for regular clothes—in direct contrast to the tailored, colorful costume of their commander, who looked very earnest and very young and—except for his clothes—didn't seem any different from the teenagers piling dirt on the dikes. "Is that a Manchu?" she asked.

Papa shook his head. "No, they're all Chinese from the garrison."

Little Swallow thought that the Rain Man could have beaten all of them with one hand.

As they neared the gates, the officer raised a hand, and his men comically bumped into one another as they came to a halt. It took a good deal of shoving and exasperated shouts from the officer to form them into four ragged ranks.

However, Uncle and the clan elders greeted them with deep bows as if they were a band of valiant heroes.

The lieutenant barely dipped his head in acknowledgment, which Little Swallow thought rather rude.

Raising his head, he announced in a shrill voice that Little Swallow would have sworn had only broken a week ago, "The magistrate has declared martial law. All military activities are to cease. We have come to take charge of your prisoners."

"To interrogate for the trial?" Uncle asked.

The lieutenant said stiffly, "The magistrate has not

yet decided that there is going to be any trial. He's still investigating who started the fighting."

Little Swallow waved a frustrated hand at the wasted ponds and orchards. "Doesn't he have eyes?"

"He sees what the magistrate tells him to see," Papa grunted.

"Let's just hope that it's not the weavers' scholar doing the investigating," Grandmama grunted.

The verdict came fourteen days later, which was lightning fast for a judicial decision. By then, Uncle had resumed operations, and though the factory grounds had been cleaned, Little Swallow saw darker stains on the bricks that could have been blood.

Uncle had the girls shut down their machines and assemble in the courtyard. He looked as pale and somber as if someone had just died, and he was leaning heavily on his cane as he walked to the stage improvised out of crates and planks.

His son helped him climb up. Then, from his sleeve, Uncle took out an official letter and gave it a token bow. It was a symbol of the emperor even if it might have been written by his representative, the magistrate. Then he began to read it out loud.

Little Swallow cheered with the others when she heard the weavers were going to have to pay hefty fines and the ringleaders would be arrested, but she couldn't believe her ears when the official decree went on. "'And,'" Uncle read, "'because they cause so much unrest, all reeling factories are to cease operations immediately.'"

"What?" Pearl said in disbelief. All around the court-yard, the girls were looking at one another incredulously.

"So we won the battles, but the weavers won the war," Little Swallow said. The words tasted bitter in her mouth.

"And the magistrate gets rich," Pearl said sourly.

Little Swallow thought of the fishponds and orchards that needed to be restored. Without the money from the factory, what would the clan do? This was a disaster. There was only one major source of money now. "I suppose more men will be trying to get to the Golden Mountain," she said. However, Lucky had said the Americans were going to make it even harder for Chinese to get into the country. The clan was being hit with one calamity after another.

Uncle let his employees complain to one another for a bit before he raised his cane for quiet. "The ban won't last. The empire needs money too bad to keep the facto-ries shut down forever, so I'm sure we'll reopen soon. But in the meantime, I'll relocate to Macau." That was a city controlled by another group of foreigners, the Portuguese. It was near the British colony of Hong Kong in the south. "I'll set up dormitories with proper chaperones, so you're welcome to come along."

"I guess I'm going to see some of the world whether I want to or not," Pearl sighed. "So much for my happy cabbage-hood."

"You'll leave the village?" Little Swallow asked, remembering that conversation so long ago.

Pearl spread her hands helplessly. "My family will starve without my salary." Suddenly she seized Little Swallow's arm. "We can go together. You're the one who wanted adventures."

The full scope of the catastrophe hit her. "Without my salary and my father's, I'll really have to go." What was Papa going to do? What were they all going to do?

Instead of heading home, Little Swallow went searching for her father and found him in the storage room, with inventory sheets in his hand. With him was Lucky, who was hobbling about with the help of a crutch. Stubbornly, he was still wearing that silly battered hat of his.

She'd been avoiding him ever since he had proposed because—torn between fear and curiosity—she still hadn't been able to make up her mind.

"How are you feeling?" she asked him.

"Much better, between the doctor and your grandmother," he said.

She wrinkled her nose when she caught a whiff of a familiar odor. "Oh no, she's been giving you one of her ointments."

"And then she comes by and sniffs me to make sure I've put it on," he laughed.

At some other time, Little Swallow might have apologized for her grandmother, but her mind was taken up with something else. "What are we going to do, Papa?"

Papa and Lucky exchanged glances. "Well, we've been discussing just that thing."

"After I'm gone," Lucky explained, "I'll need someone our business can trust to supervise our affairs here. And I can't think of a better agent than your father."

Papa knew her too well by now. "And don't worry. We're close enough to Canton so that we don't have to move."

This was all happening so fast that Little Swallow was beginning to feel a little dizzy, and she swayed slightly. "You're going to work for him?" she asked her father.

Her father put out a hand to steady her, but Lucky gripped her arm first. "That's right," he said, holding her up. "So for a while, I'll be coming around a lot." He grinned. "Especially if your grandmother makes more of her famous sticky cakes."

Little Swallow felt pleased but tamped that down quickly. Even if her father was going to work for him now, the stranger was still taking a lot for granted.

She pulled free and stepped back. "You're always welcome," Little Swallow said in a polite but neutral voice.

Her mind in a muddle, she hurried home.

CHAPTER | 43

Little Swallow

S he had been expecting Grandmama to be steaming like a pot of boiling water over the injustice of the magistrate's decree, but she barely said anything—just stood lost in thought in front of the stove.

When Little Swallow smelled the acrid odor of smoke, she hurried to her side. "Grandmama, the rice is burning."

Grandmama's head turned, and she blinked her eyes distractedly.

"A lot's happened," Little Swallow said, taking her grandmother's elbow and steering her over to a stool. "Why don't you let me do that."

Grandmama sat down obediently like a small child. As Little Swallow took over the cooking, she stole glances at her grandmother, who remained silent.

Nor did she say anything at dinner, not even when

Little Swallow mentioned going with Pearl to Macau.

It was her father who objected. "Absolutely not. I'll be working for Lucky, so we'll manage just fine."

"For now," Little Swallow argued, "but what about later? We'd be safer if there were two jobs in the family."

Papa rarely asserted his authority as the head of the family, but he did so now and vehemently. "No, no, no. I won't hear of it."

She let the matter drop, relieved in a way that she could stay. However, the worries kept nibbling just at the edge of her consciousness, so she was glad after dinner when Grandmama was still lost in thought and Little Swallow had to clean after the meal and put the little ones to bed. When Papa became absorbed in one of his philosophy books, she got ready to return to the girls' house.

Suddenly, Grandmama roused. "I feel like an evening stroll," she said coyly. "Why don't I walk you to the girls' house?"

When they stepped outside, Grandmama paused and stared up at the Weaving Maid and her sisters. "They can see the whole world from up there. I wonder what it's like?"

Little Swallow gazed at the sharp-tipped little points of light. "And if they can see the factories, what do they think of them?"

As they set out, Grandmama hooked her arm through hers. "You know, when I was small, I wanted to see the world."

"You did?" Little Swallow asked in surprise. Even if her grandmother had been born and raised elsewhere, she now seemed as much a part of the village as the walls. It was hard to think of her wandering in foreign lands in her best straw hat. Despite everything, the image was so funny she gave a giggle.

"I used to get all sorts of wild notions when I was small," Grandmama confessed ruefully.

"What happened?" Little Swallow asked.

"I had to grow up," Grandmama said, "after your great-aunt . . . well . . ." She gave a little shrug. "You know what she did for the family."

Even after all these years, Little Swallow could see that the loss of her sister still pained her. She covered her grandmama's arm with her free hand. "I'm sorry."

Grandmama nodded. "But just because I never got to travel, it doesn't mean *you* can't."

Little Swallow felt almost as frightened as when she had first seen the weaver army flooding the land. "Do you really want me to go to Macau?"

"Heavens, no." Grandmama squeezed her arm reassuringly. "But I don't want you to hide here either."

Little Swallow drew her eyebrows together in puzzlement. "What do you mean?"

"Oh, I don't ever want to let you go," Grandmama said fiercely, "but I know I'll have to sometime when you get married. And you've always been so curious about the Golden Mountain. This could be your chance to see it for yourself. You'll be able to travel like I always wanted to do."

Little Swallow stumbled, feeling as if the ground had suddenly opened. "What?" And then she realized something. "He spoke to you?" She tapped her head. "Of course he did. He's smart enough to see who's the real authority in the family."

"Yes," Grandmama insisted smoothly, "everyone knows it's your father."

As far away as Macau was, Pearl still might be able to visit home occasionally, but the Golden Mountain might as well be at the end of the world. "It's not the Milky Way, but if the Pacific Ocean's between us," Little Swallow argued, "we'll never see one another again."

Grandmama sighed. "This isn't the first time I've had to give up someone I love. But you know, the story of the Weaving Maid isn't about romance: It's about losing what you love most."

"If you really loved me, how could you think of sending me there?" Little Swallow protested. "It's dangerous on the Golden Mountain."

"True, but which is worse in the long term? Here or America?" Grandmama demanded. "Our government is full of thieves and numbskulls like the magistrate. We need more men like Uncle, and yet he's being driven out." She stared at her shoes. "My sister did what she did because the family always comes first. And I've done my best to protect this one. But after the magistrate's decision today, I can see that it's hopeless here. The family's better off taking its chances there."

Little Swallow's mouth was suddenly dry. "I'm not getting married. I'm going to be like Peony."

Grandmama pursed her lips. "You could do worse than Lucky, you know. Except for his peculiar taste in hats, he seems like a sensible young man. And remember this." She tapped Little Swallow's arm to emphasize each of her next words. "He could have fled to safety, but he stayed to defend you."

"If he was protecting anyone, it was Cousin Fortune," Little Swallow countered. "He's his friend." She clung desperately to her grandmother. "Why do we have to keep making sacrifices? I'm going to stay with you forever and ever."

"But I'm not going to be here much longer," Grandmama said gently.

Little Swallow felt tears stinging her eyes as if she were only five years old again. "Don't talk like that!"

"All right, all right," Grandmama said soothingly as she put her arms around her. "I won't scare you anymore tonight. Anyway, he's going to be visiting us a lot, so you'll have plenty of time to get to know him."

Little Swallow leaned her head against her grandmother's shoulder. It was small and bony, and yet it brought immense comfort. "It won't do any good. I'm never going to change my mind."

"Everything changes, child," Grandmama observed calmly. "Me, you, the world. When I was your age, I was reeling silk by hand. Now you do it on that big, noisy machine. Who knows what the future will bring? The one thing that doesn't change is the family. It always comes first. Keep everyone in it safe. Keep them happy."

She felt as if her grandmother were writing the words directly on her heart. "Then no matter what happens, I'll protect it just like you have," Little Swallow promised.

"I think that would please your great-aunt." Grandmama smiled as she stroked Little Swallow's hair. "And me too."

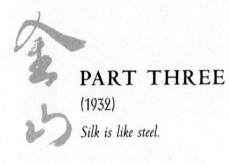

PART THREE

(1932)

Silk is like steel.

金
山

*B*y the 1880s, it was hard enough for a Chinese man to enter America because of the harsh immigration laws—and even harder for a Chinese woman. However, there were exceptions made for Chinese scholars or merchants.

Even so, by the twentieth century there were a number of small communities of Chinese American families with children born here. They no longer thought of themselves as Guests of the Golden Mountain, but as Americans.

However, in 1929 the Great Depression began, with devastating results in all parts of San Francisco, including Chinatown.

CHAPTER | 44

San Francisco's Chinatown
August 8, 1932
Seven Seven Festival

Lillian

It was hot in Chinatown. Though the tourists might not have realized it, August in San Francisco was usually cold and damp under a blanket of fog. However, today the skies were unseasonably and relentlessly clear.

Lillian walked along Grant Avenue past the empty three-story store. The tubing of the dead neon sign was broken, the metal behind the tubing pitted with rust from the moist air from the bay. Rude things had been painted on the wooden boards covering the doorway of the closed Canton Emporium, the ones in Chinese by the foreign-born boys and the ones in English by the native-born boys. Both groups had managed to misspell words, the Chinese ones with the wrong number of strokes and the American ones with the wrong vowels.

Through the dusty windows, Lillian could see the dark,

dirty interior, shelves and counters stripped clean.

Her reflection floated like a ghost upon the glass. Mommy had said that when she was old enough to use cosmetics, makeup would help compensate for her cheekbones, which were too high, and widen her eyes, which were too narrow, but in the meantime she would just have to live with that face.

Abruptly, she turned and walked away, resisting the urge to look at the third story, where her family had once lived in a spacious apartment. That was before the crash in 1929. She remembered her grandfather as a kindly man who always had some loms, preserved fruit in colorful paper wrappers, in his pocket for his grandchildren.

Her grandfather had loaned money to friends. When they couldn't pay him back, Grandpop Lucky had gone to other friends in Chinatown, but none of them would lend him money.

So he had worked twice as hard, hardly ever sleeping. And it was the effort that had killed him. On the day that the family left the apartment for the final time, he had died of a heart attack.

She quickened her steps, concentrating on avoiding the cracks in the pavement, not wanting to remember the past nor think about the present. It was the beginning of dinnertime, and the cheap chop suey joints were jammed with Americans and Chinese. The aromas made her mouth water, and she clutched the bag of groceries tighter to her stomach. It had been so long since she had tasted meat.

"Won't you buy an apple, lady?" An unshaven man in a ragged coat thrust an apple at her. His fingers couldn't quite hide the bruise on this one, and Lillian suspected that he'd scavenged it from the trash can of some grocery store along with the four at his feet.

"Sorry," she said, shaking her head apologetically, and hurried on.

Up a steep side street, she saw the line of men and women waiting patiently for a church soup kitchen to open. These were terrible times for everyone.

"Lillian," Edna said. She was a girl in Lillian's class at Francisco Junior High, and they were rivals in everything from sports to student offices. "How are you?"

"I'm fine. How are you?" Lillian asked with cautious politeness.

"We were shocked at the awful news," Edna said, but the pity in her eyes changed to curiosity, for Lillian was wearing a stylish silk blouse.

"We're doing all right," Lillian said, and silently she blessed her clever grandmother.

When they had first moved into the tenement a month ago, Mommy's cheap cardboard suitcase had split, strewing her clothing down the staircase. She had simply plopped down on the step and let out a wail. Tears pouring down her cheeks, she had sobbed, "Those vultures took everything of value, even the clothes off our backs. All we've got left are these old rags, rags. They'll call us beggars!"

Lillian had felt like crying herself, and from the wrinkling noses and squinting eyes, her brother and sister were getting ready to join her mother.

It was Grandmom who had come to the rescue, stamping her cane to get their attention. "I'll take care of what we wear. No one's going to laugh at our family." She'd motioned to Lillian and her little brother and sister, Jackie and Ruthie. "Pick those up for your mother."

The three children had gathered Mommy's scattered belongings and then Mommy herself, half carrying and half dragging her up the stairs to their one-room apartment, where they left her on the bed. Grandmom stayed to fan Mommy, while Ruthie, Jackie, and Lillian had brought up the rest of the boxes and cardboard suitcases and the sewing machine so old their creditors hadn't wanted it.

When they had finally closed the door, the room was so gloomy she felt like she was in a jail cell, so she snapped on the light. With a hiss, the naked bulb, dangling on the frayed cord from the ceiling, came on, and she could see years of accumulated dirt on the walls and the floor. She couldn't decide whether it was worse to leave the light off or on.

Grandmom had refused to let them brood about their

new home, opening up one suitcase after another until she found what she wanted. As her grandmother unwrapped the protective tissue from around the first bundle, Lillian could smell the cedar-lined trunk that had once held it.

"When we first came here, we couldn't afford to buy already-made American clothes to stock the shelves," she explained. "So I hired an Old-timer to teach me how to do it myself. I'll cut these down and sew them into new clothes. Ah, here we are." She took out a cheong-san. "The creditors said they were too Chinese so they were worthless."

Lillian had to suppress a giggle, because it was hard to picture a time when her well-rounded grandmother could ever have fit into the sleek, tight dresses, let alone shown a leg through the slit on one side of a cheong-san.

Grandmom held it out, stretched between her hands. "Touch it."

Jackie, being a boy, stood off disdainfully, but Ruthie petted the flower-patterned silk as if it were a cat. "Can you hear it?" Grandmom asked. "The silk's talking to you."

Careful not to snag the material on her calluses from violin playing, Lillian stroked it and felt it tingle against her palm.

It was the sky whispering in her ear, a ghost of wind sighing, the moon's shadow dancing across the floor.

Her grandmother saw her expression and smiled.

"Silk's in our blood, girl."

Grandmom took cheong-san after cheong-san from the suitcase. "I told Grandpop that I only needed a couple, but he said he liked seeing me in pretty things, so he kept having them made for me."

Mommy twisted a crumpled handkerchief back and forth in her hands. "I will not dress my children in antiques. People will think they're clowns."

"It's the silk we want, not the style," Grandmom said. "Silk is silk." There was just an edge of sadness to her voice.

Feeling sorry for her grandmother, Lillian tried to distract her. "Tell me all about silk, Grandmom."

So Grandmom happily showed her the many types of silk—Lillian hadn't realized there were so many—from tussah silk, shantung silk, and silk crepe to another half-dozen kinds. And Lillian drank it all in when Grandmom explained about the virtues and quirks of each type.

That had been a wonderful night, even if they were dismantling the past, scavenging among the ruins.

They had all gotten into the game of measuring and cutting. Grandmom had declared Lillian the winner because she had wasted the least amount of cloth. When Grandmom had finally set up the sewing machine, she'd told Lillian to fetch some thread from one of the boxes. Lillian had rummaged around until she found the spools. However, when she had selected one of them, Grandmom had shaken her head. "No, not that."

"It matches the color," Lillian said, clutching it in her fingers.

"Silk thread's too strong. It'll stretch the material or even tear it," Grandmom explained.

So Lillian had searched the other boxes until she found cotton thread that was close to the silk thread's hue. Then she had watched her grandmother magically produce matched blouses for Lillian and Ruthie from the scraps of her old dresses. As Grandmom sewed, she told them about their family and the silkworms in China and then the reeling machines and the fight at the factory.

Jackie had been more interested in the battle, but Lillian was fascinated by the stories, feeling a little thrill at the silken threads that linked her to the past.

After that, all three children wore silk clothes fashioned to modern styles—though Jackie had grumbled at having to wear a sissy print pattern.

Lillian clutched her groceries now as she exchanged a few more mock pleasantries with Edna and then walked away, feeling a strange satisfaction at confounding her rival.

She had always taken expensive clothes for granted, but now she reveled in the feel of the silk. It felt so cool against her skin, so light that she had to look down to make sure it was still there.

A few bars of "Chinatown, My Chinatown" floated

down from a nightclub and then stopped. The tune began over again, at a quicker tempo. Instinctively, Lillian began to work out how she would play it on her violin, her fingers moving deftly over the bag's side. It would be fun to try it on her actual instrument.

Then, with a sad jolt, she remembered that her violin had been sold with so many other of her family's precious things.

It was probably too early for the nightclub to open yet, so the band must be rehearsing for that evening's shows. Rich folk would be heading there, the women perhaps wearing silk dresses they had bought from their lost Emporium.

She turned down Washington Street. The Old-timers were gathered outside a Chinese newspaper office, craning their necks to read the news as it came in on a Teletype machine in Chinese.

Lillian wondered how the newspaper ever survived with all the freeloaders snatching the information as it came in.

Mixie and his friend Earl were on the steps of the tenement. They were both wearing short jackets of brown and tan material that made Lillian think of cowhide. Mixie had gotten his nickname because as a boy he had been a big fan of Tom Mix the cowboy. It had been cute how he'd insisted on being Tom Mix when they played cowboy—in fact, it was the only game he would play. Even now, he was usually wearing a Western string tie.

Lillian scolded herself for not having her keys ready. It couldn't be helped now.

As she reached the foot of the stairs, Mixie moved to block her way to the front door.

"Hey, doll," he said. A cigarette dangled from one corner of his mouth.

Her grip tightened involuntarily around the bag; she heard the vegetables crunch. The strong odor told her she had snapped the scallions. "I'd like to get past, Mixie," she said.

The cigarette twitched up and down. "My parents named me Steve."

"No one's used to calling you that," she said.

He spat out the cigarette. "Well, what's the rush, doll?"

"I have to make dinner for my family," she said.

Earl snickered from where he was propped against the wall. "I've seen them. They could all afford to lose a little weight."

The door opened suddenly, and a familiar cane shot out.

Whack!

Earl fell to the porch. "Ow!"

Whack! Whack!

Holding his arms up over his head protectively, Mixie scampered down the steps. "Quit it!"

"Come on, Young Swallow," her grandmother said in

Chinese. Her grandmother never used her American name but always her Chinese nickname. She hated it, especially the "young" part, but everyone in Chinatown called her grandmother Little Swallow—even though at twelve, Lillian was already an inch taller than her grandmother.

Mixie rubbed his head. "Who do you think you are?" he demanded in English.

"I know who I am," Grandmom replied in Chinese. "But do you know who you are?"

Mixie shifted uncomfortably. "Speak American, will you?"

Grandmom switched to her accented English. "I said I know who I am. But I don't you know what you are."

Mixie slouched sullenly. "Someone you don't mess with."

With the help of her cane, Grandmom stumped out onto the porch. Though she was nearly seventy, her hair was only streaked with bits of gray. "No," she corrected. "*I'm* the one you don't mess with. If a whole army couldn't tell me what to do, do you think two cockroaches can order me around?"

Lillian had never quite believed her grandmother's stories about being in a battle, but now she could picture her grandmother standing on the village walls and defying the invaders.

Mixie sneered and opened his mouth for a smart answer, but his friend was making shushing motions. "I've seen her in the square doing old stuff." His hands moved in fake Tai Chi motions. By *square*, he meant Portsmouth Square on the western edge of Chinatown.

"I didn't mean no harm," Mixie argued, but he first took the precaution of stepping onto the pavement and out of reach of her cane. His friend followed a second later, skipping down the stairs in his haste.

"Well, I do." Grandmom waved her cane menacingly. "And so will your grandmother when I tell her what you've been up to."

Mixie looked as if Grandmom had struck him in the stomach with her cane. "Go ahead and tell her," he tried to bluster, but his voice lacked conviction.

Lillian ran up the stairs, and her grandmother stepped back to let her in, hooking the curved part of the cane around the doorknob to shut the door after her. With the door safely between them and the boys, Lillian giggled with relief.

"Your bluff was magnificent," she said.

"Who said I was bluffing?" Grandmom asked, feisty as ever. "If I can't knock some sense into him, I'm sure his grandmother will."

Mixie's grandmother had arms thick as Popeye's from years of lifting crates in their fish store. "I think it'd be kinder if you were the one to beat him up instead."

The stairs were narrow and the treads creaked, but her

grandmother was tiny, so Lillian could squeeze in beside her and support her elbow as they climbed up the three flights. "It was lucky you were so near to rescue me."

"Luck had nothing to do with it," Grandmom said. "I could smell the cigarette smoke from outside, so I came down and waited." She paused for breath. "Oof. The one thing I miss most is our freight elevator," she said.

The freight elevator in their store had been built to go to all three floors before the top floor had been converted into their living quarters. However, no one had used the elevator except her grandmother—even though her grandfather had complained about the waste of running that huge elevator for just one person.

"Grandpop used to get so annoyed"—Lillian smiled at the memory—"but he never stopped you."

"He wouldn't have dared," Grandmom said indignantly, and then smiled. "That man was only scared of two things: me and being poor. Poor man. He could defend us against our enemies but not his friends."

As Grandmom trudged up the steps, she began humming her favorite old Chinese tune, which she said her own grandmother had taught her. And again, all on their own, Lillian's fingers began to move across invisible strings. She had always meant to play it on her violin for Grandmom, and now it was too late.

Suddenly Grandmom stumbled on a step but grabbed the banister in time. Straightening up, she glared at the darkness above. "When is that landlord going to replace that burned-out bulb? It's like night in here, but without the Seven Sisters. The older I get, the more I miss them."

Lillian had heard of one surviving aunt back in China, not seven. "We had a letter just last week from her," she reminded her grandmother timidly. Her aunt Wisteria had told them that everyone was worried about the threat of a Japanese invasion and then had asked them for money because all the silk-reeling factories had shut down, but of course they had none to share.

Even so, Lillian was afraid her grandmother might uproot the family and go back to China, a country she herself had never seen. And she didn't have any clue on how they were going to pay their passage back or what they would live on once there.

Grandmom snorted. "How can stars write letters?"

Lillian, used to San Francisco's bright night skies, had never seen more than a handful of dim ones so she had never understood their appeal. When she had had to learn "Twinkle, Twinkle, Little Star" in first grade, it had never made sense to her. Stars did not twinkle. They were barely there. "Oh, you mean the Pleiades," she said cautiously.

"And the Weaving Maid and all the rest. You've never seen them blazing across the night sky." Grandmom raised her hand as if she could pluck them from the air. "Back home, they're holding a festival for the Weaving Maid and her sisters today. She wove silk into wonderful garments for Heaven."

"That's nice," Lillian said without much enthusiasm.

She considered such things silly superstitions.

Grandmom didn't scold Lillian the way her friends' grandparents scolded them for ignoring the old ways, but today Grandmom looked a little sad about it—or perhaps Lillian was noticing it for the first time.

As much as she loved her grandmother, Lillian could not be totally comfortable with her either. Her single-mindedness had always intimidated Lillian. Once Grandmom had a goal, she was like a locomotive thundering relentlessly down a track, never swerving, never giving up—whether it was making sure her grandchildren got As and Bs in school, unloading a pile of outmoded red velvet cushions, or outdueling a rival store that was trying to undercut their prices.

When they were only on the landing of the second floor, they could already hear the screaming and crying from their apartment. As they set foot on the third landing, a neighbor's door opened. A bald man with glasses and a knitted vest complained in Chinese, "Little Swallow, keep your brats quiet."

Grandmom dipped her head apologetically. "I'm sorry, Ah Mo. But it's hard to confine active children."

"It's hard on all of us," Ah Mo said sourly, "especially our ears."

"I have some tea that will calm your nerves," Grandmom said, "special from Fukien. I snuck it past the creditors. I'll send you some later."

Lillian stood in admiration as her grandmother soothed her neighbor's ruffled feelings. When she had been small, she had not paid any attention to the doings of the store, but she could see now what a good salesperson Grandmom was. And yet, for all the friendliness, there was a hardness underneath that made Lillian uneasy.

The smile left Grandmom's face as soon as they reached the fourth floor and opened the door to the apartment. Lillian's little brother, Jackie, was shouting at the youngest, Ruthie, and Ruthie was wailing and rubbing her eyes with her pudgy little fists.

Grandmom stumped past them, though. "You haven't finished the blouse yet?" she said to Lillian's mother.

Mommy sat, staring helplessly at the jumble of cloth caught in the maw of the sewing machine. At her feet were sacks of precut pieces, ready to be assembled. "I'm sorry." Her fingers, the nails once immaculately manicured and painted and now chewed and plain, fluttered in the air. "But the machine ate it. Simply ate it." She leaned her head to the side and drew her shoulders up in a quick movement that little girls did in movie comedies. "The blouse was so-o-o last year's fashion anyway."

Lillian could remember a time when her mother could make her laugh, could make everyone smile. She was still as beautiful, still as charming, but the qualities that Lillian had admired when they had lived above the store now seemed like flaws in the confines of the apartment and their limited finances.

The room was a jumble of cardboard suitcases and boxes, their lives crammed into a tiny space like refugees. However, space had been found for mementos of Grandmom's two most precious people. Near the doorway hung a photograph of Lillian's great-great-grandmother, with the same round face and small features as her little sister, Ruthie, but much more mature. Before Grandmom had left China, she had dragged Lillian's great-great-grandmother into the market town to have her picture taken. And hanging from a nail next to it was Grandpop's favorite cowboy hat.

Grandmom pointed at the hot plate. They weren't supposed to have one in the room, but all the tenants had them because they hated to use the tenement's kitchen, which was dirty and full of cockroaches—though, as Jackie had joked, the bugs would be one source of meat. "Lillian, get dinner ready while I try to untangle this."

However, when Lillian raised the lid from the big pot where they stored their rice, there was barely a cupful scattered across the bottom. She looked over at her mother. "Mommy, where did you put the rice you bought?"

Guilt flitted momentarily across her mother's face, to be replaced by an apologetic little pout. "I meant to buy it, but then I saw the new *Vogue* out." Her eyebrows went up with excitement. "Do you believe the hemlines this season? I—"

Lillian cut her off. "Mommy, didn't you hear me? We don't have enough rice."

"Don't be mad, baby," Mommy wheedled. She waved a hand to indicate the apartment. "This is all just a lark. When Poppy's friends pay us back, we'll have a good laugh about it."

Poppy was her loving name for her father, Lillian's grandfather.

Grandmom took several calming breaths. Then she started to say, "Jackie . . . No, not you." She'd just remembered how he had annoyed the neighbors yesterday bouncing a tennis ball against the wall outside. "Ruthie, go next door and ask Mrs. Lai politely for some rice." As she headed for the door, Grandmom added, "And be sure to smile." She drew up the corners of her own mouth in illustration.

As Ruthie took a big bowl from a stack, Mommy fluttered a hand at her. "Oooh, see if Mrs. Lai has any coffee too."

"Forget the coffee," Grandmom instructed, and when the door closed behind Ruthie, she gazed at Mommy sadly. "Times change, and we have to change with them, even if it's not for the best. We can't waste money on luxuries anymore. Rice, vegetables, that's what we need."

Mommy stared uncomprehendingly at Grandmom as if she were speaking Martian. "You and Poppy taught me to have standards."

Grandmom's eyes gazed at Mommy as if she were a flawed bolt of shantung silk and what she saw saddened her. "I'm not blaming you, dear. We came here to give you a better life, so you're what we made you."

Mommy looked bewildered, like a child who had been slapped for simply breathing. "Poppy wouldn't be so mean to me."

"No, he wouldn't have, but Poppy's not here anymore." Grandmom rubbed the heels of her hands against her tired eyes. "He's gone, and Teddy too. There's only us left now, dear."

Lillian, Jackie, and Ruthie's father, Teddy, had left soon after the bankruptcy. No one knew where he had gone.

"Teddy's coming back," Mommy insisted. "I'm sure he is. He'll take care of us."

Lillian loved her father, from the sheen of his pomaded hair to the mirror polish of his black dancing shoes. He liked to make everyone laugh, and that was the problem. When things had turned grim for the family and there had been nothing to laugh about, he had left, dancing shoes, pomade, and all.

Grandmom pressed her lips disapprovingly. "The only thing he knew how to do was spend money."

Mommy's face screwed up even worse as she got ready to wail. Hastily Lillian took her hand before she could upset Ruthie. "I'm sure he's coming back too, Mommy.

But in the meantime, we have to learn to take care of ourselves."

"But I can't cook. I can't sew." Mommy flopped her hands miserably on her lap. "All I know how to do is be pretty."

"Silk is pretty." Grandmom pretended to tug at the ends of an invisible string. "But it's strong too. Stronger than steel. At least that's what the scientists say. You take a silk thread and a steel wire the same size, and the silk's tougher."

Lillian realized she'd been wrong when she had thought her single-minded grandmother was like a loco-motive. Locomotives didn't care about the people they were carrying in the cars behind them. No, Grandmom was like a lioness fighting to save her cubs.

Mommy threw up her hands. "It's hopeless. I can't do it."

"If I learned how to sew, so can you," Grandmom said. The friendly charm was gone. She was all iron now. "We need to deliver the blouses in two days. It's for the family's sake. We have to keep everyone safe and happy."

Mommy broke into her tears. Jackie turned his back in disgust. Mommy seemed to do that a dozen times a day over the most trivial things. "Well, I'm not happy."

"At least you're safe," Grandmom said.

Mommy shook her head violently. "I can't do it, Mama. I just can't."

"All right, pet. All right," Grandmom soothed Mommy as she guided her over to the bed. "You rest for a bit and I'll take over. Maybe I can pick the stitches out so you can try again. We can't waste anything."

As Mommy curled up on the bed, Grandmom had trouble bending her fingers to rub her eyes. Her rheumatism must have flared up again.

Lillian knew she wanted to be a lioness like her grandmother. "Teach me, Grandmom," she said, stepping forward.

Mommy sat bolt upright on the bed. "No. You're not a seamstress. Your teacher said you have a great career ahead of you as a concert violinist."

"The violin already got sold in the auction, Mommy." Lillian tried to sound as firm as Grandmom—though her voice sounded dead to her. "This is what Grandpop would have wanted."

Mommy shook her head. "No, he wanted you to think about finer things, not about vulgar things like money."

Once, Lillian had thought their mother was the epitome of grace and charm and beauty, but that was when they'd been wealthy. Now, when she said these things in this dingy little tenement, she seemed like such a silly creature.

From Ruthie's expression, she was thinking something similar.

"Mommy," Lillian asked politely but firmly, "please

be quiet and let me concentrate."

Ruthie was more to the point. "Yeah, quit acting like a baby."

Mommy opened her mouth, shut it, and then opened it again. "How . . . how dare you talk to me like that?" And Mommy flung herself facedown on the bed. "You're all just being so cruel!" Weeping, she curled up on her side.

"Well, you may have lost your violin, but you don't have to lose your music. We can listen to it at least." Grandmom turned on the old battered radio. There was an eerie whine, and then static-like noise drifted out.

"But *Little Orphan Annie's* gonna be on soon," Ruthie objected.

"Lillian's working, so we'll listen to what Lillian wants." Grandmom crouched, fiddling with the dial until she found a concert. "But the first time we get a little extra money, we'll buy some sticky cakes. All right?"

"How come we can afford sticky cakes but not coffee?" Mommy snuffled.

"Because Lillian's working for the family, and the cakes happen to be her favorite," Grandmom insisted.

Lillian tried to ignore Mommy's complaints and listen to the music instead. However, the cheap radio's speakers couldn't do justice to the sweetness of the Beethoven violin concerto. The notes should have filled her like water in a glass—just as they would have with a live performance.

But they could no longer afford tickets to a concert hall.

At least if she had been able to keep her violin, she could have continued to feel the music vibrating from the strings through her fingers and through her body. Her hands felt numb, even dead, without her violin in them.

"No one cares about me!" Mommy finally said.

Lillian swung her head toward her mother. Mommy was lying on the bed, dabbing at her tears with a Kleenex and glancing around to see if anyone was sympathizing with her plight.

Lillian gazed at her mother sorrowfully. So did Ruthie. So did Jackie. They were willing to grow up fast, but Mommy was not, as if their roles were beginning to reverse, and they were the responsible ones and she the helpless child. And that was creating a gulf separating them from their mother.

Grandmom grunted. "The first Swallow was strong for her family too. She kept them . . . well . . . not happy, but safe anyway."

Intrigued by the novelty of the moment, Lillian sat down by the sewing machine. When the violin had been her life, she'd tried to absorb everything about it from technique to traditions and history. Since sewing was going to be her life now, she would learn everything she could about that. And about Swallow, her namesake. "What did that Swallow do?"

"Let's see. She would have been your great-great-aunt,"

Grandmom said. "She sold herself to settle her family's debts."

"What?" Jackie asked, outraged.

Grandmom shrugged. "That's what happened back then." She took some new pieces from two different bags. "We'll start on these. I'll salvage what your mother did later."

It would be difficult to work by the light of the single bulb in the ceiling, but she would manage. They all would. She and Grandmom would make sure of that.

"Keep them safe," Lillian murmured to herself. "Keep them happy."

Grandmom reached her arms from behind Lillian to demonstrate what to do, and Lillian listened carefully as her Grandmom alternated between sewing lessons and the story of that first Swallow's sacrifice.

Lillian's first effort came out perfect. No matter what the calamity, her family fought back. They adapted. They survived.

As Grandmom got the next pieces, Lillian stared down at her fingers and flexed them. They were long and slender and soft. She had often pictured these same fingers wielding the bow and dancing nimbly over the violin strings, brilliant, lovely notes rising like birds to the high ceiling of Carnegie Hall, the audience in rapt attention.

As she listened to the violin soloist soaring in the sweet, joyful notes of the third movement, she felt tears stinging her eyes until the sewing machine was a dark blur.

Mommy was watching her from the bed. "See, baby? You don't want to give up the violin for that dreadful old machine. Leave it. We'll manage somehow. Maybe sell something."

Lillian thought of the first Swallow and the sacrifice she had made. As the successor to the name, Lillian could do no less.

Lillian took a ragged breath. "There's nothing left to sell, Mommy. And that includes my violin. It's gone, and so is that part of my life." She swept her sleeve over her eyes and then blinked. "Grandmom, would you turn the radio to *Little Orphan Annie*?"

"The music's free," Grandmom said softly. "What's the harm of listening?"

"Because it distracts me from sewing," Lillian said firmly. "I start remembering and imagining the wrong things. I could wind up making some mistakes, and we can't afford that now. So no more music."

And no more silly dreams.

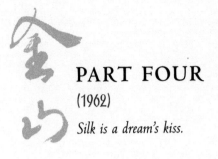

PART FOUR
(1962)

Silk is a dream's kiss.

PART FOUR

CHAPTER | 45

San Francisco's Chinatown
August 6, 1962
Seven Seven Festival

Rosie

Rosie studied the wheeled clothes racks in the Imperial Splendor Factory. It was such an impressive name for such a grubby little sweatshop. The harsh light from the fluorescent bulbs overhead brought out the grime and every shabby detail. The air was filled with the odor of the fine machine oil and the smell of new, processed cloth. Women were packed in at the tables, hunched over the old sewing machines. Cramped fingers steering the cotton cloth, eyes straining to keep the seams straight. The collective hum of the machines' needles made the room sound like the inside of a beehive.

Earl, the owner of the Imperial Splendor, had a contract for sleepwear, and the finished pajamas hung on the rack, all the same design and colors—all the pants of red cotton, tapering gradually until they would be tight around the calves, emphasizing the wearer's legs, and loose tops with red and orange blazer stripes—but in different sizes. Women came in so many heights and widths, and yet stores would be gambling that they would all want to look the same.

Next to the pajama rack was a rack of nightgowns. The design was the same as their flannel gowns but with more ruffles around the neckline. However, it was the material that fascinated Rosie. She had never seen real silk, and she felt a curiosity that was almost a physical hunger inside her. She longed to feel the fibers between her fingertips

A few months ago, she'd seen a woman in a cheongsan, a tight-fitting dress with a slit on the side like they used to wear in Canton.

Curious, she had walked behind the lady like a baby duck after its mother, but the more she studied the material, the more she felt it couldn't be silk—though she couldn't have said how she knew that. By the time she became convinced that it was some clever synthetic fabric, the woman had felt her presence and whirled around—a trick worthy of an acrobat considering she was in high heels.

The woman seemed surprised to see a girl of twelve staring at her with radar intensity.

"What do you want?" the woman had demanded.

Rosie had had her eyes fixed on the woman's shoulder

blades and back, so she looked up into a face with more makeup than she had ever seen. "I was just wondering what material that was."

The woman smoothed her hand along her shoulder. "It's silk."

Rosie's mind was so fixed on the problem at hand that she blurted out, "Um, no, I don't think it is."

"Are you calling me a liar?" the woman demanded, and stamped a foot for emphasis. There was a crack, and she started to list to her left as the stiletto heel on her shoe broke.

"Right, yes, I must be mistaken. I guess it's silk after all. Sorry." Rosie had scurried away even as the astonished lady was looking down her foot sinking toward the pavement.

However, the material of these nightgowns was far superior to the cheong-san's. Rosie drew her eyebrows together, trying to picture how it would hang on someone's frame. How would it flow when the wearer moved? she wondered, and reached out to see.

Earl slapped her hand. There was very little that owner missed in his shop. He was like the Greek myth about Argus of the Hundred Eyes. She'd read about him in a book of mythology, a prize she had won for a picture she had entered into a school-district art contest.

"Don't touch the merchandise," Earl growled. "You'll get it dirty."

From his clothes, you would never have thought Earl owned the Imperial Splendor. He wore baggy khaki work pants, a stained white shirt, and a badly knitted wool vest, as if he dressed from a thrift store's discards.

Rosie thought she was probably one of the cleanest things in this dingy shop, but she simply said, "I'm sorry."

"If you got so much time, sweep up the scraps and put them in a bag," Earl said. Though he had three apartment houses in Chinatown, he was determined to squeeze every penny out of the sweatshop and would sell the rags to papermakers.

Crash!

Her little brother, Jason, screeched like a banshee (another story in the book).

"Rosie!" her mother called.

She felt a twinge of guilt when she heard the weariness in her mother's voice. She was supposed to be watching Jason and her little sister, Mimi, instead of inspecting dresses. Mama worked so hard, and today she was under even more stress than usual. Morrie, the head salesman for the manufacturer, had come to the Imperial Splendor that morning to ask her to sew the samples that he would take around to the stores. None of the other women did such a fine, neat job as her mother, or as quick. With his usual hyperbole, Morrie had said the other women worked at their sewing machines but Mama played hers like it was a musical instrument.

All the salespeople from other clients requested that she do their samples as well, so it wasn't just flattery from Morrie.

"Can't tell stuck-up Shun-te girls anything. Do your job," Earl complained in Toisanese. Toisan was one of the Say Yup, or Four Districts to the southwest of Canton, with its own subdialect. It had been called Sunning before 1914.

Rosie's family spoke Sam Yup, the dialect spoken around Canton, but she knew Toisanese because so many other people spoke it in Chinatown.

She felt like telling him that at least they didn't live in a pigsty like the Imperial Splendor, but again she simply mumbled, "I'm sorry."

She hurried to the corner, where she heard a clinking sound. Six-year-old Jason and seven-year-old Mimi were on their knees, trying to gather up the clothes hangers that had spilled out of the overturned box and only managing to tangle them up so that they looked like a giant version of the wire puzzles sold in the Chinatown toy stalls.

"Honestly," Rosie said, exasperated. "Why do you have to make so much work for me?"

"We're sorry, Rosie," Mimi said, and she elbowed Jason.

"Yeah, sorry," Jason said.

You're mad at Earl, not your brother and sister, Rosie told herself, *so don't take it out on them.*

Rosie squatted. "I'll pick them up. Do your home-work."

Though there was no American school in August, they had Chinese lessons in the afternoon. Proper Chinese, as her mother said, because Chinese school taught the Sam Yup dialect.

"Do I have to?" Jason whined.

The fifty-year-old Morrie came over from where he had been supervising Mama. "There's a buck in it for you if you stay quiet," Morrie said, dipping a hand inside his coat. As always, he was dressed in a clean, pressed three-piece suit. Around his neck was a scarlet bow tie with white polka dots, and he always smelled of cologne.

"I have homework too," Mimi said with her hand out.

"Mimi," Rosie said, cheeks reddening.

Morrie laughed, and there was the flash of gold from his teeth. "Thanks for the reminder, honey. Got to be fair."

He pulled two dollar bills from his wallet and handed them to Rosie. "I'll let your big sister hold on to them."

Rosie would have liked to have asked for a dollar too if she knew of a way that wouldn't be embarrassing. Instead, she said, "You really don't need to."

"Your mom's doing me a special favor," Morrie said.

"I'm the one that gave my permission," Earl called across the room.

"And I appreciate it," Morrie said, tipping an imaginary hat in thanks.

Encouraged because Morrie seemed in a good mood, Rosie worked up enough nerve to ask, "Is this real silk?"

"No, it's sort of a blend, but not bad," Morrie said.

"So you've seen real silk?" Rosie asked eagerly.

"You mean you haven't?" Morrie asked, surprised, and then grinned. "Tell you what. I'll bring by some swatches."

"Maybe some tussah," Rosie asked eagerly, "and gazar, noil, organza, shantung . . ." The litany of names tripped off her tongue.

"Whoa, whoa." Morrie held up both palms. "I'll see what I can get."

"And maybe some satin?" Rosie asked, not believing her own daring even as she spoke.

Morrie rubbed his thumb against his lower lip speculatively. "You really want to know?"

"Miss Yang teaches home ec, but she's studying to be a designer," Rosie said. "She says that a designer uses fabric like an artist uses paint. And they both have to know colors."

Morrie put his hand over his heart. "Well, never let it be said that old Morrie stood in the way of your education. I'll bring by a whole bunch of swatches of all sorts of material. How's that?" He jerked a thumb at Jason and Mimi. "Just ride herd on them today." Suddenly he leaned his head to the side, noticing something. "Your dress looks sort of like my number twenty from last summer." He wiggled his fingers absently. "Not the material, but the design—except the shoulders are a little different."

Rosie had liked it and sewn her copy at home. "Yes. I liked most of it, so I made my own," Rosie confessed. She felt herself blushing.

Morrie was skeptical. "Your mama really didn't help you? You did it all by yourself?"

"I had plenty of time to study the pieces," Rosie said, and added, "I hope you're not too mad."

"Not as long as you only make one copy for yourself. And anyway, it's last year's now." Morrie folded his arms. "What did you like about it?"

"I liked its silhouette," she said, gesturing downward, "but I thought the fabric your company used was a little too stiff for the design." She touched a shoulder. "And I changed this."

Morrie laughed. "You got an eye for clothes. That was the best of the bunch, and you even improved on it." He glanced sideways at Jason and Mimi. "But those aren't from our kiddie line."

"We didn't want to steal everything," Rosie said diplomatically. She'd copied her brother's and sister's clothing from Morrie's biggest competitor.

Morrie's eyes twinkled. "You mean, you didn't like them."

Rosie shrugged but remained silent.

Morrie scratched his cheek sheepishly. "Well, you had plenty of company. That line was the brainchild of the owner's daughter. I couldn't give those outfits away." He shrugged resignedly. "And in my time, I've sold everything else—from ice-cube trays in Alaska to sandboxes in the Mojave Desert."

"Everyone's going to want Rosie's clothes," Mimi piped up loyally.

"Not me," Jason said.

"Who'd make clothes for you?" Mimi said, sticking out her tongue. "They'll just put you inside a big paper bag."

Rosie whirled, caught Jason's shoulder as he started to rise vengefully, and forced him back down. Her free hand held Mimi in her seat. "The both of you behave. Don't distract Mama anymore, okay?"

"Well," Morrie winked, "if you don't become a designer, you'll make a mighty fine prison guard."

CHAPTER | 46

Rosie

The dreary day ended at last. The machines were silent as chair legs scraped on the floor and the women stood up and began to pick up their purses and throw their coats over their arms, not even bothering to put them on before they made their escape from Earl.

Rosie shivered as she emerged from the Imperial Splendor into the alley. There was a splash of sun high up on the opposite brick wall, but the afternoon winds were blowing in from the ocean to the west, spilling down the hills into Chinatown itself. Undershirts flapped on the railing of a third-story fire escape. She didn't see how they ever got dry in the half-light that usually filled the alley—except now, when the afternoon sunlight briefly reached the upper floor.

"I'm cold," Jason complained.

"Then zipper up," she said, but instead of doing it himself, he waited like a little prince until Rosie bent her knees and did it for him. *It pays to be the only boy in the family,* she thought, and gave a harder pull than necessary at the zipper tab.

"Ow!" Jason said, rubbing his chest.

"Sorry," Rosie said insincerely, and checked her little sister.

At least Mimi had buttoned up her cotton coat, but then Mimi was a girl and could be expected to act sensibly.

As she waited, Rosie mechanically returned the other ladies' good-byes, not seeing their faces but the images in her own mind. What would she have done with the dresses' fabric?

Jason bounced up and down on the balls of his feet. "Hurry, Mama."

At last, Mama came out with Auntie Ruthie, who also worked in the sweatshop. "Be sure to stop by Kwong Joh. Jackie's going to be at the counter today, and he'll make sure we get some choice lop cheong," Aunt Ruthie said. Lop cheong were Chinese sausages and had a lovely sweet-salty taste.

"How much?" Mama asked.

"A pound will do," Auntie Ruthie said, and waved good-bye as she hurried away to her own family.

Earl came to the doorway. "Hey, Young Swallow," he

called in Chinese, "didn't you forget something?"

Mama examined herself and then the children. "I don't think so."

Earl extended a palm. "I saw Morrie give you money. I want my share."

"It was a tip," Mama said, poking a finger against her shoulder. "For me."

"You used my machine on my premises," Earl said smugly, and wriggled his fingers like hungry worms.

Rosie came back from her daydreams. Her mother looked like some little hunted animal. Even so, she was not about to give up without a fight. "It was only two dollars," she said, trying to defend every penny. In her nervousness, she fiddled with the black cord around her wrist. It used to be their father's string tie. After he had died, Mama wore it to remember him by.

"I'll take fifty percent, then," Earl said.

Reluctantly, Mama opened her purse and handed over a wrinkled dollar bill. It vanished as soon as Earl's fingers touched it.

Mimi waited until he had shut the door behind him and then made a face. "I hate him."

"Now, now, Mimi," Mama said, taking her hand. "He gave me a job."

"But he's mean. He took a whole dollar," Mimi said.

Mama swung her hand back and forth as they walked toward the alley. "Yes, but it wasn't half of the tip. Morrie gave me four dollars." She leaned over her younger daughter cheerfully. "Even small victories count."

They walked down the hill, turning onto Grant Avenue, where they headed northward, merging into the crowd of late-afternoon shoppers. The tiny Mimi would have been trampled, so they left her outside with Jason while Rosie squeezed into the Kwong Jow store with Mama.

She was tossed back and forth like a piece of driftwood on a stormy sea, but somehow she managed to keep up with her mother as she wriggled to the front.

Uncle Jackie was a bluff, friendly man who handled the horde of impatient shoppers with a mixture of teasing and gentle scolding that kept fistfights from breaking out. "Hey, how are my favorite girls in the whole world?" he greeted them, ignoring the other people shouting for his attention.

"You better not let Emma hear you say that," Mama said, grinning. Emma was his wife.

"Emma's beyond being my favorite. She's priceless, a gem beyond compare—" Uncle Jackie was capable of going on with his wife's praises for five minutes, but Mama cut him short.

"I'll take two one-pound packages of your best lop cheong," Mama said. "And mine better be nicer than Ruthie's."

Uncle Jackie winked. "They always are."

"Humph," Mama sniffed. "I bet you say the same thing to Ruthie when she's here."

"Hey, how do you think I managed to survive this long with you two?" Uncle Jackie laughed.

In no time, he'd handed them two bundles, each wrapped in pink paper. Rosie tucked them into the crook of her arm like footballs as Mama paid for them. Then, with Mama surging toward the door like a three-hundred-pound lineman, Rosie followed her.

Rosie was impatient to get home, but Mama, flush with extra funds, dawdled over the bins of fragrant vegetables and sidled down the alleys. Jason and Mimi halted periodically by some bag of treats or jar of candy as a hint, but Rosie wouldn't let them even begin to whine. She was holding on desperately to the images in her mind of blouses and dresses, but the sooner they got home, the sooner she could put them down in her sketch pad.

Her siblings only perked up a little when Mama stopped by the Far East Bakery and bought some of her favorite sticky cakes—even if they weren't as good as the ones her grandmother had made and Jason and Mimi would have preferred Twinkies.

They seemed to be walking forever in the August twilight, their purchases dangling in pink plastic bags. Rosie had distributed the load among the three children so that Mama would not have to carry anything—with her taking the most fragile things and Jason taking the vegetables, which could be washed if he dropped the bag as he usually did.

At last, they headed back along Grant Avenue, past the big building that had once belonged to their family. It was an old, boring story, so Mama didn't even bother telling it. She just paused and swiveled her head, taking in the bottom floor, which had now been divided into little stores that sold T-shirts, back scratchers, and postcards.

Then, with a little shake of her head, she continued on to Pacific Street. The pale green, impersonal walls of the Ping Yuen Project loomed over them.

Several teenage boys were pitching pennies against the wall. Their Dixie-Peached hair rose in shiny, oily cresting waves, and nearby a cheap transistor radio was playing an Everly Brothers tune.

"Hey, Rosie, the queen called," one of them said. "She wants her ball gown tomorrow."

Don't let them get under your skin, Rosie told herself. "I'm too busy," she announced, "but thanks for taking the message."

The jibes would have been a lot worse if her mother had not been there, for her mother knew all their mothers and grandmothers and aunts. The boys might be stupid, but not that stupid.

At school, though, her mother was not there to protect her, and the taunts were crueler and more pointed. She tried to give back as good as she got, tried not to cry, but there were times when she hid in a restroom stall and wept silently.

As they entered the projects, Mimi grumbled, "I wish they'd leave Rosie alone."

Mama said, quoting the proverb, "The nail that sticks out gets hammered."

"I'm not going to give up sketching," Rosie insisted.

Her mother pronounced judgment with all the finality of a court justice. "Then you can expect to get teased. That happens to anyone in Chinatown who's a little different."

"But—," Mimi began.

Behind her mother's back, Rosie turned and made a slashing motion at her throat. She didn't want to add any more worries to her mother's already heavy burden. She would handle her own battles and heal her own wounds.

The stairs were stained with urine.

"Animals," Mama grumbled.

Mimi and Jason edged away from the dark areas on the steps, but Rosie caught them. "Don't touch the walls or you'll get dirty."

Even after they had locked, bolted, and chained the door shut for the evening, Rosie could not get to her sketch pad. There was dinner to be cooked, and afterward Mimi, who was attending a Saturday arts and crafts program at the Chinese Rec Center, needed help with her project.

"Miss Okada says we have to make a wishing tree," she said, "and then put our wishes on it. Everyone does it in Japan today because it's the Tan-a . . . Tanabata. I've got to bring it in next class."

Rosie had met Mimi's art teacher and doubted that the pleasant young woman had ever laid down such laws. However, Mimi treated every word from Miss Okada as if it were one of the Ten Commandments. "Why?" she asked.

Mimi scratched her head. "It's got something to do with a weaver."

Rosie had a vague recollection of hearing that name on a radio station. "You mean the folksingers?"

"No, the Weaving Maid," Mama corrected her. "And today is her Seven Seven festival. And she's Chinese, not Japanese. She wove silk back in China a long time ago. But then she got a boyfriend and got all silly. She spent so much time mooning over him that she didn't go near her loom. So Heaven separated them, but she kept wishing and wishing she could see her husband again." Unconsciously, Mama fiddled with the cord around her wrist. "The magpies heard her and felt so sorry that they formed a bridge so she could cross over. And for one day of the year, Heaven looks the other way and allows them to meet." Mama sniffed. "The Japanese must have copied her." Mama still hadn't forgiven the Japanese for what they had done to China during World War II.

"Well, it was Miss Okada's idea. She said the tree was all about the power of wishes," Mimi explained. "I like her. She's nice. And she wasn't a soldier. She was in some kind of prison camp here during the war."

"Relocation camp," Rosie corrected her. "That's where they put Japanese Americans." Cindy Kawaguchi was her friend in class, and she had told her a little about what had happened to her family.

Of course, it didn't matter to Mama whether Miss Okada and Cindy had been born here or in Japan, because she lumped them all together. She was getting ready to give her standard lecture about Japanese atrocities during the war, but Rosie headed her off by sending Mimi to the closet to get some spare wire hangers while she went to make dinner.

A few minutes later, she heard her mother shuffle into the kitchen, her open-ended cloth slippers slapping at her heels. "I know the pliers are in here somewhere," Mama said as she began to rummage through a kitchen drawer.

Rosie paused with a pot lid in her hand. "You should rest, Mama. I'll help Mimi after dinner."

"Mimi's just as antsy as you were at that age," Mama said with a faint smile, as if she were remembering. "And anyway, I want to do more than sleep and work. It's getting so that I know that sewing machine better than I recall your faces."

It should have been easy for Mama to remember

Rosie's, because they looked so much alike with the high-boned cheeks and high-set eyes. At the moment, though, Mama looked so tired that Rosie was tempted to shoo her away, but she saw how excitedly Mimi scooted by with several wire hangers in her arms. Short with a round face and small eyes, nose, and mouth, she looked like a little elf in Santa's workshop.

Rosie didn't think she'd ever had as much energy as her little sister, who sometimes seemed as if she were plugged into the nearest electrical outlet, but Mimi had been so good today—at least for her. Nor could she disappoint her mother, so she said nothing, but went on cooking.

By the time she began serving dinner, Mama and Mimi had managed to mangle the wire into a series of progressively smaller triangles to suggest a fir tree.

"That looks pretty skimpy, if you ask me," Jason said.

"It's a modern tree, stupid," Mimi said.

Mama headed off World War III before it could start. "No name calling, Mimi." And then she fixed Jason with a stare to let him know she wanted peace tonight. "It's a modern tree for modern times."

He dropped his eyes. "I still don't think modern's supposed to be so skimpy."

After dinner, Rosie had to remind Jason that it was his turn to clean up. He did such a rush job that she would probably have to give everything a second washing, but it was a matter of principle: It was bad enough that some poor girl was going to be stuck with Jason when she married him, but Rosie was determined that at least he be slightly familiar with basic housekeeping.

"If I've got to work, at least I ought to have some music," Jason grumbled. He turned on the radio and began to fumble with the dial. Some piece of Mozart floated out of it.

"Anything but classical," Mama said. She refused to explain why, but she hated classical music.

Jason experimented some more until he found the right station. The Everly Brothers began to sing about Little Susie's unfortunate sleeping habits.

Mama rolled her eyes. "Well, I did say anything but classical." She was one of the few mothers that Rosie knew who would put up with rock and roll.

As Jason finally began clearing the table, Mimi was already cutting up a sheet of paper and handing out crayons because they didn't have enough pencils. Mama didn't look happy about putting her personal wish on a Japanese tree, but when Mimi got an idea in her head, it was like trying to stop a rolling boulder.

Rosie, of course, knew what she wanted, so she got her pad instead and sketched out that day's fashion ideas.

She was just finishing her notes when Mimi said accusingly, "Rosie, you're supposed to write your wish."

"I'm starting right now," Rosie said, and carefully

began to write out her wish. Mimi was such a perfection-ist that she would demand that her older sister use her best penmanship. When Rosie was done, she saw Mama cutting her paper into a shape.

"Such a fancy design for a wish," Rosie said to her.

Mama shrugged. "Every tree needs a bird."

Mimi craned her head curiously. "What kind of bird is it?"

Mama glanced at the fading photo of Rosie's great-great-great-grandmother on the wall, and she smiled. "I happen to like swallows."

Mimi sat back. "That's your name, Mama."

"Well," Mama argued, "there should be something Chinese about the wishing tree. After all, the Weaving Maid was Chinese."

Mimi taped her own wish to the tree. "Birds are too messy. A flower would be better."

"Don't be disrespectful," Mama told her. "A lot of women in our family have been named after that bird. The first relative named Swallow sold herself into slavery so her family could survive."

Mimi's eyes grew big as saucers. "Was she really a slave?" she asked when she came over to them.

Rosie could see Mimi was becoming upset, so she draped an arm over her little sister's shoulders. "That was back in China," she said. As far as she and the other chil-dren were concerned, China was as remote as the South

Pole, so what took place there didn't matter. "It can't happen here because there aren't any slaves nowadays." She felt Mimi relax.

Dusting his hands, Jason returned from the kitchen. "For what Earl pays Mama, she might as well be."

When he sat down, Rosie reached over and tapped his arm. "Behave now."

From the guilty expression that flickered across his features, Jason had planned to write something insulting, but he adapted quickly. "Would I do that to my baby sister?" he said, smiling. He tried his best to imitate a cherub on a church wall, even though he wound up looking more like a gargoyle spout.

"Make your wish a good one," Mimi warned as she taped her own wish to the tree. "Don't ask for just a baseball mitt."

Jason finished with a flourish. "How can I become a star third baseman without one?"

"They're expensive," Rosie warned. She'd already priced them at a downtown toy store.

"I hear they need a part-timer at the Heavenly Garden restaurant," Mama said.

"Mama, you can't take on two jobs," Rosie said. "Earl already leaves you so exhausted."

"I've done it before," Mama said defensively. Her fingertip angled Mimi's wish up so she could read it. "How else am I going to afford that fancy paint set too?"

Mimi's eyes shone. "It's got sixty colors." Then she

shot a knowing glance at her older sister. "And I already know what Rosie wants."

Jason gave a short barking laugh. "Like we couldn't guess."

Rosie picked up her mother's wish, admiring the sleek curves of the swallow's tail and wings. "Fair's fair, Mama. What did you wish?"

"That you listen to Mr. Uarte when you get back to school," Mama said simply. "I had a letter from him."

Mr. Uarte was Rosie's guidance counselor.

"In the summer?" Rosie asked, surprised.

"Mr. Uarte is very dedicated," Mama said. "When he sees you in the fall, he wants you to be prepared to talk about your future."

Rosie scowled. "He wants me to be a bank teller."

"It's good, steady money," Mama insisted, and waved a hand vaguely in the air. "This idea of being a designer is a nice daydream."

Rosie was angry enough to point out that so was being a baseball player or an artist, but she caught herself in time. It wasn't right to draw her little brother and sister into this debate as well. "I know I can do it, Mama."

"You're at an age when it's time to get practical," Mama argued.

Mama did so much for them that it was hard for Rosie to deny her . . . except on this. "It is my future, Mama."

Mama sighed. "I'm trying to keep you from getting hurt."

"By hurting me more?" Rosie pleaded. "Haven't you ever had a dream, Mama?"

"A long time ago." Mama looked down at her fingers. Though they were long and slender, years of work had left them callused and slightly crooked. Then she raised her head again. "Generations of this family have had to sacrifice what they love. Just like that first Swallow. When the moment came for me to choose, I did the right thing. Now it's your turn."

Rosie's hand shot out and she grabbed her wish. "Then there's no point to dreams." She tugged at the paper, but it had been taped so well that she knocked the tree over.

"Hey!" Mimi complained.

Rosie was crying now, and yanking so that the tree slid a few inches across the table toward her. She finally pulled her wish away, but not before she bent the wire.

"You're breaking it," Mimi said angrily.

Mama wrapped her arms around Mimi. "It's all right. It's nothing we can't fix. Jason, go get the pliers."

Rosie glared at Mama, feeling a little jealous that Mimi was getting the hug and not her. She felt the spite rise inside her, bitter and venomous. "Save your money, Mama. Jason will never be a baseball player, and you know it. And Mimi, she's going to be stuck at a sewing machine same as me."

"I am not," Mimi said, bursting into tears.

Rosie slunk away, guilty and angry and crying herself.

CHAPTER 47

August 7, 1962

Lillian

Last night's confrontation had hurt Lillian as much as it had her daughter—though even if she had been willing to admit it, she would not have known how to tell her. Chinatown parents just didn't do that sort of thing. No, you made the hard decisions for your children and steered them in the right direction even if they didn't want to go that way. Nor would they understand how much it tore you up inside when you were strict with them.

Keep the family safe, Grandmom had said. *Keep them happy.*

But it had taken everyone's combined efforts to achieve the first goal, so the second aim had to be abandoned. Nor did it sound like previous generations had been able to do any better. And now it looked as if history were repeating itself.

That morning Rosie had looked as lifeless as a zombie. She had performed all her chores mechanically, but her eyes were listless, as if her spirit were gone. Inside, Lillian felt herself grieve. She wondered if she had looked like that when she had given up the violin. Worse, did she look like that now?

In the Imperial Splendor, Rosie had sat with an open book from her summer reading assignment on her lap. She had not turned the page in half an hour. At least Jason and Mimi had picked up on her mood and were reading quietly.

Lillian thought of her grandmother. She had been so proud and yet so sad when Lillian had given up the violin. When Lillian had been Rosie's age, her grandmother had not had to tell her what to do. She had known automatically that she had to make the sacrifice. But that had been a different time, when children in Chinatown didn't celebrate the Weaving Maid with *Japanese* customs—though to be honest she couldn't remember celebrating the occasion at all. At least she had *listened* to her grandmother's stories about the old days in China.

Women in her family followed the example set by that earlier Swallow: They did their duty. If Rosie could not bring herself to do that, then Lillian would have to be strong for her and make the choices that Rosie was too weak to face on her own.

Lillian corrected herself quickly. No, Rosie wasn't weak. She took on so many unpleasant chores so her mother could concentrate on supporting them. Other women complained about how their daughters wasted time in the summer chatting, seeing movies, or sitting for hours in the listening booths down at the Music Box— girls, Lillian thought wryly, who were as spoiled and self-ish as her mother had been.

But not her Rosie. She cooked, she cleaned, and she watched Mimi and Jason all day long. Never once had she complained.

All she asked in return was that she be allowed to imagine pretty things and then draw them. Her daughter looked happiest when she was designing her fashions.

Lillian thought of a time when she had felt just as joy-ful: of the days when she had played the violin, fingers and bow dancing upon the strings, of feeling the violin wood quiver in response, of feeling the warm, golden vibrations pass into her body, of that exquisite blending with the musical instrument and her and the music, the lovely notes forming a bridge that ignored time to connect her with the genius composer.

Though she had done her best to hide it, giving up music had been like cutting off her own hands. So, once she had sat down at the machine, she had tried to turn her back on all that. However, the wounds of that sacrifice remained. Even now, she could not bear to listen to clas-sical music on the radio, could not explain the reason to her children.

Those musical dreams seemed so remote now, as if

there were a chasm between that dreamy younger self and Lillian the mature adult.

And now it was Rosie's turn to suffer through the same thing. Why did the women in the family have to keep losing what they loved?

Nor had her younger daughter been immune. Mimi had not brought along her usual pencils and scrap paper to sketch. Lillian wondered if Mimi had also taken last night's argument to heart and already given up her art.

That made Lillian's guilt all the heavier to bear. And then she thought of all the past generations who had been caught in the same pattern of sacrifice. Her grandmother had come here not only to have a better life but to escape their fate. And now her children were caught in the same trap.

She knew the Old-timers would advise her not to give in. A child had no right to be so selfish. But this wasn't China. This was America. She'd been born here just like her children. Why did this have to keep happening? When was it ever going to change?

And yet what could she do to stop it? She'd never felt more helpless. *If only I thought Rosie had a chance as a designer, perhaps I would let her follow that path. No,* she thought fiercely, *I'd do more than that. I'd fight to give her that chance.*

However, whom could she ask to judge Rosie's talent? Morrie didn't care what he sold. Morrie needed to be liked, and sales were a way of charting how likeable he was. If he were given tires, he would peddle those.

Ask Earl? She gave a derisive snort. He couldn't see beyond the price tag.

Of course, she could always ask Ruthie, but her sister would agree with her. So, without anyone else to consult, she couldn't allow her daughter to make a mistake. It was better to hold on to the sure thing, like clerking in a bank. Surely that was breaking the pattern of the past. Being a bank clerk would mean less work and more pay than laboring in the sweatshops . . . but was it worth killing your spirit?

She was so lost in these sad reflections that she barely heard Morrie's sprightly "shave and a haircut" knock on the shop's door. When Earl opened the door, Morrie clasped the owner's shoulders. "Have I got a deal for you, Earl."

"I'm not buying any more horse-race tips from you." Earl frowned.

"And I feel bad that that old nag came in last, so I'm going to pay you back with the biggest opportunity of a lifetime." Morrie picked up Earl bodily and set him on the side so he could enter the shop as he chattered on in a machine-gun rhythm. "This is the big one, Earl. If this works out, you'll have to double the staff and rent next door." He drummed his fingers against his chin as he studied one side of the shop. "I got a pal who could knock down that wall cheap."

Earl hurried after him, confused and annoyed. "I'm not tearing down any wall. I'm not renting anything more, and I'm certainly not hiring."

Morrie wheeled to his right, down the aisle between tables. "Ever hear of Giacomo?"

"No, who's he?" Earl said, bewildered.

"I'm shocked, because you're such a savvy guy about the fashion biz." Morrie rounded on his heel and flung an arm around the startled Earl. "Giacomo is the most exclusive designer in all of Frisco. He takes only the ritzy dames from Pacific Heights."

Earl was suddenly suspicious. "So? You don't work for Giacomo."

Morrie pulled him in close. "Him and me go way back, so when he got into a jam, he came to his old pal. And naturally I thought of you. Do him this favor and he'll put in the word with his bigwig fashion buddies. It could turn into big contracts."

Greed warred with skepticism in Earl. "What do I have to do?"

"You, nothing." Morrie's arms shot out wide. "Just let Giacomo borrow Miss Lillian, the goddess of the thread and needle. See, this flu bug hit Giacomo's place real bad. He's lost all his quality seamstresses right when he needs them the most."

"Who pays her salary if she's working there and not here?" Earl demanded.

"Giacomo," Morrie said instantly.

Earl got a sly look. "And what do I do in the meantime? I'll be short one person."

Morrie scratched the tip of his nose. "Earl, your perspicacity and cupidity never cease to amaze people."

Earl looked as if he wasn't sure if it was a compliment or not, but he wasn't about to ask. "Who says that?" he asked carefully.

Morrie stuck his hand inside his coat as if he were taking an oath on his wallet. "But I wouldn't let a friend suffer for doing me a favor. So I tell you what. If Giacomo won't give you a fee, then I'll pay you out of my own pocket."

Now that the last financial risk had been dealt with, Earl was feeling expansive. "Ah, we people in the fashion industry have to help one another, don't we?"

This was all very fine for Earl and Morrie, but Lillian didn't want to leave her family when they were upset with her. She had fences to mend somehow.

Lillian cleared her throat. "No one asked me if I want to go." She nodded to her children in the corner. "I'm staying with my family."

All around them the sewing machines had stilled as the other women eavesdropped. It was easy to hear Rosie's voice now. "I'll take care of them."

"And so will I," Earl declared. "At the Imperial Splendor, we're all one big happy family." He beamed at

Lillian's children. It was such an unusual sight that Mimi and Jason instinctively pressed themselves against Rosie for protection.

"We'll be okay, Mama," Rosie called. "Honest."

They were the first words that Rosie had spoken to her that day. Well, hadn't she deserved it?

"You can check on them by phone." Earl glanced at Morrie. "They'll let her call from there, right?"

"Sure," Morrie said, and he dipped his head to her. "I'd count this as a big favor, Miss Lillian. Talent needs talent. It won't do Giacomo any good to come up with designs if he doesn't have nimble fingers like yours to make them real."

Lillian had resented being loaned out like a used car, but Morrie's words jolted her. They were asking her to work for a successful designer, Giacomo, one whose opinion she could trust. If he said that Rosie had some promise, then Lillian would let her chase her dream.

She doubted she would see him, let alone get near him. But if she had the opportunity, she would seize it for her daughter's sake.

"I'll do it," she said. *Not for you, but for Rosie.*

While Morrie and Earl waited impatiently, Lillian spoke to her children. "Behave yourselves," she warned.

Jason squirmed. "Why are you looking just at me?"

Lillian hugged him. "You know why, but I love you anyway." She embraced Mimi, who told her not to worry.

And then Lillian put her arms around Rosie.

Her older daughter sat as stiff and unresponsive as a mannequin. Tears brimmed in Lillian's eyes. "You're a good girl, Rosie." It was on the tip of her tongue to say that she deserved more than having to make do all the time, but she caught herself.

She got her coat, put the pincushion that would strap to her wrist, her thimble, a small scissors, measuring tape, and other necessary items into her purse, and then followed Morrie outside and down to Grant Avenue, where he pointed eastward. "I parked in a lot on Kearny."

Lillian spun around. "I have to get something first."

"But they're waiting," Morrie objected.

"They can wait just a little longer," Lillian insisted in the same firm voice she used for Jason.

Puzzled, Morrie walked by her side until they reached the projects, waiting on the street while she went up to their apartment. The sketches were bound with red string that had originally bound pink food boxes, gifts from various friends. On the string had been taped ROSIE'S DESIGNS. KEEP OUT! THIS MEANS YOU, JASON.

She paused, thinking she should have gotten Rosie's permission. But if she had, Earl and Morrie might have forbidden her from doing this. There was no really good choice, so with a shrug she untied the bundle. There were so many designs, and she didn't have the time to go through them and select the best.

She plucked designs at random from the top, middle, and bottom, trusting to fate. Folding them up, she put them in her purse and then joined Morrie.

She felt a little pinch of anxiety as they crossed Kearny Street, which was the eastern border of Chinatown. She had been out of Chinatown many times, of course, and if she could have found a landlord willing to rent to her, she and her children might have lived elsewhere. However, circumstance had conspired to keep her and her family in Chinatown, so that was what they knew best and where she was the most comfortable.

Morrie's car was big and flashy, like his clothes. Even when her family had been rich, she'd never ridden in anything so fancy. And the polite way he opened the door for her first and then closed it behind her reminded her of the way her father had treated her mother before the money had run out.

Sitting in the front seat, she felt as grand as a queen as they drove up Broadway and through the tunnel. Usually, she just walked the few blocks south of Chinatown. For the rare grand treat, she would take the children to the Woolworth counter for turkey sandwiches and ice cream sodas. After that, the family would entertain themselves for free, taking the elevator up to the children's floor of the Sommer & Kaufmann shoe store and looking at the monkeys in the cage. Then they would squeeze into one of the music rooms at the Music Box and play sample records on the players there. For a game, they would hunt in the department stores for clothes Lillian had worked on and peek at the price tags. Though she had made them, she could never afford to buy them.

They drove past huge apartment buildings with walls so clean that they seemed to gleam in the sunlight. In front of one of them, a uniformed doorman was holding a car door open for a lady.

Small stores were on the ground floor of some of them, but instead of front windows jammed with merchandise, they had only a few tasteful things, like a pair of shoes or gilt frames. Lillian supposed that their prices were so high they only needed to sell one item per day to make their expenses. It was the kind of street where her mother would have strolled in better times.

All too soon, Morrie pulled into a space in front of an ornate building. She had to squint to see the only identification on the store. GIACOMO was painted in small but elegant gilt letters in the right corner of one big plate-glass window. Heavy lavender satin curtains discreetly hid the interior.

Morrie hopped out of the car and ran around to hold the door open for her as if he were a doorman. "Giacomo's had a lot of chances to go national, but he prefers to keep his operation small and hands-on. So he takes just the crème de la crème of San Francisco society. He's even got clients flying up from LA."

Morrie led her into a side alley, and she marveled at how clean the concrete was. No stains. No stray bits of trash. At least the steel back door was more familiar. She was used to thinking about security first and aesthetics second.

Morrie's knuckles tapped out "shave and a haircut, two bits" on the door.

A minute later, Lillian heard several locks being opened—sounds that she also knew well from life in Chinatown.

When the tall, slender young man opened the door, Miss Lillian thought he was Giacomo because he was dressed in an impeccably tailored suit and he had a ponytail. His eyes raked Lillian from head to toe. "Does she speak English?"

Her hand touched her purse where Rosie's designs sat. She had come for a reason, so she got hold of her temper and answered politely, "Quite well."

With a nod, the young man backed up. "Hurry, then. Mrs. Magnin is overdue, and Giacomo's fit to be tied."

"I got my rounds to make," Morrie said to Lillian, "so I'll come by later to pick you up." He glanced at the young man. "Hilary, when will she be through?"

Hilary shrugged. "Who knows? Whenever Mrs. Magnin shows up. She's already an hour late."

Lillian stepped past Hilary, who closed the door with a loud clang. "What is it you want me to do?"

He led her down a corridor where two mannequins

stood like sentries and then squeezed around rows of boxes with labels of useful contents like LACE or BUTTONS and the like. However, there was dust on everything, and some chips on the dummies' faces, as if they had been used once too often. Lillian began to wonder if Giacomo's best days were behind him.

At least the workroom was clean. She was so used to dingy sweatshops that the light pouring from fluorescent bulbs and the skylights overhead dazzled her. No more straining her eyes to make out details as she sewed.

It wasn't fancy—quite the opposite. It was utilitarian without any frivolous ornamentation. Bolts of material filled the metal shelves on one wall, and several sewing machines stood against another. However, what she could see of the walls was a pale cream color, and the floor was covered with practical white and black linoleum tiles in a checkerboard pattern. The two long tables in the center were basic and simple like the chairs around them.

"Wait here," Hilary said, and he returned with a barrel-chested, middle-aged man whom Lillian took for a delivery man because he was wearing a sweater thrown over a T-shirt and jeans.

"Giacomo," Hilary said, indicating Lillian. "This is the seamstress Morrie recommended."

"Can you fix this?" Giacomo demanded.

Across the table, Hilary spread a bright rose-colored sheath with a full skirt in a princess line that would move lovely on a dance floor.

"We had a temp come in yesterday, but she turned in a total disaster." Giacomo ran the dress through his hands. "The seams stretch, and there . . ." His finger jabbed at a spot. "And here it actually tore."

She didn't even have to touch the sheath to know what it had been made from. The rustle of true silk—not that blend from the sleepwear company's nightgown—was unmistakable to her ears. The sibilant whisper brought back memories of her grandmother, so sad and yet so determined as she took apart her elegant dresses to make the blouses that Lillian had once worn with such pride.

Lillian recalled one of her grandmother's first lessons about silk. Surely they couldn't have made so simple a mistake? But perhaps the temp had never worked with silk before. "May I?" she asked.

"That's what you're here for," Hilary said.

It was shantung silk, as she had suspected. With one hand on top, she slid her other hand along the length, feeling the cool electric tingle against her palms. Grandmother had said the silk was speaking to her whenever she had done that. But her hands were even more callused now from years of sewing, so she was extra careful not to snag her fingers on the fabric.

"What are you doing?" Hilary demanded.

"Just smoothing it out," Lillian ad-libbed, drawing her hand out from underneath and then smoothing the silk flat with her other.

The seams had indeed gone all crooked, and there were several holes where the stitches were. As soon as she felt the thread, she knew it was just as she had suspected. "This is silk thread."

"It's a silk dress," Hilary said. "And it was a perfect match for the dress color."

"Silk thread's too strong for the material," Lillian said, and pointed to the tear. "That's what happened there. You need to use another type of thread."

"Of course," Giacomo said, and fingered the stitches. "I should have realized that."

"You were distracted, sir," Hilary said.

Giacomo straightened. "So you've worked with silk, Miss . . . ?" He raised an eyebrow at Lillian.

"Lillian," she supplied. "Lillian Chan. And I have experience with silk." *At least until Grandmom's suitcase ran out of dresses.* She remembered what her grandmom had often said. "Silk's in our blood."

"My dear Lillian," Giacomo said airily, "I need a sheath, not a transfusion."

"I can fix the tears," Lillian said, "but wouldn't it be better if I could replace this torn section with a new one?"

"Don't question Mr. Giacomo's orders," Hilary scolded.

Giacomo held up a hand and glanced over his shoulder at Hilary. "Do we have more material?"

"Not very much," Hilary said cautiously.

"I was taught to waste as little material as I could when I cut," Lillian said, remembering what an effort it sometimes took to create a piece of clothing from her grandmother's hand-me-downs.

"Can you do it quickly?" Giacomo asked.

Lillian nodded. At least, she hoped so.

"Then go ahead," Giacomo said and started to turn away.

"Excuse me," Lillian said, hardly believing her own daring, "but I was told I could call and check on my family every now and then."

"We made no such promise," Hilary said stiffly.

A smile teased the corners of Giacomo's mouth. "Hilary, my lad, you like to live dangerously, don't you? Do you know the first rule of survival in the fashion industry?"

"No, sir," Hilary said warily.

"Never try to keep salesmen from the buffet table or a mother from her children," Giacomo said placidly. "If Mrs. Magnin comes in the meantime, I'll stall her with chitchat and champagne. Hilary, chill a bottle, quick."

"Thank you, sir," Lillian said to his back as he left.

Hilary came back a while later with a small rectangle of silk, which he spread on the long table over a paper pattern. Then he hovered nervously nearby. "I don't know if there's enough."

"We won't know until we try," Lillian said. Lillian had brought her things in her big purse, but Hilary set out a small sewing case that belonged to the store. She supposed that they would be more comfortable if she used their tools, which would be a known quantity, but she touched her purse. "I brought my own things," she said.

After she had carefully marked the material, she took out her grandmom's scissors. Though old, they were of the finest German steel, and she'd kept them sharp and clean all these years. Deftly, swiftly, she began cutting, the scissors shearing through the silk as if it were tissue paper. She knew how much was at stake, but that didn't reduce her pleasure. Such fine silk.

Her grandmother would have been purring with happiness. No, she would have been humming her favorite tune. It was something about the Weaving Maid, which seemed appropriate for the moment.

Then Lillian began to sew, her fingers moving instinctively as her mind drifted back to those lessons from her grandmother. The Weaving Maid's song was woven as tightly through those memories as the threads of the cloth.

She found the notes rising into her throat unbidden, and before she knew it, she was humming them. It had been a long time since she had done that or hummed any music.

And yet it seemed the right thing to do just now when she was thinking of Grandmom. Strong, feisty Grandmom, who had kept her family safe and tried to keep them happy.

Just as Lillian was trying to do now.

CHAPTER | 48

Lillian

As soon as she had tied off the last thread, Hilary seized it and ran from the room. She sat back, satisfied. It had been a long time since she had felt challenged.

She tidied up her work space as her grandmother had taught her, and then, with nothing to do, just sat there. A half hour went by and then an hour, and she heard a woman's voice at the front of the hall but could not make out the words.

When she heard footsteps coming toward her in the corridor, she got to her feet and went to the doorway. Hilary was going into the room next to the workroom. "Excuse me, but I want to call my children."

Hilary seemed to be trying to decide how to treat her. He didn't want to be too closely associated if Lillian failed, but he also didn't want to be too distant if Lillian succeeded.

He compromised on a pleasant nod of the head and a polite gesture. "There's a telephone in the office." He motioned for her to follow him.

The little office was crammed with ledger books, the kind of boxes in which accounts and files were kept, and various scrapbooks from which dangled the tail ends of various articles—probably about Giacomo. A small refrigerator sat in one corner, and from it Hilary took a bottle of champagne and a plate of fruit, cheeses, and crackers.

Lillian, who'd had no lunch, heard her stomach growl, but she had more urgent things on her mind.

"Make yourself comfortable," he said, nodding to the black telephone on the desk. Then, with two flute glasses in one hand, the bottle tucked under an arm, and the plate held in the other, he scurried away.

She got Jason first at the Imperial Splendor. "We had chili dogs, Mama."

Lillian blinked. "Where did you find those in Chinatown? And who bought them?"

"Earl," Jason said. "He went up to North Beach." That was the Italian district to the north of Chinatown.

Apparently Earl was determined to keep her family happy for the chance of future business with Giacomo. "Don't overeat," Lillian warned.

Mimi had liked the cannoli Earl had bought them, but at least she remembered to add that she missed Lillian.

When Rosie came on, she gave a practical report on the family's activities in the same listless voice she had been using that day. It was on the tip of Lillian's tongue to tell her that she had borrowed the designs, but she was not sure how her daughter would react. All Lillian could think of to say was, "Thank you, dear. I'll be home soon."

She went back to the workroom to wait, rummaging around in her purse until she found a roll of mints. Putting one in her mouth, she crunched it with her teeth. She was just finishing her skimpy meal when Hilary summoned her. "We need some alterations."

Lillian selected some spools with threads of the proper colors and then picked up her purse. "I've got everything else I need in here."

She followed Hilary to the showroom in the front of the store. Lillian had once visited a friend who worked as a maid at the posh Fairmont Hotel, and this place was as luxurious—plush cream carpets, oak paneling, and brass electric fittings.

Against one wall were several full-length mirrors forming the three sides of a box so that a customer could see herself from all angles. When Hilary pulled at them, they swung away from the wall as a unit.

Behind the doorway was a private fitting room, just as elegant as the showroom. The buffet table still had plenty of tidbits on the platters next to an open bottle of champagne and the flute glasses.

Giacomo had changed into a blue sports coat with a white silk scarf that fluffed out beneath his neck like a mound of whipped cream.

A slender woman was smiling at him. "This is all your fault for stuffing me with those goodies," she said playfully.

She was in her thirties, with her brown hair cut and styled like the president's wife. From her ears dangled simple earrings in the shape of crescent moons, with a large diamond on the topmost tip of each. She was twisting her head, checking how she looked in the silk sheath.

"Now, my dear, if you'll just stand still for a moment," Giacomo coaxed.

When the woman stopped moving about, Giacomo gestured to Lillian. The diamonds sparkled even more the nearer Lillian got.

As Lillian bent, the woman smiled briefly at her. Then, under Giacomo's professional eye, Lillian made some quick marks with chalk, and the woman slipped into a changing room. She came out a moment later in a blouse and tailored slacks, and Lillian took the sheath into the rear to make the alterations.

When she brought it back again, the sheath fit the customer like a sleek glove. The woman pressed her cheek against Giacomo's as she kissed the air, thanking him.

"I'm only too happy to please," Giacomo said smoothly. They forgot about Lillian, who retreated into a corner and then did her best to be inconspicuous. When the woman had removed the sheath again, Hilary took it away to give it one last ironing and then wrap it up. Giacomo and the woman chatted, mentioning people whom Lillian would never meet. When Hilary returned, the sheath was in an elegant black box with red and gold lettering and stripes. The two of them escorted the woman from the building.

When Giacomo returned with Hilary, they seemed surprised to find Lillian still in the showroom.

Hilary frowned. "That's all. You can wait in the workroom for Morrie."

Because Giacomo was feeling relieved, he waved a hand expansively at the champagne. "Have some champagne first."

Lillian's heart was pounding as she shook her head. "No, thank you."

Giacomo unwound his scarf and scratched his throat. "Can't stand the stuff myself, but it goes with the image. I drink it because the customers expect it, but I prefer beer. Would you like one?"

"I don't drink," Lillian said.

"A wise choice." Giacomo saluted her with the scarf. "And thank you for your help. You saved the day like a knight errant with a needle instead of a lance."

Nervously, Lillian fingered the cord around her wrist. This was all for Rosie's sake, one way or another. So she snapped open her purse. "If you really want to thank me, would you look at these?" She took out the folded designs.

Her hand trembled. The precious pages fluttered. "My daughter wants to be a designer. Her name's Rosie."

Hilary tried to snatch them from her fingers. "Mr. Giacomo doesn't have time for someone's scribbles."

Lillian thought of how those other Swallows had fought for their families. And even if she had resisted the nickname, she was a Swallow too. That gave her courage now. Years of battling for the best items at the Chinatown fruit stands and delis had honed her technique, and she hipped Hilary easily out of her way. "I need to know if she's making the right choice."

The grin had left Giacomo's face, but he extended his palm. "You may not like what I have to say," he warned, all warmth gone from his voice.

"I just want the truth," Lillian said, hardly daring to breathe.

He unfolded the pages and then leafed through them. Lillian's hopes rose when he paused once, but then fell when he only gave a noncommittal grunt and went on. Finally he handed them back. "Her designs are all over the place—a little bit of everything. What she needs to do is find her own voice, her own vision, but yes, there's a spark there." He laced his fingers together. "However, I can't use her."

Had Giacomo praised her daughter just to get rid of Lillian? "I wasn't asking you to employ her, sir." Lillian folded the designs back up, still unsure of what to do about Rosie.

"Then why did you waste Giacomo's time?" Hilary demanded haughtily.

Lillian restored the designs to her purse. "I wanted to see if I should encourage her to be a designer. You see, her guidance counselor says she should be a bank teller."

From the plate on the table, Giacomo took a little poppy-seed cracker and popped it into his mouth. "Banking's a very steady profession, much steadier than being a designer."

"Anyway, what would she know about fashion?" Hilary scoffed. "She'll be better off in a bank."

Lillian rounded on her heel. "Who knows a car better than the mechanic who can take it apart and put it back together? Mr. Giacomo might set the trend, but it eventually comes into shops like ours, maybe changed a little and with cheaper fabric. And my daughter's there, studying everything. She not only understands the design and all its variations but also how you make it."

"A gown is not a car," Hilary argued. "It takes . . . well, good taste to create fashion. Refinement. A sense of style. Your daughter's probably a nice girl, but she won't have a clue about those things."

"Neither did I when I started out." Giacomo popped the cracker into his mouth.

"But you were born with the right instincts, sir," Hilary protested.

"Nonsense." Giacomo dusted some crumbs from his palms. "My father was a simple tailor with a tiny shop in

New York. And so was his father back in Palermo. And on and on. For all I know, one of my ancestors was sewing furs together with animal sinews and a needle of bone. But none of us had the first notion about fashion. I just knew I wanted to be part of it."

"I wasn't aware of that, sir," Hilary said, chastened.

Giacomo folded his hands in front of him. "Well, it's not part of the official biography that I want my clients to hear. My father pounded the pavement through the entire garment district until he finally found this one tiny designer who was willing to take me on as an office boy."

"You repaid his devotion, sir," Hilary said.

Giacomo turned to Lillian. "He had the same determined look that you have." Steepling his fingers, he rested his chin on them and became lost in thought for a moment. "So I'll do this much in memory of my father. I'll let your daughter come in after school. It'll be strictly as a gofer, fetching things and filing and such—at minimum wage, of course."

This was far more than Lillian had hoped for. "I don't know how to thank you."

"Don't. I'm running a business, not a classroom." He smiled at Lillian. "However, if she keeps her eyes and ears open, she'll learn a few things. The rest will be up to her."

"She'll soak up everything like a sponge," Lillian promised, "just as you did."

She didn't know the future, but she did know her daughter.

CHAPTER | 49

Rosie

That was very kind of you, Mama," Rosie said with the formal politeness of a rich old lady, "but I'll tell him no thank you. I can't do it."

Mama fingered the cord around her wrist. "I thought this was what you wanted." When Rosie remained silent, her mother nudged her insistently. "Go on. Tell Mama what's the matter."

Rosie gave an exasperated sniff. "You don't want to know."

"Of course I do," Mama insisted.

Well, Rosie thought to herself, *Mama asked for it*. She stared directly into her mother's eyes. "Who's going to watch Jason and Mimi?"

Jason glanced up from his comic book. "I'm already nine. I don't need a babysitter."

Mimi looked upset. "Why are you sending Rosie away?"

"It's just for part of the day," Mama said. "We can manage."

Mimi folded her arms with a harrumph. "You're always too busy."

"Who do you think used to watch Rosie when she was your age? And she survived." Mama sat back, hurt. "You act like you don't think I'm competent."

"She wasn't saying that, Mama," Rosie said hurriedly.

"Rosie does almost everything." Raising a hand, Mimi began to tick off the items on her fingers. "She does most of the shopping and the cooking. And she does all the laundry—"

Rosie grabbed her little sister's hand and forced it down before Mimi could get into further trouble. "Don't exaggerate," she said with a nervous laugh.

"Big sisters always take on a lot of responsibility," Mama said, and drummed her fingertips on the kitchen table. "But if we all pitch in, Rosie won't have to do as much as she does now."

Mimi broke into tears. "I don't want Rosie to leave."

Even Jason's upper lip was beginning to twitch, as if he were getting ready to join Mimi, so Rosie assured them, "I'm not going anywhere."

Mama threw up her hands. "But this is an opportunity."

Rosie dropped her eyes. "There'll be others," she mumbled.

Mama's fingers cupped her chin and forced her head back up. "Sometimes there aren't. That's why you're accepting this offer."

"But it's so far away," Mimi wailed.

Mama rubbed her temples as if she were getting a headache. "It's downtown, silly. You've been there before. And anyway, if your great-grandmother could leave China for the rest of her life, Rosie ought to be able to leave Chinatown for a few hours."

"But not every day," Rosie fretted. "What if something happens to one of you while I'm gone? I could never forgive myself."

"You're not going to the end of the world. If something went wrong, we'd telephone you. If you ran, you could be at home before you knew it." She added quickly before Mimi could cry again, "Not that anything bad is going to happen." Mama studied Rosie thoughtfully. "Why are you making up all these excuses? Are you scared?"

"I can handle anything," Rosie said indignantly.

Mama folded her arms. "In Chinatown. But that's the problem. We're used to Chinatown, but not to the outside, no matter how many times we go. Even today, when I first left Chinatown, I felt a little nervous. Is that it?"

Rosie had not been able to name the source of her uneasiness until her mother put her finger on it. Now her hesitation sounded foolish, and yet she could feel the fear creeping around inside her like a little mouse. "You were the one who told me we do what we have to so the family can survive."

Mama reached across the table and took both of Rosie's hands in hers. "This family has always survived by changing as the world changes. So maybe this time that change means we have to stop being practical and do something wild and impossible instead."

Rosie drew her eyebrows together in confusion. "I thought you wanted me to be a bank teller."

Mama squeezed her fingers. "And you may still wind up doing that, but you're going to try this first." She looked from Rosie to Jason and Mimi. "Children need to have dreams. Oof."

Rosie had jumped up and wrapped her arms around her mother tight. Her mother was small, but there was a solid core to her, so it was like hugging a rock. "I love you, Mama."

Her mother patted her forearm. "Yes, yes, I know. Now shouldn't we get dinner started?"

Rosie let go. "And maybe while we're doing that, you could tell me some of the old stories?"

PART FIVE

(2011)

Silk is in our blood.

CHAPTER | 50

New York
August 6, 2011
Seven Seven Festival

Rosie

The lecture room was standing room only, and the professor had trouble keeping students and faculty from completely filling the stairs and violating the fire code. The ones who were allowed to stay counted themselves lucky, and they murmured excitedly to one another while the tall blond man tapped keys on a laptop on a table by the lectern and then looked behind him at the pictures appearing one after another on the large overhead screen.

Satisfied, he tickled a few more keys, and the screen went blue, but the laptop was ready to begin the slide show. Nodding to the professor, he said in a slight Texas drawl, "Everything's ready to go."

Then he squeezed his long frame into a desk in the front row next to a little girl with hair to match his but with high cheekbones and high-set Asian eyes. Bored, a small Chinese American boy with blue eyes drummed his heels on the floor until his mother, a Chinese American woman with brown hair, stopped him. One look at their faces and it was easy to tell they were related to the little girl.

The crowd fell silent when the professor stepped to the lectern and began his introduction.

In the hallway behind the rear of the lecture room, Rosie waited impatiently. She was dressed in a stylish red silk blouse and light blue slacks that she had designed. On her blouse was her trademark logo, a swallow.

She was studying her speech when a woman said timidly, "Excuse me."

Rosie turned, annoyed at having her focus broken. "Yes?"

A Chinese woman stood there in a navy blue pantsuit. On the lapel of her jacket was a brooch set with pearls in the shape of the Pleiades. Perhaps she'd worn it in honor of the Weaving Maid and the sisters, and Rosie felt herself softening a bit toward her.

The woman nervously presented her card. "I'm Miss Lin. I think we might be related." She had a slight British accent.

People had made that claim before—usually when they wanted a favor or even a loan—and Rosie got ready with her standard polite refusal, but then the woman added breathlessly, "I wasn't sure I'd have the nerve to speak to you. I think my ancestor Swallow was a sister of your ancestor Lily. Was she a Lee from Bird Hill in Shun-te District?"

"Yes, I believe so." Rosie glanced at the card. Miss Lin's first name was Lily. "You're from Singapore?"

"Yes," Miss Lin said. "My family never moved after she settled there."

Rosie checked on the professor, but he was still listing her early accomplishments, so she had time. He made her success sound so easy, but it had taken a good deal of struggle, tears, and anxiety to achieve anything. "I thought Swallow was in the household of a merchant."

Miss Lin smiled. "She fell in love with the merchant's steward, and together they scrimped and saved so they could buy her freedom. After they were married, they set up their own business."

"Really?" Rosie felt so elated by the news about that first Swallow. She wished she could have told her mother. "And how'd they do?"

"Extremely well," Miss Lin said. "According to the Singapore histories, she was a formidable person."

"From what I've heard, so was my ancestor, her sister," Rosie said. "According to the family stories, she tried to find out about your ancestor."

Miss Lin drew her eyebrows together. "And according to our family stories, once she was married, Swallow wrote to her sister."

"I don't think my ancestor ever got the letters," Rosie

said. "But, of course, she would have changed her name when she got married and moved. And then she moved a second time, to Nam-hoi to take care of her grandchildren. So it's no wonder the letters never found her. As far as my family knew, your ancestor stayed a slave."

Miss Lin shook her head. "That's such a pity. My ancestor loved her sister so much that she named a daughter after her. And the name's been handed on through the generations along with this brooch." She touched the stones for a moment. "I happen to be the current one."

They were both silent for a moment as they considered how sad it was that one sister's letter had never reached the other.

In the other room, Rosie could hear the professor saying, ". . . but I know you're here to listen to our guest and not me."

"Can you stay afterward?" Rosie asked.

"I came tonight to hear you, Ms. Bouvier." Miss Lin nodded.

"Call me Rosie." She slipped the card into a pocket.

"Then please call me Lily," Miss Lin said. "Do you ever come to Singapore?"

"Often," Rosie said. "In fact, I was just in China, but only in Hong Kong and the New Territories. I didn't get that far south."

"Have you ever tried to find Bird Hill?" Miss Lin asked.

Rosie laughed. "Well, I went to an area that my guide said had been Bird Hill, but it was all factories and apartment houses by then."

"The next time you're in Singapore, please call me," Miss Lin urged. "We know all about you and have followed your career, of course. But we've been very curious about the rest of your branch."

"I will," Rosie said to her . . . ? She was sure Chinese had an exact term for their relationship, but she didn't know what that was. English, on the other hand, being less precise, was more convenient, so *cousin* would do. "My family's here, and I'm sure we'd all like to find out about your branch of the family, Lily."

Miss Lin pressed a hand beneath her throat. "I'd be delighted to meet them too."

"Then we'll talk later." Turning, Rosie grasped the door handle.

In the other room, the professor was finishing. "We're lucky to have such a special speaker today. As a designer, she reinvigorated American fashion and has continued to do so decade after decade, fusing Asian and Western ideas into her own unique vision. As an executive, she has served as a role model for a generation of entrepreneurs. I give you now that visionary, that fashion icon, Rose Bouvier."

Humming her mother's favorite tune for luck, Rosie stepped through the rear door into the brightly lit room. The spectators applauded so enthusiastically that it was hard to hear. Cameras and cell phones flashed, and stars momentarily swam before her eyes. By now, such things didn't faze her, and she continued on across the floor.

As she set her prepared speech on the lectern, her eyes drifted upward to the ceiling. Some of the ceiling lights had gone out, so the lit ones formed a pattern that reminded her vaguely of the Pleiades, the Seven Sisters, which she took for a good omen.

"Good evening," she said. "I think it's fitting that people interested in fashion meet today, because in China they're celebrating the Weaving Maid's festival."

"Are they, Granny?" her granddaughter piped up, and then shrank as everyone began to laugh.

Rosie smiled at her. "Yes, dear."

The boy, her grandson, gave her the thumbs-up signal, so she knew the microphone was projecting her voice clearly through the packed room. Even speeches were a family effort.

She gazed at the crowd for the first time. Each row of desks sat on a raked slope that ran all the way up to the tech room, so that it seemed like a tidal wave of faces rising before her: Men and women, young and old, Asian, Caucasian, Latino, African American, they were all represented and dressed in everything from trendy suits to leather jackets with metal studs.

It was the youthful, hopeful faces that held her attention the most, and she found herself suddenly drawing inspiration from them. "I'll talk to you about design in the twenty-first century in a moment, but first I want to say that if you remember one thing from tonight, it's that no one achieves success on their own. Success is a joint accomplishment."

She motioned to the blond man who'd been setting up the computer. "So I want to thank my son-in-law, Robert, for helping with the technology." She smiled at the older Chinese American man and woman in the second row. "And my brother, Jason, and my sister, Mimi, who are the brains and heart of our company." She inclined her head toward the young Chinese American woman in the front row who resembled her. "And I'm always grateful to my daughter, Lilith, my grandson, Bobby, and my granddaughter, Rosalie, for keeping both me and our company on a straight course."

She paused while they stood up sheepishly to the polite applause.

High up in the room, she saw Lily squeeze through the crowd as adeptly as any Chinatowner would have and slip into a seat that another Chinese woman had saved for her.

"But there's one person without whom none of us would be here—someone who isn't with us anymore." Rosie swallowed, feeling a twinge of grief and nostalgia. "My mother fought for the opportunity that let me learn about the fashion industry from the ground up. Later, when I started out on my own, she sewed my samples. I should also add that she was my harshest critic."

There was sympathetic laughter at that.

Feeling her mother's invisible presence, Rosie paused to smile. Jason and Mimi grinned back at her, as if they were reading her mind. Even in later years, after Rosie had begun gaining some fame and success, Mama had hated any public acknowledgment. If she had been here in body right now, Rosie was sure she would have been getting ready to pinch her and tell her to get on with the speech.

"She was hard on me because she knew she was standing in for all those earlier generations who sweated and sacrificed and shed tears for my sake—even though those generations did not know me personally, even though I was a mere abstract concept in an unknown future." Her words rose, as if those ghosts from the past were adding their strength to her voice. "For centuries, my family has worked in the silk trade. We've raised the worms that spun silk. We've reeled that silk into threads. We've then sewed clothing from those threads of silk. And now we design clothes of silk."

She waited to let the next thought fix itself into her listeners' minds. "Silk is in our blood. . . ."

AFTERWORD

The Silkworms

The Kwangtung silkworms described in this book are different from the ones in central China or Europe—and it's the latter that are usually described in the reference books and on the internet. Not only were the Kwangtung silkworms smaller, but their growth cycle was a little less than half the growth cycle of the larger species. As a result, the Kwangtung silkworms produced seven crops each year as opposed to the single or double crops of the larger silkworms. The silk strands that these or any other silkworms produce are also stronger than strands of steel of comparable size.

As part of its exhibit on the Silk Road, the American Museum of Natural History posted a video on YouTube called "AMNH - Silk Road - Making Silk." The tools that the demonstrator, Michael Cook, uses are made mostly of metal and synthetic materials, such as plastic and nylon, but I believe they're essentially the same.

The Myth

The Weaving Maid was the star Vega, and the Cowboy was the star Altair. I'm aware that the Pleiades have seven stars, but the story of the Weaving Maid only has six sisters. However, according to the *Encyclopedia Britannica*, sometimes only six are visible to the naked eye, so perhaps that's why there are only six sisters in the tale.

Readers will note the many different dates for their special day, the Seven Seven festival. This is because the Chinese use a lunar calendar, which does not match the Western solar one. Sometimes, in order to bring the two types of calendars more into alignment, the Chinese introduced an extra, or intercalary, month such as in 1835.

Part One

The Sam Yup, from the Three Districts around Canton, is the dialect that I tried to learn in Chinese school, even if my own family came from Lucky's area, Sunning, or Toisan, as it was later renamed.

Silk production had long been the main industry in the area around Canton, with much of the land devoted to mulberry trees by the early nineteenth century. The farmers had created their own remarkable closed-loop ecology employing pigs, fishponds, mulberry trees, and silkworms.

The customs and practices for girls in the Sam Yup

area were quite different from the traditions of northern China. It was also customary in the Sam Yup districts for girls of a marriageable age to live together in a separate house. Women from these places were famous for being independent-minded, and a number of them swore they would never marry.

For the laborious process of raising silkworms and reeling silk, Howard and Buswell's *A Survey of the Silk Industry of South China* has been invaluable. They went into painstaking detail about the care of mulberry trees, the harvesting of the leaves, the tending of silkworms, and reeling, both by hand and by steam-driven machines.

They traveled by boat up and down the Pearl River Delta, observing numerous farms and factories, so their descriptions are all firsthand.

Joseph Needham described the silkworm nets, and though Howard and Buswell agree that nets would have made for better crops, they noted that such things were luxuries for the average farmer, who had neither the time, money, nor spare labor to employ the method.

Part Two

As noted above, the descriptions of the factory building and life inside were drawn from Howard and Buswell's invaluable book.

Uncle is based on a remarkable man named Ch'en

ch'i-yüan, who saw a picture bigger than his own imme-
diate profits. Having failed the government exams, he
went to French Indochina, where he became a merchant
with his brother. There, he became fascinated by the silk-
reeling factories the French had built. Having made his
fortune, he returned to his native village in China and
opened his own factory in 1874. Foreign companies had
previously attempted to start factories and failed for a
variety of reasons.

Ch'en involved his clan in the ownership of his factory,
setting a pattern for other clans, with whom he shared his
technical knowledge because he wanted to encourage the
creation of a new silk industry. As a result, these clans
subsequently built and owned their own factories. So the
majority of silk-reeling factories in southern China were
owned locally rather than by foreign companies.

Unlike other factory owners, though, he also provided
medical services and food and goods at prices cheaper
than in the towns, and he gave money to widows, the
elderly, and public works.

In October 1881, the male weavers looted and then
burned down one factory for the reasons described in the
novel. They then attempted to do the same to Ch'en, but
his clan's militia, stiffened by mercenaries, was able to
repulse them in two battles. All the reeling factories were
closed down, but China sorely missed their revenue, and
in just three years Ch'en was invited back to reopen his

factory. In 1888, there was another battle with the weavers, so, in order to ease hard feelings, Ch'en helped invent a foot reeler that was cheap, easy to use and maintain, and made the weavers more competitive with his factories.

Part Three

My maternal grandmother, like the heroes of this novel, belonged to a long tradition of women skilled in using a needle. She held many jobs, trying to support her large family. Among other things, she learned how to use a sewing machine to support the family and sewed clothing in the sweatshops. My mother told me that my grandmother was so skillful that salesmen asked her to do the samples that they would show the store owners—just as Morrie asks Lillian to do.

While I never saw my grandmother at work, I can remember as a boy passing by the Chinatown sweatshops, where, on a hot afternoon, the doors would be open and I could hear the rattle of the old sewing machines and loud Chinese music playing.

Readers who are interested in learning more about silk might want to read some of the books that I used for research.

PARTIAL BIBLIOGRAPHY

Eng, Robert Y. *Economic Imperialism in China: Silk Production and Exports, 1861–1932*. Berkeley: Institute of East Asian Studies, University of California, 1986.

Feltwell, John. *The Story of Silk*. New York: St. Martin's Press, 1991.

Finnane, Antonia. *Changing Clothes in China: Fashion, Modernity, Nation*. New York: Columbia University Press, 2008.

Howard, Charles Walter, and K. P. Buswell. *A Survey of the Silk Industry of South China*. Hong Kong: Ling Nan Agricultural College, 1925.

Li, Lillian M. *China's Silk Trade: Traditional Industry in the Modern World, 1842–1937*. Cambridge, MA: Harvard University Press, 1981.

Marks, Robert B. *Tigers, Rice, Silk, and Silt: Environment and Economy in Late Imperial South China*. Cambridge:

Cambridge University Press, 1998.

Needham, Joseph, and Dieter Kuhn. *Science and Civilisation in China*. Vol. 5, *Chemistry and Chemical Technology*. Pt. 9, *Textile Technology: Spinning and Reeling*. Cambridge: Cambridge University Press, 1988.

So, Alvin Y. *The South China Silk District: Local Historical Transformation and World-System Theory*. Albany: State University of New York Press, 1986.

Stockard, Janice E. *Daughters of the Canton Delta: Marriage Patterns and Economic Strategies in South China, 1860–1930*. Stanford: Stanford University Press, 1989.

Wright, Grace. *Sericulture: The Proper Employment of Women in 19th Century China*. Lulu.com, 2006.

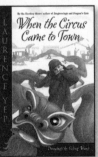